Lady
Catherine's
Coil

Also by Shirley Marks

REGENCY ROMANCE SERIES

The Dueling Season

Meant to be read in order of publication

Book 1: Honor of a Lady
Book 2: No Higher Opinion
Book 3: Matter of Affection

The Gentlemen of Worth

The Suitor List
Perfectly Flawed
A Grand Deception
The Duke Dilemma
An Elaborate Hoax
A Rogue Reformed

REGENCY ROMANCE

Miss Quinn's Quandary
An Agreeable Arrangement
Lady Eugenia's Holiday

Lady Catherine's Coil

SHIRLEY MARKS

ISBN-13: 978-1-946314-12-3 (paperback)
ISBN-10: 1-9494314-11-0

ISBN-13: 978-1-946314-13-0 (epub)
ISBN-10: 1-946314-13-7

Photographs provided by Unsplashed.com
Daniel Robert - Pergola
Background provided by BookBrush.com
Public domain:
Portrait of a Young Lady by Eduard Friedrich Leybold

www.ShirleyMarks.com

Dedication

Paula S
for your inspiration

Rachel, Jenny, Linda, and Kim for their
comments, suggestions, and time

Lady
Catherine's
Coil

One

"Needs must, Kitty. I could not remain in that house a moment longer—else I would have gone mad." Lady Catherine Jessup leaned back against the squabs of her uncle's fine traveling coach and stared out the window. "I cannot say that I am sorry to leave London. Good riddance!" Kate couldn't imagine a duller, more mundane purgatory could befall her than the last few months attending her first, and hopefully only, Season.

"If you had not been so obtuse and contrary, Kate." Kitty Matthews sitting across from Kate—her school friend, now abigail and companion—had an entire bench to herself. They were dressed in similar travel cloaks and bonnets. For it would not do to have one dressed plain or shabby and the other very fine. She crossed her arms and shook her head. "I do not believe I've seen you behave worse in all our years spent together. What did you *do* to vex Lady Bradford so?"

"As my aunt tells it—I *defied* her," Kate said in harsh tones. "She *wished* me to marry. I do not believe she cared *who* I married, she merely wished to be rid of me." Lady Bradford was not related by blood to Kate and never truly cared for her. "My aunt and uncle have inherited my parents' titles and estates—and they may have also acquired their position in society, but they cannot touch the fortune. *My* fortune. It is completely separate from the entails."

Kitty rolled her eyes. "I know *that* cannot be true. You are her family … perhaps only by marriage. But she must care about you."

"No. No, she does not." From what Lady Bradford, Kate had *always* been a burden … tiresome and difficult.

Her Bradford cousins, a bit younger than she, were raised at the country estate with their own nannies and governess. Kate, who would have been considered a *bad* influence, was enrolled at Miss Maddingly's Academy for Young Ladies in Sussex. To her mind, that was the best outcome she could have imagined. Her aunt and uncle's neglect gave Kate the opportunity to make many friends and it was where she met her lifelong friend Kitty—Catherine Matthews.

"But we have been *sent* away! Your aunt was very angry. I do not believe I've ever seen anyone in such a temper."

"I have given my aunt the disgust of me," Kate confessed. She would, of course, need to tell Kitty all—when did they ever hide anything from one another?

"Where is it we are being sent to, again?" Kitty could not have forgotten. Over the last few days before their departure, tempers were running high and it was such a relief to quit the place.

"We are being sent to Lady Bradford's sister's country home in Wiltshire—Grimshaw Court."

The farther away, the better.

"*Grims-shaw* Court?" Kitty uttered the name somewhat distastefully. "That sounds like a dreadful place."

"It will be a vast improvement if you ask me. It is not London … it is not Bradford House. My aunt will not be in residence nor will there be any unwanted visitors *dropping by* at all hours—suitors who were thrown underfoot." Kate thoroughly despised the lengths in which her aunt dangled her unwanted niece in front of any eligible young man. "I can honestly say I do not know Lady James from Adam ... perhaps I should say from *Eve...* I am sure she will be some poor relation for whom Lady Bradford cares nothing."

"But she is a *Lady* ... that must be of some consequence ..." Kitty pointed out.

"Just because one holds a title does not mean one is someone."

"You have never met Lady James ... ever?"

"I may have when I was first orphaned but I was not much more than a babe then. My uncle George became the Earl of Bradford after my father died and his wife, the new countess. I cannot believe she understands that she has benefited from my tragedy." Only then did it occur to Kate how wretched and unfeeling her aunt had been. "She could not touch my fortune—held safely in trust for me. My father's brother George and a solicitor, who was a good friend of my parents, were left as co-guardians."

"You have never spoken of this before, Kate."

"I really did not understand the whole of it while at school. I was a child, the same as every other student in attendance." She treasured her years spent at the Academy. But now her time there was over and her first step out into the world had not been anywhere near a success. "Thank goodness *she* is not my guardian —I would be left without a feather to fly with. I shall keep my fortune, thank you very much—for if I should marry, it will all be handed to my *husband* ... again, leaving me *without a feather to fly with.*"

"Is *everyone* trying to take your money?" Kitty had no money nor position so it would be difficult for her to understand.

"The money is not the half of it—everyone always wants to *tell* me what to do." Kate could recall as far back as she could remember. "Dictate my actions—where I should go—how I should behave—what I should think— Really ... am I not allowed some privacy? What goes on in my head is *my* business, is it not?"

"I should think so." Of course, Kitty *had* to agree.

"My aunt may believe as if *she* were in charge … of me … but she is not. My *uncle* is my guardian."

"Is that not the same thing?"

"No, it is not. But he has handed over my care to his wife without thought—allowed her to make the decisions … and it is *she* who sends me to *her* sister Lady James and her husband Lord James Emerson of Grimshaw Court. She has quite washed her hands of me." Kate could not imagine her situation being any worse in the country than spending time in London. She hated the city—the crowding, the smells, the unpleasant *people.*

"Do not fret, Kate. We will manage," Kitty said in a bracing, uplifting tone.

"There is nothing for it… I *must* go and I'm afraid you have been sent packing as well … but …" Kate was struck silent as an idea came to her. She gazed across at Kitty, staring at her intently.

"What is it?"

"I've just been inspired …"

"Oh, no… I don't like the sound of this."

"It is true that I must go to Grimshaw Court, there is no doubt," Kate began. "But there is no reason I must submit to the daily drudgery of family matters which do not concern me."

"What does that mean?"

"That means, dear Kitty, that since my aunt Lady Bradford's sister Lady James and her husband are not familiar with me, there is no reason *I* need to present myself as *Lady Catherine.*"

"If you are not *Lady Catherine*, then who are you?"

"I will be *Miss Matthews* … the companion to Lady Catherine."

"But—you cannot pretend to be *me!*"

"I must be you if you are to fill Lady Catherine's shoes."

"*Me*—pose as Lady Catherine?" Kitty's mouth moved in protest without words emerging.

"You must, Kitty… I am tired of it—and I cannot tolerate to be so any longer! I shall pose as you and you can assume my place while we remain at Grimshaw Court. Who will ever know, I ask you?"

"I … can … not …"

"Yes, you can—you must." It was the only way Kate could endure. "If I do not have a moment of solitude to myself I vow I will go mad!"

"It is impossible, Kate. Seems like a fool's errand to me. I, for one, will not be a part of your scheme. I refuse."

"You *never* refuse, Kitty. You are always amenable." Kate was taken aback by Kitty's staunch rejection of their simple exchange. She meant no harm … it was an innocent act. Who was to know?

"Not this time. You cannot ask this of me—it is too much."

Kitty was uncooperative and looked away, refusing to speak further, leaving Kate cross and frustrated. They hadn't traveled too much farther before the motion of the coach, in their mutually agreed upon silence, soon lulled the two to sleep.

Some hours later, the bumping of the carriage down the hardened dirt road woke Kitty. She rocked from side to side as much as ever, proving the roads had not improved. Glancing out the window, the landscape did not appear much different from the rural scenery beyond the tollgate outside London.

Kitty allowed her friend to sleep … considering what they had been talking about … *Kate's scheme* … it was best to leave her dreaming, lest the same disagreement arise again. Kitty did not wish to revisit that topic.

Kate had always been more than generous with Kitty, never treating her as if she were a servant. She clothed her, fed her … she even provided Kitty with pin money. As an attendant to Kate in a *customary* capacity as a maid, companion, or friend was more than acceptable to Kitty but what Kate asked of her—to step into her shoes was outside of enough.

Kate soon opened her eyes, drew in a deep breath, and stretched as much as she could in her confined area of the coach. "I don't expect I missed a stop, have I?"

"No. One of the footmen would have alerted us, I'm sure."

"Lady Bradford was quite explicit about this being a full day's journey. There would be no stopping for our comfort—sounds as if it will be harder on the horses than it will be on us."

"Not to mention the coachman, footmen, and outriders accompanying us." Kitty caught sight of one of the outriders every now and again and felt sorry for their onerous burden to oversee the travel.

The coach turned off the main road and rolled down a wooded park, approaching nearer and nearer to some structure in the distance. Soon, out their window, it became clear that it was a grand house. They kept watch out their window, noting how the vertical lines grew tall and its reddish color deepened.

Passing through a pair of iron gates, Kitty thought they looked not as grand as she once thought but a bit … *tired*. Drawing nearer and nearer, both she and Kate sat more erect in their seats anxious for their arrival.

"Oh—look! I think we are almost there." Kitty gazed out the window, staring at the pile in the distance. "That must be it. Grimshaw Court may not sound idyllic but it looks to be quite magnificent."

"We are still some distance away." Kate stared out the window. "You haven't changed your mind about my *suggestion*, have you?"

"No, I have not. I still cannot believe you would propose such a thing. " Kitty had already made up her mind and had no intention of changing it. "You may have concocted some schemes in the past that I may have gone along with but that was when we were mere schoolgirls—but no longer, do you hear me? We are young ladies and should behave as such."

"I feel quite desperate about it all—" Kate leaned forward in her last plea to Kitty.

"This is nonsense! *Do* give it up, Kate." Kitty had had enough. "And do not ask me again!"

"Oh, pooh, Kitty!" Kate remarked just before the coach came to a complete stop.

Outside the coach were the butler and several footmen stood ready to receive them. A few moments later, the steps were let down and the door opened. Kitty could wait no longer and stepped out before Kate could say anything more. Once in the company of others, there would be no more discussion of the topic Kitty did not wish to hear.

She readjusted the bonnet on her head and straightened her skirts, waiting for Kate to disembark. A glance from the butler to one of the footmen was silent instruction to direct the coachman to the back of the house to unload the luggage. The coach, with its outriders, pulled away and rounded the corner of the house.

With Kate now standing beside Kitty, the butler bowed to the ladies and opened the front doors to Grimshaw Court, revealing their hostess Lady James, stepping forward to greet the guests. The two made to enter but ... Kate hesitated, allowing Kitty to be the first to enter, stepping toward Lady James. Etiquette rules dictated that Lady Catherine would have been ... *should* have been.

What Kate's wayward step had done was wordlessly indicate that Kitty *was* Lady Catherine. Lady James extended her arms welcoming her sister's niece to Grimshaw Court.

"Welcome! Welcome to you, Lady Catherine, and your" — Lady James stared at Kitty, addressing her, then glanced at Kate— "Abigail? Companion? Surely you are too young to have a companion."

What was Kate doing? Without Kitty's consent, her *friend* had taken the step—and *not* stood alongside her. With that one action, Kate had reversed their identities ... their positions—and there was nothing Kitty could do about it. Not unless she called Kate an out-and-out liar right there in the open—causing a scene in front of Lady James and the staff of Grimshaw Court.

No, Kitty could not do that.

"As you see ..." Kitty motioned to Kate who was now behind her.

"*Ehm—Miss Kate Matthew*s. How do you do, Lady James?" Kate curtsied.

It was all Kitty could do to keep her composure. She willed herself not to shake with anger and kept her breathing slow and even as not to display her exasperation with her *friend.*

"My gracious... *Miss Matthews* does seem a cut above what one would expect of an abigail," my lady commented.

"Yes, Kate is almost *quality* herself." Kitty smiled ... inside, she was seething.

"And she goes by *Kate* ... as in *Catherine?* You both—"

"I am accustomed to being called *Kitty*." Kitty smiled, hoping to put her ladyship at ease.

"Oh, I beg your pardon... Lady Bradford has always referred to you as Lady Catherine."

"It can be quite confusing because we both are *Catherine*—our names were decided long ago when we were at school," Kitty explained. "I expect that is a story in itself ... for another time perhaps?"

"We will show you to your rooms where you can have some time to rest before we have tea." Lady James motioned them forward and waved a footman to help with their outer garments.

"That sounds lovely," Kitty remarked with a smile. "It will be very nice to sit on something that is *not* moving."

"That is exactly how I feel after a long journey—no matter how comfortable the traveling coach. Do allow me to show you to your rooms." Lady James lifted the hem of her skirt to pivot and led the two toward the main staircase. "If you ladies will follow me ..."

Why Lady James did the lowly deed herself and not regale it to a servant, she did not know. Kitty glanced back at Kate, who would now trail her mistress, followed her ladyship to the staircase, up the stairs, and off to the left, the west wing.

"You'll be staying in the Floral suite." Lady James stepped inside. "For you, Lady Catherine, and the connecting one, right through the dressing room next door, is for your companion, Miss Matthews."

Kitty, followed by Kate, entered. The bedchamber was beautiful. As the name indicated, the room was decorated in light green with floral accents in pink, yellow, and peach. It was still spacious with its four-poster bed and two skirted chairs set before a metal-grate fireplace. Next to the bed was a dressing table and between the two sash windows sat a writing table.

"This is very fine. Thank you." Kitty had never stayed in a lovelier bedchamber.

"The footmen should deliver your luggage shortly. We shall have tea in the front parlor when the two of you are ready."

"Yes, indeed." Kitty held her smile without difficulty. "We shall be down after we have had a chance to rest and freshen up."

With that, Lady James retreated, pulling the door closed behind her, leaving the two young ladies.

When Kitty turned to address Kate, she found her friend was gone. She soon reappeared, standing at the door to the connecting room.

"That room is so much smaller than this one!" Kate remarked, sounding shocked that there should be such a difference.

"I expect *you* will manage," Kitty retorted rather pointedly.

"*Me?*" Kate sounded quite displeased. "Why should I take the smaller bedchamber?"

"Because *I* am Lady Catherine or have you forgotten? Might I remind you this *was* your idea?"

"*You?*" It could not have escaped Kate that *appearances were everything*. "But you are not—"

"How would it appear if they should see *Miss Matthews* occupying the grand bedchamber and *Lady Catherine* reside in the smaller?"

Kate's expression said it all. *She had not realized.*

"I see that there are some advantages to being *Lady Catherine*," Kitty mused.

"I would gladly accept the smaller bedchamber if it means I need not put up with the formality of the family belowstairs" — Kate widened her eyes in realization— "And I need not bother with the servants of the household because I am a guest—I am the *companion* of a guest which elevates my position amongst the staff and I should not be expected to light the fires, empty the chamber pots, or scrub the floors."

"That is true," Kitty agreed.

"Take the grand bedchamber!" Kate announced. "I shall make do with the cozier quarters. I shall have food trays delivered to my room for every meal! I can lounge and nap to my heart's content. This is going to be Heaven, Kitty!"

"Oh, Kate! I could just shake you! How could you? How *could you?*" Kitty could not believe her friend had managed to get her way. "How could you allow them to believe that I was *Lady Catherine?*"

"I *had* to, Kitty. I had to. I told you I am desperate." Kate did not seem the least bit sorry. Did she really not care who she *lied* to … for this was much more than a mere deception.

Kitty closed her eyes and shook her fists. She wanted to scream.

"Please … *please,* Kitty. Do not be angry with me."

"*Angry?* I have no wish to—" she needlessly glanced around before whispering, "*pretend* to be you."

"What will it matter? Nothing, really." Kate shrugged and waved away any concerns Kitty had. "In a fortnight we will be somewhere else, doing something else. Hopefully, I shall have a plan for us by then. I do not know exactly what but it is upper-most on my mind. We cannot return to the Academy and I have no intention of ever stepping foot again in London."

There was a knock at the door announcing the arrival of the luggage, bringing all conversation to an end. Once the footmen left, the unpacking began.

"Like it or not you must keep up appearances. You cannot always remain alone as you would wish." Kitty opened a portmanteau. "We are expected to take tea with Lady James, whether you are *Lady Catherine* or merely her companion."

"I do not mind in the least." Kate set aside the frock she had pulled from her trunk. "I am famished, to be honest. We haven't eaten a thing all day."

"We don't want to be late for tea. Let us freshen up and we shall unpack later."

"Good idea, Kitty." Kate sounded far more anxious to venture below.

"Oh, Kate—" Kitty dreaded interaction with the family. Nothing good could come of this ruse—no matter her friend's intentions, good or ill. "I wish we would have *never* come to Grimshaw Court!"

"I could be very happy here, Uncle," mused Lord Stephen Emerson. "There is nothing better than languishing next to the gently flowing river at Grimshaw Court." He'd abandoned his jacket and waistcoat, opting for shirtsleeves, and stretched his buckskin-clad legs out before him, reclining against the base of a large tree.

"You'd better be doing more than *languishing*, lad." Lord James nodded at his nephew's idle fishing pole. "If you want dinner tonight, you'd better get busy—and mind you don't frighten the fish away."

Stephen's friend, and future vicar, Tobias Drayton had rolled up his shirtsleeves to the elbow and went straight to work, casting his line into the water.

"We'll want plenty so we have something to barter in the village," Lord James reminded them. "Fish is a precious commodity if it's *fresh*. We'll be able to come away with some red meat."

"A man could survive on fish, don't you think, Toby?" Stephen appreciated his friend's efforts toward the goal.

"Fish is versatile and nourishing. It can be prepared in many ways. I have no complaints," Toby replied.

"That may be true—but my uncle's guests may become weary of eating fish day in and day out of their stay."

"A guest that would dare complain about their meal is a guest you wouldn't want to return," Toby remarked.

"Easier said than done, I'm afraid." Uncle James kept his eyes on his fishing pole and the tension of his line. "Seems we have all sorts of relations dropping in on us." He laughed in good humor, knowing that Stephen was exactly the person to whom he referred. "Food ain't free, lad … whether you pay coin or hunt for it yourself, some effort must be made."

"You aren't serious about that are you, Uncle?"

"I live here on your father's, my elder brother's, largess but he don't feed me … that I must do on my own. I need to keep good relations with the tenants, make sure they're happy … and sometimes I barter for goods. It's all work one way or t' other."

"It looks as if you avoid one dire situation only to become embroiled in another," Toby teased his friend. "You can hardly claim that *this* is not preferable to side-stepping the many snares your mother's laid out for you at Woodley Towers."

"Oh, good Lord, no … *that* is a far more dire situation …" Stephen sighed before continuing, "She has done her utmost to relocate those I most wished to avoid from London to The Towers for a country house party—lasting a fortnight. We managed to escape, Toby, thanks to Lord James, here. Why does she wish to torture me?"

"I do not believe it is *torture* she is inflicting on you … it is her fervent wish that you marry," his uncle said.

"Why should I marry? There is no need for me to provide an heir … that's Greg's onerous task, he's in line to inherit, not I. Nor would I wish to."

"True, she's already got him wed … but you're still next in line … it only goes to figure. Until your brother fills his nursery, Lady Woodley will not rest."

"I'm certain Greg will not disappoint. This time next year he'll have pushed me down the inheritance line. I'll never have a chance to inherit the title nor make Woodley Towers my home."

"I can see you're broken up about that." Toby chuckled, recasting his line.

"You laugh now, Toby, but what of my future? Where shall I live?" It wasn't a concern Stephen took seriously, after all, he was not even twenty, and life after University was quite a ways off … why did he need to worry about it now?

"I'll request that Grimshaw be left to you, what do you say?" Lord James proposed.

"What's that?" Stephen wasn't certain he heard what he thought he'd heard. He sat up a bit, resting his elbows on his knees.

"Your father is the one who bought the property … I only have use of it. Why could it not be for your use as well?"

"What about *your* family?" Stephen could not take away his uncle's home. "Do they not need to be provided for?"

"*Girls*! I have only daughters—they'll all marry in time and fly the nest. Grimshaw will still be standing—vacant, most probably. Someone should live here."

"AH!" Toby's pole bent, its tip arcing downward, and he turned the reel, wrestling the fish to shore. There was a flash of silver of its side as it wriggled and trashed, fighting to escape. Toby was then confident to announce. "Got one!"

Stephen hoped it was a *fine* catch and could be traded for either mutton or several good-sized fowl. That would be a nice meal at the dinner table this evening.

Toby landed the water-borne animal onto the grassy riverbank where Lord James quickly approached to subdue the catch with the net.

"Well done, Mr. Drayton!"

"Thank you, sir." Toby appeared quite pleased with himself. Fishing was relatively new to his city-raised friend and his enthusiasm was second to none. Stephen could see he was taking to it … well … like a *fish takes to water.*

"There will be no white soup for us tonight," Lord James announced, approving of the catch.

"I thought the white soup last night was splendid." Toby would never complain … about anything … ever … it was not in his nature. He was a truly kind, grateful man, and a most faithful friend.

"Along with the brace of fowl it was fine," Stephen added. He admitted that he could never be as kind or as grateful. Growing up privileged had made him a bit more self-indulgent and entitled than the rest.

"Well … last night was the last of the fish—bartered half my catch from the day before when I learned you and Mr. Drayton were to stay with us."

"I hate to be a burden on you, Uncle."

"You need to put some effort in, Nephew. Lend a hand," Lord James urged. "If Grimshaw Court is to be yours someday, you need to learn how to run an estate. It is not simply strolling the grounds and fishing all day. There's more to do here than meets the eye."

"What is it you're saying, sir?"

"What I'm saying, *boy*, is that there is much more to taking part in living in a grand house besides the care of the house, the surrounding land, and the estate itself. There are those around you and your household that you need to think about—there's the farmers, the millers, all those in the village."

"Seems like *work*." It was all sounding a bit scary.

"It might be just that. If you wish to eat tonight you'd best take up your pole and employ it with some purpose!"

"I cannot see a better purpose than wishing to eat tonight!" Stephen confessed. Collecting his long, wooden fishing pole next to him as he got to his feet. He walked a ways down the bank to a calm, dark-colored area where he'd always had good luck.

He glanced over his shoulder at his uncle nurturing Toby's interest as he had Stephen when he was younger. Sure ... that's how it all started ... take a lad's curiosity and give him a few pointers and then foist the responsibility of running the grand house on him. Toby was the lucky one. He could merely enjoy the sport of fishing and eat what he's caught.

Not Stephen. Uncle James might have given him a firm nudge to turn his well-practiced hand to fishing but the next thing he knew, his uncle would be having him pick up a pitchfork and muck out the stables. It seemed there was more to living on the estate than trotting one's horse along the edge of the river to admire the view.

Two

Kitty, followed by Kate, was led by a footman to the drawing room for tea. Approaching the doorway, she spied Lady James inside, speaking quietly with a young lady who moved about, making minute adjustments of throw pillows on the sofas.

"All you need do is be yourself," Kate whispered to her friend. "Your behavior is always above reproach and ladylike, you do not need to do more to prove yourself."

"Thank you, Kate. That is very kind of you to say." Kitty could not help but feel nervous because she was in a house she had never stepped foot in, associating with people she did not know, with an identity that was not her own.

"All *I* need do is remain silent and keep my opinions to myself," Kate announced. She had always been outspoken. Perhaps it was due to her privilege and position that made her so.

"I daresay you have a more onerous task than I," Kitty replied and could not quite bring herself to feel sympathetic.

"Oh, *Kitty*!" Kate groused. "You needn't be rude."

"It just so happens I agree with you." Kitty readied herself and led the way.

They entered the sitting room that was decorated in comfortable soft, pastel colors, much resembling Kitty's bedchamber, instead of the formal, garish interior as some of the houses in London they'd seen in the last few months. That was a style that had, thankfully, not yet spread to the country.

"Do come in, ladies," Lady James greeted them when she noticed their arrival. "Lady Catherine, may I present my daughter, Miss Alicia Emerson."

"How do you do, Miss Emerson?" Kitty had never seen anyone with such red hair—what she would describe as ruby red. It was glorious! The vivid color with the striking green of her eyes were further contrasted by Miss Emerson's flawless, creamy skin. What true beauty she was.

"Alicia, this is Lady Catherine Jessup and her companion Miss Matthews."

The young ladies acknowledged one another with shallow curtsies and softly uttered, *"How do you do?"* to one another all around.

"You are my *cousin* Catherine, are you not?" Miss Emerson smiled and curtsied to Kitty.

"Yes, that's right. I suppose I must be." Kitty returned her smile. She thought carefully before speaking. "Your mother and Lady Bradford are sisters."

"Who is also my Aunt Bradford as well as yours," Miss Emerson amended.

"That would, indeed, make us cousins, Miss Emerson." Kitty had to remember that Kate's relations were now *hers*.

"Then you must not address me as Miss Emerson … do call me Cousin Alicia." The young lady's shy, timid smile had much to recommend her. Any gentleman would be delighted to be its recipient.

"If you wish." But Kitty could not quite bring herself to think of her new acquaintance as *cousin*, she insisted, "Please… I know it is not quite the thing but you must call me *Kitty* for I hardly answer to *Lady Catherine*." Kitty exchanged glances with Lady

James and decided an explanation was needed. "My companion and I have only just recently come from the schoolroom. Well, we are both *Catherine,* you understand, and since our schoolroom days, she has been known by *Kate,* and me as *Kitty.*" Kitty smiled at the ladies. There was no need to change or embellish for it was the truth.

'It is your proper name and you must grow accustomed to answering to it!' Kitty had heard Lady Bradford raise an angry voice to Kate on more than several occasions. Kate tolerated the use of *Lady Catherine* but to Kitty's knowledge, never truly became fond of being called that.

"*Cousin Kitty* it shall be, then." Miss Alicia's bright smile shone in her eyes and they creased at the outer corners.

That wasn't exactly what Kitty had in mind but it was an improvement from being referred to as Lady Catherine.

"Let us be seated, shall we?" Lady James and Miss Alicia sat upon one of the two matching needlepoint-covered sofas while Kitty and Kate made themselves comfortable on the other.

Kate was unusually quiet, blending into the background … as she would want. Kitty knew her friend was there only because her presence was required. Kate would have been satisfied with a lukewarm cup of tea next to her as she hid behind her reading glasses, losing herself in a book, sitting blissfully alone.

"Excuse me for staring but… I find your appearance striking, Cousin Alicia. You are quite beautiful." Never had Kitty seen any young lady with coloring quite like Miss Alicia's—and coming from an all-girls' school that was saying quite a bit. She had seen all sorts of natural beauties.

A flush of color washed onto Miss Alicia's cheeks and she turned away with a shy smile. Either she was tired of hearing the compliment or had never heard such praise, which Kitty could not bring herself to believe. For gentlemen would be bound to say much the same thing for years to come.

"But red hair is so out of fashion, I hear." Lady James sounded as if she were trying not to raise her daughter's expectations.

"I do not believe anyone would think her *ordinary* when they set eyes on such a beauty. She will bring Titian hair quite into fashion again—and there is no artificial method to imitate her appearance." Kitty had never seen anyone with such coloring. How could Miss Alicia not be the envy of all?

"You must not say such things, Cousin." Miss Alicia turned her head, facing away, nearly blushing as deep red as her tresses.

"Will you bring her to Town for a Season?" Kitty could think of no one who could cause a larger sensation. London Society did like to make such a do over the unusual.

"I rather doubt it … you see …" Lady James glanced at her daughter who looked away.

"Can you not appeal to Lady Bradford to help launch her into society?" Kitty thought for certain her own family must come to her aid. "She is your sister and Miss Emerson's aunt."

"Yes, well … she is not *exactly*—how shall I put this …" Lady James paused while lifting the teapot to pour. It also might have been a useful excuse to pause and choose her words carefully so as not to speak ill of her sister.

"Say no more, Lady James, I completely understand," Kitty whispered and there was a very soft comment uttered from Kate that Kitty could not make out, an unflattering assessment of her aunt, most probably. It was clear that they *all* understood.

Miss Alicia passed the filled cups to Kitty and Kate before taking her own.

"You should help yourself to a biscuit." Lady James gestured to the small plate with four treats, identical in size and shape, sitting on a lovely, small floral-gilded plate. The offerings were not plentiful but looked very nice.

Kitty noticed Miss Alicia's delicate fingers were positioned, rather deliberately on her teacup, but there were too many small chips she could not hide. Kitty noted only a bit of wear on the gold gilt on her but nothing significant. They would place their best set before the guests, wouldn't they?

After a day's travel, both she and Kate were peckish. Kitty gave her friend a surreptitious glance before replying, "I thank you but we are used to having only tea in the afternoon." She smiled and lifted her saucer. Kate mimicked the motion and did not indicate anything to the contrary.

Knowing the tea table set before her meant something but she was yet unsure of its full meaning, Kitty sipped from her cup and stilled … something was amiss here.

"What of your other children, Lady James?" Kitty knew there were younger daughters.

"Cindy, Sandy, and Candy," Miss Alicia spouted gleefully. "They also have hair of various hues of red."

"Red hair runs in my family," said Lady James whose auburn-colored curls peeked out from under her lace cap, framing her face. "Cynthia will soon be sixteen, Sandra, twelve and Candice, eight."

"Candy only has a hint of red in hers … my hair was the very same when I was at that age."

"As all the females in the family, our hair usually darkens with age," Lady James smiled when she informed the guests. She must have been very proud to pass on such a delightful trait.

Kitty thought how pleasant it would be to see the four together … and who knows, perhaps there may come a time during her stay when that would happen.

"I understand that you've just finished attending your first Season." Lady James had gently yet skillfully altered the topic from her family to Kitty … or should she say, *Lady Catherine*.

First and only Season, Kitty imagined. Kate would not be returning for a second if she had her way.

"You have just had your Come Out … how did you find London? Did you enjoy yourself? Did you find any particular gentleman who interested you? More than one perhaps?"

"I'm afraid city life is not for me. There are too many people about for me to really feel comfortable."

"I know exactly what you mean," Lady James mused, sipping from her cup. "One becomes lost amid the sea of souls." After taking the time to compose herself she continued, "Lady Bradford asked that she be allowed to send you to us here at Grimshaw Court but did not exactly elaborate on the reason why—and she did not so much *ask* but *inform* me that it was her wish to do so. Knowing my sister, I believe she might have been somewhat *annoyed? Put out?* Can you shed some light on what exactly has transpired?"

"Did Lady Bradford not tell you?" Kitty did not wish to speak out of place because it was not her story to tell, it was Kate's.

"No, she did not," Lady James replied with an arch of her brow. "I am finding you all that is kind and amiable. I cannot conceive of what you might have done to be at odds with my sister. I must confess one does not need to do much to be in her black books."

"How kind of you to say." This was an area that Kitty best not be creative. The truth she was told by Kate might have been a different truth Lady Bradford recalled. It was best Kitty keep quiet about it.

She was not *Lady Catherine* then and those actions during the London Season belonged to Kate. A quick glance at her friend told Kitty that since it was *she* who had assumed the role and currently inhabited *her ladyship's* shoes, it was at her discretion what could be relayed to their company.

"I expect you understand why I might hesitate to approach her about Alicia," Lady James commented.

"I believe we all have the measure of Lady Bradford, do we not?" Kitty said amicably and around her the nods among the quartet said that everyone was in agreement.

Again … they *all* understood.

"Lord Bradford was kind enough to ensure our safe passage to

Grimshaw Court," Kitty began. They were here now because of a quarrel between Kate and Lady Bradford but they could not remain here forever. "You wouldn't happen to know when he plans to send his coaches to retrieve us?"

"I beg your pardon … but she did not say." What was not said relayed more than her answer itself. Perhaps the elder sister might have not harbored warm feelings for the younger.

"We will be here as long as that, will we?" The idea was terrifying. Kitty dare not turn and look at Kate. Kitty felt quite *abandoned*. She could not imagine what her friend must have felt. The only home Kitty and Kate ever knew was the boarding school and they had left that months ago, knowing they could not return.

"Certainly, we can accommodate you for as long as your stay may be," Lady James told her—them. "We should be delighted to have just us ladies about … as it should be *us* most of the time. I don't expect you would see much of the gentlemen about."

"Gentlemen? What gentlemen?" Kitty did her very best not to react outwardly but could not help but steal a glance at Kate whose dearest wish was, especially after her failed Season, to remain as far from the opposite sex as possible.

Lady Bradford could not have been so underhanded as to send her niece to Grimshaw Court only to trap Kate into some kind of marriage by isolating her with *another* young man.

"Not that Lady Bradford would have told me of any other visitors who might reside at Grimshaw Court but …" Kitty had hoped she could learn more of these *gentlemen* with whom she would soon become acquainted—rather, foisted upon her. "It is only that… I had not expected …"

"Nor did I," Lady James confessed. "My sister could not have known. Lord James' favorite nephew, Lord Stephen, and his friend arrived on our doorstep only two days ago—now we have four guests staying with us."

"I hope our visit is not inconvenient." Kitty suddenly realized what had been bothering her—the meager offering of edibles, the worn and slightly damaged porcelain tea set, and the less than exemplary quality of tea served came to her—although connected to aristocrats of some means, the Emersons were not well off and no matter what Lady James said, she could not turn her sister's niece away any more than she could turn away Lord James' nephew.

"It was quite unexpected. They arrived unannounced, you see," Miss Alicia declared with discomfort.

"Your visit we had planned for, theirs—well, it is not the thing to speak of it in such harsh terms, really. It does sound so very *unfeeling* but Lord Stephen is family, his friend Mr. Drayton is not."

"True. Mother, but you cannot mean to say our cousin Stephen, or his friend, is not welcome."

"Well, of course, they are welcome, Alicia." Lady James stated in all kindness. "I only mean that their unscheduled visit has set us all to sixes and sevens. Do not worry yourself, my dears, you know how it is ... we hardly see the gentlemen ... and they spend the majority of their time with Lord James."

"Are they schoolboys?" —and needed to be supervised? Kitty's curiosity was piqued by discussion of the other two guests.

"Heaven's no ... unless you consider Oxford a school for *boys*." Miss Alicia giggled. Her humorous quip made her cheeks flush a most becoming shade of pink.

"You will meet them this evening before dinner, I expect." Lady James glanced off to the side where one of the housemaids stood in the doorway.

"I beg your pardon, my lady." The housemaid bobbed a curtsey.

"I believe I am needed" —Lady James set her cup on the low table before her— "If you will excuse me. Alicia, do entertain our guests."

"Yes, Mama." The three watched Lady James quit the room, following behind a housemaid.

"Now that Mama has left and I see we have finished with our tea," Miss Alicia set her teacup upon the low table. "Shall we stroll in the back gardens?"

"I think that would be lovely!" Kate voiced without any other encouragement. Kitty knew that there was nothing better than a sturdy walk outdoors for her friend.

"Very well, then." Miss Alicia stood and straightened her skirts while she waited for the other two to join her. They walked toward the back of the house and then through the door to the … oh, my … this was not at all what Kate had expected.

"It is our habit to stroll out in the back garden after our evening meal, if weather permits." Miss Alicia stepped through the back door with Kate and Kitty close behind. "Although there isn't much of a garden *per se*, much of the land behind the house is rather unkempt …"

Instead of a neat and tidy terrace and gardens with sculpted greenery and well-tended walkways, the steps from the house led to a disorganized mound of weeds and brambles of vines that stretched out from behind the house. Upon careful inspection, there was a path … a dirt path, not lined or paved, that meandered from the terrace.

"There is a picturesque trail that we keep trimmed. It meanders out from the terrace, around the tall shrubbery, around the old oak tree, and back toward the stone folly."

"You have a folly?" Kate enjoyed a nice ruin. It held secrets, mysteries but not true nor very serious ones for a folly was a *false*, decorative building, not an ancient structure that had fallen into ruin with real ghosts.

"Yes, there is a lovely folly … although we do not usually venture out that far … it is quite a ways away."

"Perhaps we can look forward to visiting *later*," Kitty said, encouragingly.

"Yes, we can plan an outing. I admit that the garden is a bit of a tangle," Miss Alicia confessed, perhaps a bit shy and embarrassed about its condition. "But we think of it as our *jungle*."

It did look like some sort of a jungle, Kate had to admit. It might be a bit frightening if there were not enough light to see where one could take their next step. With the late summer sun still riding high in the sky, that would not be considered any kind of threat. She was certain that Miss Alicia would not think it so because she was familiar with the path.

Miss Alicia braved the way, she stepped forward first. "Come now, it's perfectly safe."

"*Safe*... I'm certain it is," Kitty, the more timid, uttered, yet hesitated to move forward.

"Oh, go on," Kate urged and touched more than prodded Kitty's shoulder, teasing her with, "Are you certain there are no tigers or lions out here?"

"*Tigers*?" Miss Alicia giggled. "Heavens no!"

Kitty laughed at the jest but kept up with Miss Alicia. Kate was certain her friend was not about to let down her guard on the off-chance there should be some fierce wildlife about.

They walked along for some minutes while Miss Alicia provided narration for their journey. She told of how she and her sisters played and made up stories in their wilderness. Cindy's tales were of wild horses that galloped through the long grasses, Sandy's were of monkeys swinging through the trees, and Candy was frightened of all things ... real or imaginary.

"See there" —Miss Alicia pointed up toward the house— "That is the nursery window, the large one, on the left is the children's library."

"Your sisters have their very own library?" Kate thought that was the most wonderful thing for children to have as many books as they could ever wish to read. How lucky her sisters must be!

The three walked on for a few minutes more. Miss Alicia pointed out items of interest to Kitty, Kate did not pay much attention to the whispered stories and lagged farther and farther behind.

"And in that direction" —Miss Alicia pointed away from the house— "There is a rotunda ... or rather ... our folly."

"Where is it?" Kate rushed forward. She ventured out a few steps ahead of Miss Alicia and stood on her tiptoes to catch a glimpse of it herself.

"It's just there—do you see?" Miss Alicia took a few more steps to the left and pointed. "Off to the right ... the area around it has been kept clear just so we may gaze upon it from the end of our walk."

"*Gaze upon it?* Can we not go see it for ourselves?" Kate was quite eager to investigate, no matter how large or small it was.

"Oh, no. As I said, it is much too far to walk there. It does take quite some time ... although it does appear closer."

"Oh, that is disappointing." Kate had hoped to see it today ... or get a closer look at least.

"I cannot imagine starting a journey only to fall short to reach the destination. It is tempting but I can see how it would be a horrid disappointment if we fail." Kitty might have been of two minds about it. However, Kate took this as a cautionary warning from her friend to her. "To undertake a long trek by foot would not be what I wish after our journey from London."

"It truly is not advisable to attempt such a thing now. It is best if we make plans and leave very early in the morning." Miss Alicia was the voice of reason that Kate did not wish to hear. "We should also invite my sisters. They have not been there in a very long time. Perhaps we should plan a picnic!"

"I think that would be lovely!" Kitty had been convinced they should wait. "It will give us a chance to become acquainted with your siblings."

"Exactly," Miss Alicia continued and appeared gratified that her suggestion had been well accepted. "I know they would wish to meet the two of you. We have so few visitors and fewer still are appropriate company."

The three set off again. The decision—*all* the decisions were out of Kate's hand. She simply followed where she was led. Again she lagged with growing disinterest. She caught a word here and a word there. At the moment, Miss Alicia chatted about her *Cousin Stephen* to Kitty who would naturally fill Kate in on the important details at some later time. The topic of *the gentlemen* was not of primary interest.

There was a slight rise in the landscape and soon the old oak tree with its weathered wooden bench wrapped around its trunk came into sight. From what she understood it was the halfway point. To *sit* there—even *worse*—to have to *stand* idle next to the bench as the others sat, passing time would be unbearable for Kate. She could not remain still, she must have something or other to occupy her.

Kate's attention was immediately drawn off to her left. *Oh, look there!* She wasn't certain what she saw out of the corner of her eye. It was something colorful that flew by and disappeared into the fork of a tree standing quite near to the house. This diversion she would use to her advantage.

"I beg you excuse me, ladies. I should return to the house to unpack before the wrinkles in our clothing are firmly set." No doubt Kitty would have seen through that bouncer for what did Kate know of *wrinkles*? "I will retrace our steps and return to the house. Thank you for your hospitality, Miss Alicia."

"Don't mind Kate," Kitty said to Miss Alicia as the two watched Kate leave. "I'm certain she's seen a butterfly flutter by or some such that has distracted her."

Or some such… Kate gave the two not another thought as she jogged back to the house, happy to abandon them.

After a very successful morning's fishing expedition on the riverbank in the upper meadow, Stephen had washed up, changed his clothing, and retreated into his uncle's library. Uncle James had inhabited the cavernous room but did not take full advantage of the space it offered, ignoring most of the vast area.

Lord James had never paid any interest in the books that inhabited the house before he lived there. All that interested him was the desk and a few shelves—the ones within arm's reach for he was not about to leave his chair to retrieve anything farther away. The rest—floor-to-ceiling bookshelves that covered the remaining walls he had left untouched since moving into the house some decades ago. Stephen was the only person, that he knew, who had delved into the books that lay beyond his uncle's domain.

What Stephen searched for now was one of his favorite stories. It came in two volumes and so far they were not to be found. He expected they would be sitting together on some high shelf and imagined them to be easily found. It was not so and, as he recalled, it had been some time since he'd seen the two volumes.

Still, he was here now and he had the time to start with one bookcase and methodically work his way, shelf by shelf then move on to the next, and eventually, he would find them, for they could not have strayed far. Perhaps along the way, he would find something to interest him, he always had. There were a few places he had favored for a hiding spot, and he would begin his search there.

Stephen pulled the library ladder from where it rested, at the farthest point of the north wall, then pushed it to the other end of the wall. With its inability to move freely, he could tell it had *not* been moved in a very long time. It could do with a bit of oil on the wheels and the rails. When he had the ladder in the right place … where he *thought* was the correct spot—or one of them, Stephen stepped on the first rung.

It seemed to hold him well enough. He pushed off the floor

and placed his foot on the next. It creaked with his added bulk accrued over the years from youth to adult. The ladder was old and it was probably only complaining, not truly decayed enough to break under his six-foot frame.

He stepped up and up and up, only glancing to the floor in cursory consideration of the damage that might occur should he fall. Stephen reached the third shelf from the ceiling, because his six-year-old self had decided that no one would climb beyond this great height and here his books would be safe.

Stephen took his time. He had not meant to read each and every spine. However, he hadn't planned to come all this way just to miss a title because of his carelessness. He came across many books about traveling—through the Continent—and several others on the same topic—travels to the Orient—another about travels to the west. He stacked one book on the other along one arm, pulling those from this current shelf, and holding several in his hand from previous shelves.

There were far too many books he found interesting and looked promising to read. Standing on the ladder was precarious enough without the complication of balancing the armful of accumulated books. He'd best set them aside before some sort of mishap occurred. Holding the small pile firmly to his chest, Stephen readied himself for the journey down. The door, that he had not completely closed when he entered, burst open.

"Stephen! *Stephen*?"

The disruption broke Stephen's concentration, sending the books from his arm into the air and sent them flying and upon the unsuspecting visitor who'd entered.

"*Oi!* What's—" Toby cried out, fending off the rain of books from above and he lifted his arms over his head for protection.

"Sorry... Sorry... Toby, you startled me." Stephen realized that his friend's outburst meant he was unharmed, but the condition of the books ... they may not have fared as well. How many old, brittle spines had been broken?

"Where are you?" Toby bent to retrieve the fallen items.

"Up here." Stephen, who managed to hold on to only one tome, descended from the ladder.

"What are you doing up *there*?"

"Looking for some books. What is it?" Even from his elevated distance, Stephen could see Toby was bothered. Abandoning his search, Stephen finally stepped onto the carpet.

"*They're* here. Lord James says—"

"Who's here?"

"The *girls* ... no, they're not girls ... t—they're women," Toby stuttered "... they're *ladies*."

"*Ladies?* Females?" It came as a shock to Stephen. "Not sent from Woodley Towers? Do you mean my mother has impressed upon my uncle to—"

"No, Lord James has nothing to do with it—it's your aunt Lady James ... it's her niece, or some such, who's come." Toby moved about, continuing to retrieve the books from the floor.

"I wouldn't have thought Lord James would scheme behind my back." Stephen felt almost betrayed at the thought that his favorite uncle would turn against him.

"Lord James scratched his head and mumbled *summin'* about not knowing anything about *other* guests. Lady James was quite cross with him and she said he had attics to let."

"So where are the female guests? Are they here now?" Stephen wasn't particularly interested in making their acquaintance, he only wanted to make certain he did not run into them.

"They arrived while we were out this morning." Toby had gathered the books into a tidy pile. "I don't expect we'll need to see them much ... mealtimes and such ..."

"It almost makes me want to take my dinner on a tray in my rooms." Stephen expected contact with them might be neglectable.

"No need for that." Toby was attempting to assert a calming influence over him. "I don't expect they'll put you off your food."

"How many arrived exactly?"

"It's some relative of Lady James ... her sister's niece? And a maid? Abigail? Chaperone?" Toby squinted, trying to recall. "Couldn't be five of them, I don't think. We shan't see any of her servants at any rate, I expect."

"True." Stephen motioned to the books. "Here, let's have those."

"What are all these?" Toby handed the lot over to him.

"Just some titles that looked interesting." Stephen glanced about and added, "You might want to have a look. I'll wager there is nothing new but still something of interest. You can make some rare finds in this old place."

"Very well." Toby nodded, glancing around taking in the sight of the volumes around him. "I shall do so."

"If I had wished for female company, Toby, I would have remained at Woodley Towers." Stephen shook his head. He had believed that he had found the perfect escape from the parson's mousetrap. "My mother made certain every acquaintance of mine, those whom she approved of, mind, would be in attendance—that's why we left London in the first place, or have you forgotten?"

"That's right ..." Toby shook his head. "I have forgotten. What will you do ... now ... here?"

"If it is only a few females ... and by the sounds of it that there is only one lady among them. Male and female pastimes are so varied. I cannot see that our paths will cross ... except at meal-times, of course." Stephen exhaled heavily, realizing the news was nothing to concern him. "You've nearly given me an apoplexy."

"I do beg your pardon, Stephen. I did not mean to do so."

Stephen clapped a hand on his friend's shoulder and smiled. "No, you wouldn't. You haven't a malicious bone in your body."

Toby smiled. "You're very kind to say so."

"I expect the new visitor will make very good company for

Cousin Alicia. Unless you would care to step in, perhaps. Do you fancy her?" He waggled his eyebrows.

"NO! Oh, no!" Toby recoiled. "She *is* pretty ... very lovely ... *most striking* but I believe women with red hair to be most temperamental. In any case, she is not for me."

"Really?" This was something Stephen did not know about his friend.

"Oh, yes. I believe they are far too spirited for my tastes. Haven't you noticed?"

"No, I can't say I have." Stephen could honestly say he could not think of one red-headed female who was inordinately quick to anger than any other of their sex.

"I share your feelings regarding marriage—I am not looking for a wife."

"Good man," Stephen congratulated his friend. "Now that I've found several books to enjoy, I plan to take in the solitude of the morning room, or the sunshine outside, or claim an armchair in this peaceful library in the evenings."

"Sounds like a most agreeable plan."

"I would share my company with you if you'd like."

"Perhaps later, eh?"

"Have no worries, my friend." Stephen set his small stack of books on a table where he would, at his leisure, browse through them. "I have every confidence we can peacefully coexist with the ladies at Grimshaw Court. With the exception of coffee in the morning and dinners in the evening, they will have their distinct areas of occupation and we have ours during the daylight hours, where I expect never our two groups shall meet."

Three

After making a successful escape, Kate felt quite pleased with herself. Kitty and Miss Alicia would spend a pleasant few hours strolling, chatting, and whatever else they might choose to occupy their time together. Kate continued to Kitty's bedchamber, just as she had promised, but she ducked into her own little room first. She tied on her apron, and collected her pencil and sketch pad before making her way to the upper floor.

Where had that flash of color she's seen that flew by her disappear to? She believed it was into the tree next to the house. She also thought she might be able to see the fork in the tree from above.

Kate wanted a vantage point that was high—one of the windows that Miss Alicia might do. The nursery, schoolroom, or the *children's library*—that was a room Kate dearly wished to see. Stepping onto the third floor landing, she glanced about looking for anyone who might object to her presence. She saw no one. Walking softly from the staircase, she continued down the corridor in the direction of the rooms on the south side of the building.

Glancing into the first room with the open door, she spied

three desks in a line. Opposite the desks was a long table. Kate knew a schoolroom when she saw one. Peeking inside the next room, Kate saw that it held short, child-height bookcases along two walls.

This must be the library. Kate stepped inside and walked to the window. There, to her left in the distance was the distinct dome of the rotunda. It looked very grand from this perspective, but wasn't that a function of a folly? Something ornamental and a bit unexpected?

Out of the corner of her eye, Kate spotted movement. The darting of a bird—that splash of red she had seen earlier. This time it had flown *from* the tree and not toward it. She moved to the right side of the window and stared, trying to discern whether this bird had a nest tucked into a crevice. In a small recess she saw it—the rounded shapes and cream-ivory coloring of two, three, maybe four eggs. She'd need her spyglass for a closer view of the exact number of eggs and finer details of the nest to do a proper sketch.

Kate spent the remainder of her time in the library glancing from the rotunda on her left to observe the nest, waiting for the bird's return. Farther on the ground level, she spotted the garden path stretching from the back terrace. All were visible from this vantage point. She needed to keep watch for signs of Kitty and Miss Alicia's return to the house.

Glancing about the room, Kate allowed her gaze to roam one of the bookshelves. She noticed a familiar title on the spine of a book: *Goody Two-Shoes.* How it brought back fond memories of the first time she'd come across that story! She did not even think twice before removing it and reading the first page, which led to reading the second and the third … then the next, and the next. Before she knew it Kate had finished the entire book.

Well … it wasn't very long and, to be honest, it was a chil-dren's book. She returned it to its place. How many of these books had she already read? What would the Emerson children think if they knew a stranger had helped themselves to their literary treasures?

Kate had never owned more than a few books at a time. She'd limited herself to only two—one, the current book she was reading and the other, what she would read next. It was difficult to part with the books once she'd reached the end of the story. Once she had finished with the first, it would be left behind or given away. Kate had nowhere to keep them.

Kitty, on the other hand, preferred poetry. She carried with her three books at a time. She kept one book, her *favorite*, while the other was the current book she enjoyed, and reserved the third for the future. Although a slimmer volume one could easily consume in a short period, Kitty would take her time, reread, and ponder the writings.

Kate preferred long, epic tales—ones with adventure and of exotic, far away places. They were worlds that she could only dream of visiting. It had taken her years to travel from London to Sussex and back to London. There was no hope that she would ever leave England.

But to have a library such as this—filled with all her books … could be an achievable dream.

She would like to keep them. The idea appealed to her very much. Yes, she wanted that more than anything. Kate hadn't realized it until this very moment.

She would like to live in a house *someday*—a fine house of her own where she would never need to move. It would not need to be grand, something modest with a good-sized library would suit her. It would have many shelves and many books. Kate thought she might have more than enough funds to do so, thanks to her parents. *Someday.*

She would live there and, of course, Kitty would share the dwelling. Kate would fulfill her friend's dearest wish of a pianoforte of her very own in a music room. No more would Kitty need to choose between an extra chemise or another selection of sheet music that would need to be stored at the bottom of her portmanteau.

They would employ a cook, a maid, and a footman … and perhaps a groom for a horse or two. Oh, dear … the household was getting larger by the moment. Society would call Kate a spinster but she would be a happy, wealthy spinster doing whatever she wanted, in the company of her best friend where they could read, talk, and laugh together.

First, she needed to get through this visit with the Emersons and then, Kate expected, there would be at least another round with Lord and Lady Bradford—clashing over their expectations for her versus what she wished to do. She had no intention of allowing herself to be subjected to a repeat of the matchmaking schemes of this last summer. When, she wondered, would they leave her be and allow her to run her life the way she wished to?

Gad… Kate hoped she wouldn't need to wait until she reached the ripe old age of thirty. This was when she made up her mind that it would not be so. Kate fully intended to take charge of her own life. As it was now, she could not take any actions … but she was determined that she would make her own decisions about her future.

After their stroll, Miss Alicia very graciously led Kitty through the main floor: the withdrawing room through the long gallery to the morning room, which apparently was not the normal route. The more time Kitty spent with her, the more agreeable and good-natured the red-haired young lady appeared to be. Kitty thought it was too bad that the delightful Miss Alicia would not have her chance in London. She was more convinced than ever that her new friend would make a tremendous society splash if given the chance.

"Goodness—a *grand* pianoforte!" Kitty could not restrain herself and immediately moved to the instrument upon entering the music room. "How very lovely it is." It felt as if it had been a very long time since she had been able to touch a pianoforte such as this and she gratefully allowed her hands to rest upon the solid wood lid.

"It was here when we came to the house," Miss Alicia replied.

There had been a square pianoforte at Bradford House in London. Kitty could only gaze at it longingly from a distance. She had no knowledge if anyone ever played for she never heard the tremor of a single note much less an entire chord during the time she resided there.

"*This* is truly magnificent."

"Mama has it tuned every now and again in hopes that I will play," Miss Alicia sadly confessed.

"Do you play now? How much do you practice?" Kitty was very much interested. It was her notion that the repetition of finger movements was key to precise playing. It had been forever since she'd played. At the Academy, she had practiced for hours and hours every day in between lessons and in her free time.

"I'm not very good. I have had some lessons when I was young, years ago. I really can't ..." Alicia glanced at Kitty with her wide, green eyes. "Can you play?"

"Playing the pianoforte is my greatest joy." It was not so of the real *Lady Catherine* but the words came spilling out of Kitty. "I haven't had a chance to sit at the keyboard for months."

"You should perform for us ... all of us. Mama will be thrilled when she learns of it. I cannot wait to tell her."

"I would like to practice first." Kitty could not imagine anyone would wish to hear her when she had not touched the keys for so long. "As I said, it has been quite some time."

"Feel free to play when you wish," Miss Alicia encouraged her. "I expect you will have plenty of time on your hands during your stay."

"Thank you, Miss Alicia, I shall." That was the most joyous thing Kitty had heard in … a very long time. This was certainly one of the benefits of taking on the role of Lady Catherine.

At the end of their leisurely tour, Miss Alicia suggested they part to begin their evening's toilette. Kitty returned to her bedchamber and, as Kate was not truly an abigail, Kitty need not wait before beginning her own preparations to dress and style her hair for dinner.

It was fortunate that her wardrobe was near-equal to Kate's. At her insistence, and expense, she wished that her friend enjoyed the very same luxuries she had herself. Kitty could not have been more prepared to step into Lady Catherine's shoes.

Kitty and Kate met during their first year at Miss Maddingly's Academy. Kate had lost both parents when very young and knew nothing of them. In contrast, Catherine Matthews was orphaned in her fifth year while attending school and had been left with no relatives and without a penny.

The headmistress allowed her to remain, taking on chores and tending to the other students in the capacity as maid. Kitty helped the other girls dress and braid their hair besides tutoring the younger girls in music. It was Kitty's exceptional talent that allowed her to continue her studies.

Near the end of her last term, Kate's aunt and uncle, Lord and Lady Bradford, recalled her to prepare her for the London Season, when she was ready to leave the schoolroom. They left the task of informing Kate of her title and position to Miss Maddingly. That was when Kate learned that she was *Lady Catherine Jessup* and not *plain* Miss Jessup. Not an onerous task by any means, and Kate had been informed that she was better than well-to-do but quite a wealthy young lady. The news had come as a shock.

Kitty thought back to those few days, right at the end of school, it seemed as if it had happened so long ago. Kate adjusted swiftly and before her departure, announcing that she would take Kitty into her employ, removing her from the school and bringing her to London as well. Kitty was ever so happy not to have lost her very best friend.

When they had arrived in London before the start of the Season, Lady Bradford discovered: first, that her niece needed a full wardrobe now that she had come to Town, and second, that Kate had brought with her a *companion*. Kitty, who had been raised alongside Kate at the Academy, was far more knowledge-able in ladylike accomplishments than employable skills as a maid. She was proficient in plaiting hair and showed minimal skill with a curling iron.

Mrs. Dobson, Lady Bradford's lady's maid, had taken Kitty under her wing—and Kitty had been more than eager to learn. With a bit of instruction, a few lessons on how to care for the mistress' hair, clothing, footwear, hats, bonnets, and assorted accessories, She became quite adept at caring for the new wardrobe she and Kate had acquired. Never did Kitty believe she would be applying her newly learned skills on herself—for she was both the maid *and* the mistress.

This afternoon at Grimshaw Court, Kitty had to make her own decisions. She narrowed her choices to a few dresses for dinner this evening. She felt that somehow her actions, as Lady Cather-ine, reflected upon Kate. If—*when* the story of Lady Catherine's stay was relayed to Lady Bradford, and Kitty could almost guar-antee that it would, she wanted Lady James to honestly tell her sister that Lady Catherine had been a most considerate and splendid guest.

After spending some time with Miss Alicia this afternoon, Kitty was of the opinion that the Emerson household was not as well-off as they might lead visitors to believe. As such, she had no wish to display any ostentatious tendencies.

Kitty had already curled and pinned up her hair to cool while she considered what she should wear for dinner. She stared at her two choices, either would suit, but one did not have a second chance to make a first impression.

How she wished Kate was here to help her to choose. Kate was so much better at this sort of thing.

What to do? What to do?

A hasty knock at the door was followed by an immediate entrance.

"Oh—you are already here!" Kate declared and swung into the room and peered into the open clothespress, being nosy. "And you have already unpacked and arranged it all just so."

"Someone had to unpack our clothing."

"And you are so much more accomplished at the task than I," Kate said with a nod.

"What constructive activity did you occupy yourself with after you excused yourself and left me with Miss Alicia?"

"I returned to the house, collected my sketchbook, and ventured to the upper floors to see if there was a better vantage point to see the folly."

"And did you find that view?"

"Yes, I did." Kate pulled her sketchpad from under her arm and turned to the page where she'd drawn the rotunda.

"It's not much different than what we saw from the path." Kitty studied the illustration.

"No," Kate admitted, not too disappointed in her effort. "But there will be more detail when I am allowed to inspect it further."

"That will give you something to look forward to." Kitty motioned Kate closer. "Would you give me a hand? I need help to fasten my gown and—"

"It will be just as it was at school … you fasten my gown and I fasten yours." The reminder of happier days during their childhood brought a smile to Kate's lips.

"And my hair?" Kitty returned the smile but she appeared skeptical.

"You dress my hair—" Kate began, "And then you dress *your own hair.*"

"Exactly." Kitty giggled. They both knew that was not where Kate's talent lay.

"Well, I wish you to look your best and if I styled your hair you would not."

"I could not agree more."

"I will, however, brush the back and help by putting it up. It would be quite presentable and you may do the front." Kate set aside her sketchpad and motioned Kitty to the dressing table. "Do sit and you can tell me all the interesting bits Miss Alicia said after I left."

"Do you mean after you *abandoned* us?" Kitty settled herself at the dressing table.

"I'm sorry I left you with Miss Alicia, Kitty." Kate felt a bit self-conscious about her poor behavior and, as ever, her friend was so very tolerant. She did know better than to behave in that manner and in the future she would need to improve... Kate would try. "I was growing bored strolling aimlessly about. I needed something to do."

"No apology necessary, Kate. I know how taxing it is for you." Kitty was beginning to feel sorry for her friend. "Perhaps I have been a bit harsh—I'm not condoning your actions—exchanging places is not right at all ... quite *dishonest* actually."

"I understand ... and I agree, but ... I did warn you, I was feeling desperate."

"It is of no import. What's done is done." Kitty sat straighter and still for Kate to begin work on her hair. "Miss Alicia says her cousin Lord Stephen Emerson and his friend Mr. Tobias Drayton are the two gentlemen who arrived a few days ago."

"And what of Lord Stephen and Mr. Drayton? Does Miss Alicia think either of them as suitable *parti*?" Kate glanced from her hands, unpinning Kitty's hair, to her reflection in the glass, meeting her gaze.

"I understand that it is acceptable for cousins to marry, but she feels that they are too familiar."

"I see." Kate imagined Miss Alicia considered Lord Stephen almost a sibling, far too close to consider marriage. "And Mr. Drayton? Does Miss Alicia think him agreeable?"

"She thinks him *quiet* and told me he *actually* recoils when he gazes upon her."

"Oh, dear." Kate paused, holding a lock of Kitty's hair in one hand and a brush in the other. "That does not sound at all nice. Poor Alicia."

"No, there will be no match there. I think she is determined to become a spinster."

"But I think she will make some gentleman a delightful wife. She appears neither extravagant nor proud." It was Kate's initial impression of her cousin. She could not say for certain she was correct about her character.

"I agree but how is she to *find* a husband unless one arrives on her doorstep?" Kitty went on to elaborate, softening her voice unnecessarily, and appearing pained as to admit, "I believe they are not very well off."

"But *this house* … the servants …" Kate imagined the size of the dwelling and surrounding estate substantial. "Does this all not belong to them?"

"It is somewhat of a show, I'm afraid. The Emersons do not live in poverty but they make do with the largess from his brother the marquess, which includes this house, and occasional kind offerings from Lady Bradford, though I am less certain what that entails. Lord James is a younger son with no money to speak of and no property."

"I— I do not quite know what to say. Do you believe Lady Bradford is aware of the Emersons' situation? How could she deposit us onto her sister's doorstep with little warning?" Kate would believe it of her aunt. "I do not believe she knows… I don't even think she even cares about her sister's situation."

"Perhaps Lady James feels her sister does enough for her family that Lady Bradford can ask anything she likes. I cannot say." Kitty lowered her gaze, unable to meet Kate's eyes. She must have felt embarrassed to bring up such things, or embarrassed for Lady James and Miss Alicia but continued in a quiet voice, "Did you see the state of the china service this afternoon?"

"The *chipped* set?" Kate had not wished to mention it. "Not our dishes but theirs… Yes, I did."

"And the meager biscuits?" Kitty continued.

"And the disappointing tea?" Kate concluded. "I do not wish to sound ungrateful but it was almost not palatable."

"Yes, well… I did not wish to take food, or tea, out of their mouths." Kitty sounded quite sorry for them.

"It does seem as if they are trying to keep up appearances." They seem to be a very nice family. Kate felt sorry for them as well. As it turned out, both hosts and guests might be employing a bit of deception.

"It does, doesn't it? I should not care to prove them otherwise. They are going along the best they can. Who am I to accuse them of deceit or chicanery? I, who have nothing …" If Kitty went on like this she would soon turn into a watering pot and then her face would grow puffy and her eyes would grow red.

Kate could not see that this would be conducive to an agreeable impression and Kitty needed to stop thinking along those lines at once.

"Lady James has been everything that is kind and we should be on our best behavior and treat her and her family with gratitude," Kate uttered sternly.

"I agree." Kitty looked into the glass, staring at Kate's reflection. "I have no wish to cause her to feel ill at ease."

"Very well, then. What do you think?" Kate had finished with Kitty's hair and moved from her side.

Kitty patted the back of her head, checking the size, shape, and tightness of the bun. "It is very nice. I shall arrange the front after I don my dress." She stood from the dressing table and moved to the bed, staring between the two gowns she'd laid onto the counterpane. "Do you have an opinion on which I should wear this evening?"

"Does it matter?" Kate wondered aloud. "This is precisely why I have no wish to play your part. What a waste of time ... *which dress shall I wear?*"

"Really? I would think you would wish me to give some consideration to my appearance since I am to represent you. Your opinion would be greatly appreciated, Kate."

"Hmmm ... what would *Lady Catherine* care to wear?" Kate moved toward the bed and glanced at the light blue and the rose gowns Kitty had chosen.

"She should like to make a good impression ... without appearing too flamboyant." Kitty voiced her reasoning.

"Never *that*," Kate agreed and laughed.

"I wish to make a good impression ... for *both* our sakes," Kitty added, seemingly quite sincere.

"Are you certain there is not a third choice?" Kate was well-aware that her ... or rather *Kitty's* conduct would be reported to her aunt. And Kitty's behavior was far more acceptable than Kate's, thus the details would be positive.

"Well, of course. I have very many lovely gowns but I thought — What can you mean, Kate?"

"I think perhaps your puce silk or the drab with the spotted overskirt might be a better alternative."

"*Drab?*" Kitty made quite an unpleasant expression ... as if she had bitten into a lemon or some such. Apparently, she did not care for Kate's suggestion. "But that is so dull."

"It is not as if they are *old* ... both are stylish and fit well. Dull might be preferable." *As not to draw attention to one's self.*

"In what way?" Dear Kitty was trying her best to make the most agreeable impression, which a young lady might wish to do ... under normal circumstances.

"The two visiting gentlemen will be attending this evening, will they not?" Kate reached for the hair brush.

"Oh, yes. I nearly forgot." Kitty's eyes widened. "I suppose I shall make their acquaintance when we gather in the front parlor, before dinner. It will not be as comfortable as keeping company with Miss Alicia."

"Did you wish to catch the eye of either gentleman in attendance?"

"Oh, no. Of course not." Kitty was well aware of Kate's predicament over the last several months. She headed to the wardrobe to find a few alternative choices—the silk puce and the beige with the spotted overskirt. They were nowhere as nice as Kitty's selection.

Kitty settled on the puce lest the diaphanous overskirt be construed as *attractive*. Kate finished fastening the back and swung around to look at the overall effect.

"You needn't look at me like that—" Kitty's hands went to the clips on the sides of her head. "I haven't finished my hair yet."

"It's not your hair. It's your… your… You know what you need?" Kate stepped away, leaving Kitty for just a moment, just long enough to collect… "Here. This should do very well." She drew out a necklace made of pinkish-colored matched pearls. In one fluid motion, she unfastened the clasp and drew it around Kitty's neck.

"Kate—" Kitty placed a protective hand to her throat. "These are your mother's."

"And she would be so very glad to see *Lady Catherine* wear them." Kate smiled. "You will make us both proud, Kitty."

The dinner bell sounded and Stephen left his bedchamber on his way down to the front parlor to meet the others. He met Toby in the corridor and the two walked toward the stairs.

"Blasted waistcoat is riding up," Toby grumbled. His steps

were staggered as he reached under his jacket to pull it down in the back. "We wouldn't need to dress so formally for dinner if it weren't for the *new* guests."

"How easily we slide into informality of country life, eh?" Stephen fell into step with his friend ... actually, moved ahead of him during the battle with his clothing. "We've been here less than two days and already you have difficulty donning a pair of breeches?"

"It ain't the breeches I mind ... although I don't recall them fitting as snug." Toby inhaled and ran his hand under the waist-band, around his midsection.

"This cravat feels excessively tight." Stephen pulled at the neckcloth around his throat with two fingers, hoping to stretch it, if only slightly. "And this is completely adjustable, yet I feel as if I am being strangled."

"Had Warren tie it for you, did you?" Toby seemed to have straightened himself out and once again walked unencumbered.

"He is hardly to blame. I should have spoken up before I was robbed of breath." Stephen had the benefit of his uncle's valet services, as did Toby, so neither was about to complain.

"Your fault then ... only yourself to blame," Toby replied.

"Happened so suddenly. Should have been paying attention ... my mind wandered," Stephen replied, making his way down the stairs with his friend not far behind.

"We must do the pretty, Stephen." Toby caught up with him once they reached the main floor and they strolled toward the corridor together.

"I know, but I had my fill of females when we were in Town."

"We need only observe the formalities tonight, then we may be comfortable once again," Toby said reasonably.

"You have the right of it, my friend." Stephen clapped him on the back and did the brave thing by stepping into the parlor first.

There stood his aunt, uncle, and cousin. "Ah, there you are, *gentlemen* ..." Lady James motioned them into the room. "You've arrived before our new guest."

"I was afraid we might be late." Stephen still fidgeted with his neckcloth.

"Father was just telling us about this morning's fishing expedition," Cousin Alicia said brightly. "Twelve trout ... *twelve!*"

"I do not believe they were *all* trout," he corrected his cousin. Stephen could catch fish. He enjoyed fishing but he did not keep account of how many of which type was caught.

"You cannot tell me that your skill is not equal to Lord Stephen's, Mr. Drayton." Lady James' tone was quite complimentary.

"That may well be, my lady, but my friend's enthusiasm for the sport is far greater," Stephen remarked then turned to Lord James. "Aren't you doing it a bit too brown, Uncle?"

"Nonsense! We wouldn't have caught near as many if I had gone by myself," Lord James declared.

Toby's brows lifted in surprise and he whispered to Stephen, "One only has to do the sums."

"Indeed ..." Stephen was not about to argue with either of them and glanced off to the side, turning his head toward the door once he saw *her.* She was dressed in a fashionable but dull-colored frock. Would not something lighter, perhaps *white* be more appropriate?

"Welcome, Lady Catherine—" Lady James smiled and extended her hand to welcome the young lady who approached. "I hope you are finding your accommodations adequate."

"They are quite splendid—beautiful as well as comfortable. Thank you."

"Do allow me to make you known to our other recently arrived guests," Lady James offered.

"It would be a pleasure, Lady James," the young lady replied.

"This is our nephew Lord Stephen Emerson and his friend Mr. Drayton." The two bowed after the introduction. "This is my sister, Lady Bradford's niece, Lady Catherine Jessup. She arrives from Town just this afternoon."

"Lord Stephen, Mr. Drayton," Lady Catherine acknowledged them with a curtsey. "How do you do?"

"Gentlemen" —Lady James motioned to the young lady— "Lady Catherine."

"How do you do, my lady?" Stephen and Toby bowed in unison.

Lady Catherine Jessup. Stephen allowed her name to linger some moments to see if it sounded familiar. He didn't think so. If she were in London for the Season, as was he, it seemed they could have previously met *somewhere*. London Society was not so large, one would have thought... Then again, perhaps not. It may be that they circulated in different circles.

"My goodness, how lovely you look." There was not a detail Lady James overlooked. "Are those—those your mother's pearls?"

"Yes, they belonged to the *previous* Lady Bradford." Lady Catherine touched the necklace at her throat. Her reference also meant that her father, the *previous* earl, was now deceased. How sad for her to be orphaned at such a young age.

"I am quite honored that you should wear them this evening. I know you have little that belonged to her." The catch in her voice told of the lingering sadness she felt for the young lady's loss.

"Yes ... and I am quite fond of these." Kitty touched the pearls at her throat. "I hope they are not too elaborate for this evening and I have not overdressed."

"You look lovely, *Kitty*," Cousin Alicia said to the newcomer.

Kitty? Is that what she was called? Perhaps Stephen thought the earl's daughter might have a more dignified diminutive. And it appeared to Stephen that the two young ladies were already fast friends. But isn't that the way it always was with young ladies?

The butler appeared and announced dinner. Stephen met his

uncle's gaze and stepped to one side, allowing him to escort Lady Catherine.

"Aunt?" Stephen offered his arm to Lady James, who accepted.

"Miss Emerson?" Toby offered his arm to the remaining lady.

The three couples entered the dining room, making dinner a small, cozy affair.

"I see that your companion is not joining us this evening." Lady James gazed around the table with some satisfaction.

"No, Kate is happy to take a tray in her room this evening," Lady Catherine told the hostess. "I believe she did not wish to make an odd number at the table but I'm sure she would have happily dined with us if she were needed."

"Well, there is that. What good sense she has," Lady James replied as the soup was brought out.

"Yes, she is all consideration." Lady Catherine smiled, then reached for her spoon.

Four

After Kitty had left, Kate retrieved her spyglass from her room then collected her sketchpad and pencil before seeking the children's library. The books, although quite a bit young for her, were a great draw but her primary interest was the nest in the tree outside. Had the mother bird returned to her eggs?

Setting the pencil and pad on a nearby table, Kate extended her spyglass to its full length, nearly twice its smaller, compressed, traveling size. She held it up to her eye and focused on the nest ... the eggs in the nest, for the mother bird was not present. The small yet substantial bird's home appeared cozy. There were five eggs in all. Light-colored with tiny, reddish brown flecks. Kate wondered how long they'd been there and when would they hatch?

On the left, a blurred image partially appeared, mostly brown. She could make out the round black of an eye and the surrounding orange of the head. Moving before the lens, then between her vision and the nest, the mother bird looked as though she was checking the condition of her eggs. Now Kate could see that it *was* clearly a robin—the brown body and orange-red of the breast, covering the throat and face.

The mother hopped around before settling on her clutch of eggs.

Kate brought her sketchpad quickly before her and made a rough drawing, catching as many details as she could while Mrs. Robin sat patiently on her eggs. The orange-red feathers of her face surrounded the round, black eye and the small pointed beak. Brown feathers on the top of her head spread down her cheeks toward her back to the long brown tail sticking out behind her.

She would note the colors if she decided to create watercolors later, when she had more time to devote to a more detailed illustration. Kate looked forward to it now that she resided in the grand house in the country. Feeling more hopeful than she had in months, she felt as if there was much to look forward to in the coming days and weeks ahead.

At Grimshaw Court, the ladies did not remove to the drawing room after dinner while the gentlemen remained in the dining room to enjoy their wine. Stephen had learned the normal practice was for Lady James and Cousin Alicia to take the air, strolling down the path from the terrace in the rear gardens. Since arriving, he and Toby joined the ladies, offering their arms.

"I will leave you two gentlemen to escort the young ladies for this evening's promenade." Lady James rose from the table. "I hope you all find that agreeable."

"Delighted, Aunt," Stephen said with a slow nod of his head. "Lady Catherine, would you care to join us?" He thought better of his request and added, "It is a place you would not wish to venture off on your own for it is a *wilderness*."

"*A wilderness!*" Lady Catherine's small mock-gasp of horror was followed by a chuckle. "You make yourself sound positively heroic, Lord Stephen."

"May I escort you for this evening's promenade, Miss Emerson?" Toby's opinion regarding ladies with red hair did not deter him from being a thoughtful guest and doing his due diligence. He pushed away from the table and stepped toward her, holding her chair as she stood.

"I would be delighted to walk with you again, Mr. Drayton," Alicia replied. "Thank you."

A stroll after dinner, while the sun hovered higher than one would wish in the sky, was as worthwhile a diversion before the long hours they would spend indoors once darkness descended.

The four left the dining room, turned into the corridor, and headed to the back of the house. Stepping onto the back terrace, Stephen offered Lady Catherine his arm and they stepped onto the path, beginning their journey.

"The fish was very nice this evening and the meat pie, quite splendid." Lady Catherine's high praise appeared to be genuine and heartfelt. "The blancmange was exceptional."

"Lady James prides herself on their meals. You won't hear complaints from me."

"You must be an excellent house guest, my lord."

"Doesn't one always wish to be?" Stephen pointed at an oversized stone that was dangerously close to the side where she walked. "Do take care that you do not step on that stone and turn your ankle."

"Heavens—I did not see that earlier this afternoon." Lady Catherine drew closer to him, pulling her skirts to one side to avoid the hazard. "I had no idea the dangers of walking two abreast." She flashed him a smile of gratitude.

Stephen had the oddest feeling. If he hadn't known better, he might have thought this was all planned. His mother's wish would have him marry. To have him leg-shackled to Lady James' sister Countess of Bradford's niece, who happened to have a disaster of a first Season, might have worked out just as well for both managing parties. He did not like it. The elements that had brought both him and Lady Catherine to Grimshaw Court ... it seemed too far-fetched ... but was it a coincidence or a carefully laid out plan?

"I hope you are finding Grimshaw Court to your liking," he said to Lady Catherine. "It is a comfortable old pile, and I've spent many hours tucked away in its dim corners, ensconced in chairs, reading, dreaming, just idling away great amounts of time in my youth."

"I have hardly had time to form an opinion, my lord, having only arrived some hours ago," Lady Catherine replied. "I have spent most of my childhood at Miss Maddingly's Academy for Young Ladies until I came to London a few months hence. *Everywhere* seems a bit unsettling for me. I understand that we—*I* am to remain here for some time ... weeks? I dare not think *months*."

"I came here quite unexpectedly—my aunt and uncle had no idea. I believe you had a proper invite."

"I believe my stay here is due to my behavior during the Season." Her stern delivery told of strain and discomfort. It sounded as if neither aunt nor niece found her London stay to be pleasurable.

"Did you not enjoy your Season? Was it not *worthwhile?*" Was Lady Catherine Jessup so disagreeable she could not find a husband? It was Stephen's experience that those who could not find a husband were ... antidotes, those caught up in scandal, and those who did not wish to find a spouse.

"*My* expectations had nothing to do with it. Lady Bradford, however, was not pleased with the outcome."

"You are being rather harsh, don't you think?"

"I have given Lady Bradford a complete disgust of me."

Stephen was curious as to which category applied? The female who could not snare a husband or one who avoided such entrapments? He peered at her as they walked ... she did not appear unattractive nor very old. Her name, as far as he could recall, had not been the Town's *on-dit* during his stay there. Could it be that

she shared his opinion about matrimony? It was of no matter…
Stephen was not searching for a wife. He had no interest in
marriage then, now, or in the foreseeable future.

"I am certain you are mistaken, Lady Catherine …"

"*Please* …" she said in a pleading tone. "You must not call me
'Lady Catherine'… I realize it is not customary to address one
another by one's Christian name on such a short acquaintance but
I am not in the habit to answering to—"

"Oh, Cousin Stephen … you do wish *Kitty* to be comfortable
with us," Alicia said with the most pleading tone.

"I do, certainly." Stephen glanced over his shoulder. The four
came to a stop and turned toward one another to properly
converse.

"She wishes you would call her *Kitty*—it is just as she has
always been addressed," Alicia told him.

Stephen shifted his gaze from his cousin to Lady Catherine
whose woeful expression told him all he needed to know. "Uncus-
tomary as it seems, if I am to refer to you by your schoolroom
name … as is your preference, then I shall do so. Is it permissible
if I address you as Lady *Kitty*?"

"As you wish … but a simple *Kitty* would suffice, thank
you." Lady Cath— Lady *Kitty* went on to explain, "The young
ladies at the Academy were all treated the same, regardless of
our rank. There were so very many *Catherines* in residence. We
all had variations on the name: Cat, Cathy, Kay, I was *Kitty*, and
my friend—eh, my *companion*, is also Catherine and known as
Kate."

"But *Kitty* … not even *Lady* Kitty?" Stephen shook his head in
disbelief. Habits, his as well as hers, would be difficult to amend.
"I hope you will forgive me if I find it difficult to make the
concession."

"That would sound incongruous, do you not agree?" Kitty
insisted. "You cannot expect me to change a habit that was years
in the making."

"Do you hear that, *Toby*? We are to address *Lady Catherine* as *Kitty* from now on."

"Understood, Stephen." Toby nodded and gave *Kitty* an extended bow of his head with an agreeable smile. "It will be as you wish, my lady—*Kitty.*"

"*Toby?*" Alicia repeated, quite taken aback by the escort's moniker, having only been known to her as *Mr. Drayton* ... all this time.

"I daresay my cousin has never heard your Christian name—*Tobias.*" Stephen informed the ladies.

"I believe *your* cousin, Miss Alicia, is attempting to shock us all!" Kitty teased. The pronouncement made Stephen laugh out loud.

"Shall we continue our promenade, ladies?" Stephen suggested, The other three fell into their previous positions, once more, moving forward toward the large oak tree that marked the end of the tamed jungle and the place where they would begin their return.

"What are you doing here?" A small girl dressed in a nightgown stood at the threshold of the children's library. "Are you my cousin Lady Catherine?"

"I am Lady Catherine's ... maid *Kate,*" Kate replied, collapsing the spyglass and sliding it into her pocket, hiding more than just her identity. "And who might you be? I don't think you're supposed to be walking about at this time, are you?"

"I'm supposed to be in bed but I can't sleep ... not with all that talking and laughing coming in through my window." The girl must have decided Kate was not a threat and moved closer.

"You must be one of Miss Alicia's sisters. Are you Cynthia, Sandra, or Candice?"

"I'm Candy!" The girl giggled. *Candice.* She had very light reddish-blonde hair that was plaited, draped over her left shoulder and she ran her fingers through the end. Kate recalled the tale Lady James recounted at tea that afternoon about the hue of her daughters' hair. "What are you doing?"

Candy had her gaze directed at Kate's sketchpad. "I'm drawing Mrs. Robin and her eggs."

"Eggs! Where?" Candy ran past Kate to the window to peer out. "How many are there?" Kate placed her head next to Candy's, guiding her to the secluded location in a whisper.

"You can't see the eggs now because the mother is sitting on them." Kate hadn't received the enthusiastic reply she thought there would be. "Do you see Mrs. Robin?"

"I see her! I see her! *Oh … shhh!*" she hushed herself.

"I saw them earlier … would you care to see my drawing?" Kate turned back to the first sketch she'd made.

"Oh, yes, please." Candy, while watching Kate, also kept an eye on the robin sitting on the nest. "How many eggs did you see?"

"I believe there are five. And here is the one I made of Mrs. Robin earlier."

"Look—you've got her tail just there." Candy pointed at the picture with her chubby finger. "I like her long tail."

"Yes, I do too." Kate smiled at the excitement.

"Will Mrs. Robin fly away when she hears the people on the path under the tree?"

"Are they *that* boisterous?"

"I think they're noisy. Perhaps they will make their way to the folly and not bother walking back to the house." Which was quite wishful thinking on Candy's part.

"Maybe you only wish for them to do so." Kate pointed out. "I've heard it is far away. Much too far to attempt a journey in the evening."

"I suppose. I don't want them to frighten Mrs. Robin," Candy told her. "I've been to the folly lots of times. It *is* far! It takes a long time to walk there. Sometimes we take the pony cart… Well, we take the cart only because we use it to carry the hamper for our picnic."

"A picnic at the folly?" Kate recalled that notion being proposed that very afternoon. "I believe your sister mentioned something about arranging one for us."

"That would be famous! I would talk to her right away about it except—" Candy's eyes grew wide.

"Except?" Kate widened her eyes, wondering what could be the cause for alarm.

"I think Alicia is out there" —Candy softened her voice, as if she might be overheard, and pointed out the window— "And I'm supposed to be in bed."

"There is that …" Kate agreed, somewhat relieved. At least *she* was not the only person who had the potential of stirring up trouble.

"Now that you have learned what has brought me here, my lord, might I inquire the same of you?" Lady—*Kitty*, as she had asked to be addressed, spoke quite directly. "Presumably, you attended the Season for the same reason as I? Yet, you have *escaped* some horror, from my understanding and found a safe haven at Grimshaw Court."

"Well-spotted, my lady." Stephen nodded and could not hold back a smile. She was not one to be underestimated. "I must confess… I believe I share similar sentiments as you regarding the London Season."

He felt her grip on his arm ease as they walked, the smooth, solid ground beneath their feet must have helped her keep her equilibrium. The tall hedge came into sight and just beyond they would be rewarded with the view of the folly.

"Do you not think it was odd that we did not meet in Town?" He still was not completely certain it had not happened.

"Not so odd, I think," Lady Cath—*Kitty* replied. "One thinks of society in London as fairly small but it's not so. How can it be unexpected that we have not shared an acquaintance when, if I am correct in my belief, we have both done our best to shun society?"

"How right you are." Stephen could not find fault with her reasoning.

"However, if we have been introduced, I shall do my utmost to recall when and where we were first acquainted. Is that agreeable to you, my lord?"

"Most agreeable, Lady Kitty." He acknowledged with a slight incline of his head. Stephen had no wish to further tax his memory, feeling quite sure they could not have met previously and he allowed their conversation to lull.

"*Goodness, me*... Is that not an impressive sight?" Toby declared when he caught sight of the folly in the distance.

The stretch of shadow across the grass from the columns and the dust motes dancing in the early evening sun was an image worthy to be painted.

"I do not think there is a finer one in the county," Alicia stated proudly.

"I cannot say I could make a fair judgment since I have only seen it at a distance but it appears to be very fine, indeed," Toby added. Stephen wasn't certain if his friend said this because it was his honest opinion or that he did not wish to incur his cousin's wrath that he alleged she had as a result of her red hair. However, the vicar-to-be was not prone to telling falsehoods.

"If the sun were a bit lower in the sky" —Lady Kitty began— "And the right side of the columns was just a bit more shadowed ... it would give the pergola greater definition and it would sit quite prominent on the hill amongst the trees ... almost like an oil painting."

"It seems you have an artist's eye, Lady Kitty." This was from Toby who apparently could not bring himself to relinquish the formality of her status entirely.

"That is most kind of you to say, Mr. Drayton," Alicia replied. "Now that we have seen the folly, shall we return to the house?" The abrupt change of topic had Stephen thinking ... had his cousin said such out of kindness or jealousy?

It was just as if she had never left Miss Maddingly's Academy. In the children's library, Kate sat on a child's chair near a low table with her knees close to her elbows, nearly reaching her ears. Next to her, Candy employed a pencil on her sheet of paper. The two whispered to one another, not secrets but in a shared, casual conversation. Kate offered gentle instruction and much encouragement to her new acquaintance. It was as if the two had already become fast friends.

"*Here you are!*" another red-headed girl, scolded upon seeing Candy. She turned her head to call down the corridor, "*Cindy*! I've found her!"

"We ain't doing nothing wrong, Sandy," Candy replied.

Sandy—*Sandra* strode into the room and eyed Kate. Her pear-red colored hair was a few shades darker than Candy's light rhubarb-red.

"When Miss Fawcett discovers—" Sandy stopped once she noticed Kate.

"What ..." Cindy—*Cynthia* appeared a moment later at the doorway. Immediately noticeable to Kate was the elder sister's hair—the color of beetroot. It was much darker than that of her two younger sisters and very near that of Alicia's. "You must be Lady Catherine's companion, Miss Matthews."

Kate nodded. She was not as discreet as she had hoped but her true identity had remained hidden.

"This is Miss Kate, Cindy. We're drawing pictures of the folly," Candy told her sisters. "See here ..." She held up her paper and pointed at it with the end of her pencil. "I put in the ducks."

"The ducks?" Kate had watched her drawing companion hard at work, making small, dark ovals on the paper but had not a clue as to the subject. Of course, they were ducks.

"You haven't nearly enough of them." Sandy approached her sister, settling on a chair next to her. "And I do not think the pergola is that small."

"It only looks small because *this*" —Candy indicated her drawing— "Is closer to the lake. You can't see the pond from this —but you can see the pond on the *other* side."

"Is there?" Kate would love to sketch that—it would be a different aspect of the familiar, well-known structure—only seen from the walking path and the house. The notion intrigued her.

It wasn't much longer until Cindy joined their conversation with her own opinions on the folly, pond, and ducks. Soon she sat with them at the table with her pencil and paper in hand.

It was interesting to watch as the sisters said each was more familiar with the folly than the other. Candy drew a half circle for the dome and two lines for the columns, she concentrated on the pond and the ducks. Sandy's sketch had no pond but the decoration on the dome and of the columns were quite elaborate. Cindy's illustration seemed the most realistic of the three. The true appearance of the folly and pond could only be determined once Kate saw the construction for herself.

"My goodness—this is quite the gathering." A woman, some years older than she, with a rather stern-looking expression, appeared. There she stood with her arms folded in front of her, holding a book against her chest.

"Miss Faw-cett!" The girls cried out and launched to their feet before into three separate strings of excuses why they were out of bed and now in the library.

"Is this an art lesson?" The governess craned to see what lay before them. "I see I have been remiss about your artistic education. Reading, writing, and sums are apparently not sufficient." The only response was silence. "I certainly hope Miss Matthews can spare some of her time to devote a lesson or two while she resides with us. I do very well at teaching academics but I'm afraid I am quite lacking at the arts."

The girls' eyes went wide at their governess' invitation. Was it that she had confessed to not being adept at all things?

"I would be delighted," Kate replied. "Thank you for asking, Miss Fawcett."

"Well ..." By her tone, the governess made it sound as if this was the evening's swan song. "I think we should set aside our work and head back to bed."

"Yes, Miss Fawcett," the girls chorused, picking up after themselves.

"You can return to your drawings in a day or two." She stood there, waiting for them to comply. "I will make certain your draperies are drawn properly and light shan't peek through to wake you. Shall we go to bed now? Bid goodnight to Miss *Kate* and we will be on our way. I shall be but a moment."

"Yes, ma'am. Goodnight, Miss Kate." The girls bobbed curtsies and scurried out of the room. There must have been something to be feared whilst left alone with the governess, Kate imagined ... somewhat as if one were left to speak to a headmistress.

When the two were private, Kate stood and did her best to speak these difficult words without glancing away. "I do wish to apologize for intruding. I have no right to encroach ..." She did not suffer remorse easily. "All I can say is... I simply could not help myself. I found the lure of all these volumes" —she glanced at the wall-lined shelves in the room— "Quite tempting... I could not resist having a look myself and reminiscing about my child-hood favorites. I truly am sorry for trespassing."

"It would be beyond all endurance for you to disregard every fond feeling you have to relive your childhood recollections. I could not ask that of anyone, for we all have participated in unfor-tunate actions in our lives." Miss Fawcett's small smile forgave all.

The governess' stern expression and exterior melted away to reveal a kind, understanding female who must have had similar experiences and understood Kate's impulse.

"You are quite welcome here … although I cannot imagine what you might find of interest in this old room with its old books. They came with the house, belonging to the previous owners." She strolled from the table along the wall of bookcases, stopping where Kate had retrieved the single book she'd removed, read, and replaced as if she knew every book in its place and immediately recognized that their order had been disturbed. "Since the shelves were filled, Lord James had thought there was no need to purchase new reading material for his children."

"This very much reminds me of the book room at the Young Lady's Academy where I attended. There were many girls and thus, we had a great many and some of the same books."

"As needs must, I expect." Miss Fawcett broke the brief silence that settled between them by clearing her throat. "I bid you a good day and look forward to the next time we meet … for a drawing lesson, perhaps?"

"If you like." Kate collected her sketchpad, preparing to quit the room.

"The girls seem very excited to take up the pencil under your instruction and complete their sketches." Miss Fawcett glanced at Kate. "I will direct your attention to the library on the main floor to search for any future reading material."

"Oh… I will not be intruding there, will I?" The Grimshaw library should be more of a hallowed domain than the children's library.

"I expect not. You are a guest and not a servant in this house. Lord James would not mind if you browse through his collections in the least."

"Thank you, Miss Fawcett." Kate nodded and turned to leave. She had just begun to feel a bit better about her situation and would do just as the governess suggested.

"If I may ask a favor of you before you leave?"

"If I am able, certainly." Kate turned to face the governess once more.

"Would you be so kind as to return this book?" Miss Fawcett offered Kate a slim volume. "I have finished. You might wish to have a look at it yourself. It might be of interest."

"Really?" Kate gladly accepted. The book was old, covered in reddish, thin leather.

"If you like tales of shipwrecks, strange people in strange lands, and intrigue this might appeal to you. I found it quite compelling."

"That does sound nice." Kate turned the spine towards her to read the title in raised gold leaf: *Gulliver's Travels, Vol 1.*

"If not, then you can simply return it for me. Should you happen to come across the subsequent volume, I would be interested in reading the conclusion to the tale. I have a feeling that someone has placed them in an isolated spot for safekeeping for I found only the one." There was a tinge of disappointment and frustration in Miss Fawcett's tone.

"I will certainly keep that in mind," Kate replied.

"Thank you, Miss Kate. In any case, I feel confident you will find something more to your taste there." The governess sounded most optimistic.

Kate left the children's library. She would take Miss Fawcett at her word and spend some time with *Gulliver's Travels* to form her own opinion before returning it to the main library. If the tale was interesting enough to hold the governess' attention surely it would be of some interest to Kate. Whether or not she would seek out the remaining volume remained to be seen.

Kate made her way down the staircase one floor and entered Kitty's bedchamber, passing through to her own little room. Inside, on a small table, sat a dinner tray. She lifted the corner of the cloth cover to see a bowl of soup with a slice of bread and butter and a piece of cheese. It was hardly anything to tempt her from the book in her hand.

She was, however, reminded of Kitty who had made the greater sacrifice by keeping company with the Emerson family and the other guests. What was her friend doing now? She hoped there was some enjoyment to be had for Kitty was always the more outgoing of the two.

Kate pulled a hard, straight-backed chair next to her window and lowered onto it. Her back could not get quite comfortable and the light wasn't quite right. She tried shifting the chair a few inches one way and then moved it a quarter turn anti-clockwise, angling it so that the light came more directly through the window onto the pages.

That did not satisfy Kate either.

She relocated to Kitty's room where the southern exposure directed the sun's light straight through the window, providing excellent illumination. Kate moved one of the chairs from the corner fireplace to the window. She settled into it and opened the front cover of the book. There, an inscription, filled the page from top to bottom and right to left:

Stephen
Emerson

It took real arrogance to deface a book. By the look of the large script, it appeared to be written by a juvenile hand. No matter, Kate would ignore it and continue. She bypassed the author's note to the reader and the *LETTER FROM CAPTAIN GULLIVER TO HIS COUSIN SYMPSON*. She would read both later... Kate wanted to start the novel straightaway.

Chapter One, Part I A Voyage to Lilliput

And she began:

My father had a small estate in Nottinghamshire...

Five

The two couples returned to the house, making their way to the drawing room where Lord and Lady James waited.

"Did you enjoy your walk?" Lady James clasped her hands in front of her and approached Kitty.

"It was very nice." Kitty smiled. She had not had the chance to speak to Mr. Drayton since his friend had been her escort. "Lord Stephen seemed very knowledgeable of the landscape and he even pointed out the folly in the distance."

"Yes, our rotunda is the envy of the area," her ladyship modestly admitted.

"I am told there is a plan for a picnic there one day." Kitty actually had looked forward to the outing. As Miss Alicia told her earlier, there was little to do in the country and they needed to take every opportunity that arose to fill their days.

"That will be pleasant, indeed," Lady James replied. "We have the remainder of our evening where we could play cards or... I had hoped ... my daughter tells me you are quite proficient on the pianoforte."

At this Miss Alicia's cheeks flushed and she turned her face away. She behaved as if it was a betrayal of confidence but Kitty thought of it as nothing of the sort.

"I have taken the liberty of airing out the music room and having it cleaned in hopes that you would grace us with a small selection," Lady James said with great hope. "This evening perhaps?"

"I don't know—" Kitty sent Miss Alicia a look of panic. She could not help herself. Under normal circumstances, it would not trouble her but now … she felt so ill-prepared, ill at ease.

"Mama dearly loves music and we are so lacking in…" Miss Alicia pleaded, and Kitty did not wish to disappoint either lady.

"Very well … but you must give me a half hour to warm up my fingers, decide what I am to play, and—" Kitty sighed in disbelief. Was she truly going through with this? "I need some time to—I beg your pardon, but I am woefully out of practice, you see. It has been some months since …"

"Will you favor us with a few selections this evening? *After* you take some time to prepare."

"I would be happy to play for you then." Kitty pasted on her best smile and tried not to display the dread growing inside her. Although with a searching glance, from face-to-face of those around her, it was clear they all had hoped she would accommodate them.

"Oh, yes, dear," Lady James replied. "Take as much time as you need. Alicia—" she waved her daughter near— "Do go along with Lady Catherine to the music room and make certain everything is to her liking."

Miss Alicia brightened. It seemed her mother was not the only person who harbored enthusiasm for music, however good or bad. Kitty's new friend led the way. Miss Alicia chattered about her family's excitement at the opportunity of the impromptu concert.

"I would hardly call it a concert. I need to bring to mind any pieces I have memorized … and by my current recollection, I cannot recall a single one." Kitty did, indeed, find this a bit unsettling.

"Oh, Miss Kitty, you are bamming me!" Miss Alicia chuckled as they walked into the large room they had visited earlier.

Once again Kitty found herself face-to-face with the grand pianoforte. It was a magnificent instrument. It was situated in a place of prominence, surrounded by a semicircle of floor-to-ceiling windows behind it and five chairs for the spectators. She felt as if she would be quite in the center of attention sitting at its keyboard.

Kitty squeezed her hands tightly into fists then extended her fingers, working the idle muscles. This she repeated several times. She bent each finger separately and then rubbed her hands together.

"Will this chair do? Or shall I find another?" Miss Alicia glanced about, searching for a substitute.

"This will be fine." Kitty rotated her wrists before sitting at the keyboard. Once seated, she bent her head, stretching her neck muscles—left ear to left shoulder then her right ear to her right shoulder in an attempt to ease the tightness.

"There are some music books if you prefer to use those." Miss Alicia moved to a drawer, it must have held sheet music and Kitty could hear the shuffle of various papers within.

"I do not think this is the time to attempt a new piece. Allow me to warm up my fingers and bring some memorized pieces to mind." Kitty raised her arms over her head—rotated her shoulders forward a few times then backward. "I'm certain it will be fine," Kitty murmured to herself. She hoped so. Certainly, all she need do was clear her mind and all would be well.

At one time, Kitty knew, or had known, dozens by heart and could perform them without thought. At this moment, any and every tune she had known seemed to have flown from her head. She needed to allow her fingers the freedom to move and it would all come back.

Just place your fingers on the keys and play.

As nervous as she felt, it amazed Kitty that her hands did not shake and her fingers did not tremble. She began by progressing up the keyboard, slowly. Then returned to middle C. Repeated the exercise in half notes ... then again in quarter notes ... the final run in eighth notes. Then she would move on to playing chords. By that point, she hoped, some of the music she'd forgotten would return to her.

As far as Stephen understood, the guests were to wait until Lady Catherine ... *Miss Kitty*, as his cousin referred to her, had practiced until she felt comfortable enough to perform in front of an audience. It was to be a relatively short interval since she had left before there were lilting sounds of music ... no, not *music* precisely but very pleasant-sounding notes. Although very soft in volume, they sounded as if they were played with confidence by an accomplished musician. He came to notice his aunt's agitation.

What was it causing her such distress? It was enough to distract him from carrying on a conversation with his uncle and Toby.

"It does sound very nice," Lady James murmured to herself then stood and began to pace. "I must get just a bit closer," he heard her say. She inched toward the door, growing closer and closer until she soon hovered about the doorway, glancing into the corridor. It was all too evident it would be mere minutes until she would escape.

Stephen stood at his aunt's exit. "Excuse me. I think we should accompany Lady James," he muttered to Lord James and Toby. He followed her out the door, leaving the other gentlemen, and glimpsed her rounding the corner at the far end of the corridor. It did not take long for him to catch up to his aunt for she had come to a stop at the open door of the music room and stood there, merely observing.

"Oh!" Lady James whispered. "It is a Bach *partita!*"

Cousin Alicia had followed her mother as well. She moved past Stephen, approaching her parent. "Shhh—Mama, you must shush. Miss Kitty is practicing." She silently ushered them into the room, gesturing at the prearranged chairs where they eventually settled, not as unnoticed as one would have hoped.

The music came to an end and Miss Kitty—*Lady Catherine* turned toward the small gathering at the door. "None of you were meant to hear any of this." She could not meet the gazes of her admirers and averted her eyes. A most becoming rose-color flush washed across her cheeks, whether from vexation or embarrassment, he did not know.

"I do beg your pardon, Lady Catherine," Lady James sounded most apologetic. "I know I should not be here but—"

"This is your home, you should be allowed to go wherever you wish." The young lady removed her hands from the keyboard and rubbed them together gently. Stephen recognized the signs of impatience when someone's focus was disturbed. He had to admire her restraint for she was most tolerant, far more polite about the interruption than he would have been.

"But it was agreed you should have some privacy," Alicia unnecessarily reminded her.

"Pray, please continue, Lady Catherine," Lady James urged. "I am quite content to hear you practice."

"Should I make a mistake … which I fully expect will happen" —She made excuses before there was a need— "I will remind you that I am unpracticed and quite unsure of what I am to play."

"You shall not hear an unfavorable remark from my quarter, I can assure you." Lady James lowered onto a seat. An air of anticipation swirled about her now that her presence had been accepted, she need not make excuses for her early arrival.

While Alicia seated herself to her mother's left, Stephen, with

Toby now by his side, quietly occupied the two chairs to Lady James' right. Lord James, who was the last to arrive, settled into the remaining chair.

Lady Catherine faced forward, ignoring the other unwanted visitors. Stephen watched her settle her hands on the keyboard and close her eyes. It seemed that she drew down a blind, screening the onlookers from her view to help her concentrate. He had no true knowledge of her skill and expected that being observed might hinder her performance. From the promising measures he had heard previously, he assumed she had some talent. Her hands lowered. Her fingers lightly brushed the keys before she began to play.

Cousin Alicia could barely contain her joy and clapped to the lively music. "I know that piece!"

"Oh, yes, dear—it is Haydn!" Her mother laid her hand on her daughter's forearm.

"Did you notice how she has altered?" Toby remarked, whispering to Stephen. "The music has quite transformed her."

"You don't say?" Stephen glanced at his cousin. Alicia's gleeful smile bordered on laughter. Her delight was evident and had indeed animated her entire countenance. "Both she and my aunt admire music greatly ... it is unfortunate that neither is accomplished at the pianoforte."

And why exactly was that? Stephen did not know.

"That is odd," Toby reflected. "It is a common accomplishment for most ladies. I would expect they had acquired the skill years ago ... Lady James, before she was married."

"If I recollect" —he leaned toward his friend to confess— "I cannot think I've ever heard either play ... nor have I ever seen either sit at that instrument. However, I must confess the occasions I have been in residence have been, for the most part, spent outdoors—not tied to the apron strings of the females."

"I cannot imagine you restricting yourself to the house when great open spaces beckon to you," Toby agreed. "Lord James is a great one to encourage sport, not to mention he's mad for your company." He nudged Stephen and with a certain finality murmured, "We should be silent now—bad manners to whisper during a performance—especially when there are those nearby who wish to listen."

"To be sure." Stephen quit all manner of communication with his friend. Toby turned his attention, as did the others, to the music.

Did he and Toby not experience the very same only a few weeks ago? They attended countless evenings with many accomplished young ladies, displaying their musical skills. Perhaps too many. Stephen recalled his friend who sat next to him, just as he was now, and observed with equal tepid regard, and both remaining unmoved. That was not so this evening.

Stephen gave his friend a silent nod and a smile of curiosity. Had Toby developed a sudden *tendre* for Alicia? This was quite unexpected—considering Toby was set against all females with Titian tresses and her hair color had remained unchanged. Did that no longer matter to him?

If Stephen were seated with a book in hand, entrenched in a story while music lilted in the background, it would make his time here more than tolerable. It would border on sheer perfection. But to sit upright in a chair and struggle to remain awake made the exercise tortuous. He would endure this out of civility of the other guests and Lady Catherine who, he suspected, at this moment performed under duress.

The first piece ended to small but enthusiastic applause. Lady Catherine's next choice, Bach—theme and variations, Stephen felt, was conventional and safe. Every young lady must have had this memorized, a perfect performance piece to demonstrate skill. It was familiar and lively for any listener's enjoyment. Although he had to give her credit that what she played was from memory, without sheet music before her. And then she began to play—*practice*, she called it, but to his amazement, with all the disruptions and not quite ideal conditions as she would have wished, she did so without a noticeable flaw.

Stephen's primary enjoyment came from watching Toby. Not only did his friend seem to enjoy the music, more than before, there was a newfound delight when watching the red-headed beauty. Toby's gaze spent the majority of the time alternating from the musician to the smiling, cheerful Alicia.

"Marvelous, my dear, simply marvelous. *Brava!*" Lady James blotted her tears between her generous applause.

Kitty straightened and leaned away from the keyboard. She was glad her performance had pleased her hosts but she could not be satisfied with herself.

"How I have missed having music in the house. I never knew our own pianoforte could sound so splendid." Her ladyship held her clasped hands over her heart. "I do not regret the unnecessary expense of having it tuned all these years."

"Quite, quite splendid," Lord James proclaimed, rising to his feet. "I do not know why you think there is need for additional practice. You are most accomplished."

"Thank you, sir. You are too kind." Kitty felt the high opinion of her performance was unwarranted. Under normal circumstances, her skill might be considered superior, at best, but without practice … her errant fingers felt lethargic … and she *sounded* clumsy to her ears. She only had an audience of Miss Maddingly and residents of the girls' school to measure her ability. On occasion, there had been visitors, but those instances occurred very infrequently. "I believe my performance was satisfactory," she murmured in discomfort.

"Come now, do not claim false modesty," his lordship

declared. "You must know that your playing is quite beyond the ordinary."

"Oh, yes, Kitty, Father has the right of it," Alicia added. "How I wish I had a small portion of your talent."

"Such beautiful playing, my dear! So lovely! It brought me to tears," Lady James said, sniffing into her handkerchief.

"I dearly wish I had continued my lessons," Miss Alicia confessed in a whisper. "I feel quite ashamed."

"Do not despair, daughter. Your lessons were very many years ago, you were only five or so at the time. We had not the means to — You had no notion of—" Lady James stopped abruptly and her smile waned. Her gaze darted to the guests in an awkward manner. From Kitty's observation of the family's present financial position, it would not be unexpected that music lessons were a luxury they could no longer afford.

Was Miss Alicia only in want of lessons?

That was something Kitty could easily remedy, and would be very happy to do so. Music lessons should be a much welcome occupation for everyone. In turn, her ability to be of some service, by way of music lessons, would be Kitty's pleasure.

"Oh, fiddle!" She thought this the most ridiculous thing she had ever heard. "There is no reason why you cannot learn—*continue* to learn, that is. If you have the mind to apply yourself then there is no reason you should not." These were not empty words. Kitty was willing and more than capable.

"We have no access to a music teacher here," Lady James was quick to explain.

"Yes, I understand but I must let it be known that at the Academy, I tutored girls and young ladies on the pianoforte," Kitty announced with much pride. "I believe I have more talent in teaching than performing."

"Do you mean *you* can—you will instruct me?" Miss Alicia gasped in delight.

"If you, and your mother, will allow it." Kitty could not go along, willy-nilly, taking on pupils and offering her musical instruction as if she passed from village to town, along the length and breadth of England!

"I should like that above all things!" Miss Alicia turned to her mother for approval. Kitty did not think they would find her opposed to the suggestion.

"What about singing?" Lady James interrupted, smiling at Kitty. "Do you also teach singing? Do you happen to have a fine voice? It would be wonderful if you could accompany yourself and sing!"

Kitty could not help but stare wide-eyed at Lady James. No, she did not sing. Well ... she did not sing *alone*. She sang with a group or lent her voice in harmony where hers was not the predominant vocal.

"Oh, no, I dare not before an audience. However—" Kitty wasn't certain she should mention it but... "I do accompany my friend ... er ... *companion* Kate. *Miss Kate* ... she has the voice of a songbird. I shall ask if she will perform for us."

"Do you think she would?" Lady James did her best to insist without sounding overbearing. "I do not wish to impose but... I would dearly wish to hear her ... if she would care to join us one evening."

"I will do my best to persuade her." Kitty smiled and would be more than delighted to relay the request to display Kate's talent.

"I am certain you can convince her." Lady James was all smiles when contemplating the boon of entertainment that was bound to follow.

"You make me wish we could begin at this very moment!" Miss Alicia sounded eager and ready to commit to the new task before her.

"Tonight?" Kitty was taken aback. Why must this family insist all their requests be granted at a moment's notice? "Perhaps you might give me until tomorrow to come up with a study plan. It would be very nice to evaluate your skill and contemplate a course of instruction. I believe that best be done after a good night's sleep."

"That will give me some time to find my lesson books. I know exactly where they are." Miss Alicia announced with confidence. "We should start at the very beginning, shall we not? First thing tomorrow morning."

"That might prove best." Then Kitty thought better of the suggestion when recalling they now kept *country hours* because they were no longer in London. That meant rising very, very early.

"I shall not sleep a wink tonight!" Miss Alicia proclaimed. "I am far too excited."

Kitty could see that, although she had remained silent, Lady James was thrilled for her daughter. One glance at her ladyship reminded Kitty of her curiosity about Miss Alicia's singing potential.

Kitty glanced at her new pupil and asked, "Tell me, Miss Alicia … are *you* in the possession of a fine singing voice?"

She stared back at Kitty with a blank expression. Her beautiful green eyes went wide. The sudden shock made her creamy white complexion lightened a tinge paler.

"I cannot say," she replied. "No one has ever told me— I have never attempted to sing—alone, you see. I suppose I shall wait until … until you and Miss Kate present your opinions. Then we shall all know."

Six

"Morning, Kitty!" Dressed much the same as she had been the day before with her work apron over a simple day dress, Kate swept from her small room through the connecting dressing room doors into the next bedchamber. With her sketchbook in one hand, she snatched up a piece of toast from her friend's breakfast tray for a quick bite, lifted the cup of chocolate to her lips, and returned it to its saucer with a slight clatter.

"I beg your pardon—that's my chocolate!" Kitty complained, turning from her portmanteau, lying open on her bed. Not one for sleeping late herself, her hair had been put up and she wore a day dress fit for the company she would keep this morning. "There is plenty to eat in the breakfast room, I am sure."

"Don't have time for breakfast." After a second bite of toast, Kate abandoned it on the plate. "I have an art lesson scheduled."

"You've received the note I passed on to you, I see." Of course Kitty had been the one to slide the message under Kate's door late last night. "Is that what it was about?"

"From the governess Miss Fawcett. Thank you." Kate offered a curt nod. She'd read a good portion of *Gulliver's Travels* last night and wished to continue after she'd finished the current book. This novel was a tale told in four parts, two volumes. That would mean she needed to find its missing volume as Miss Fawcett had asked. She, too, wished to read the end.

"And what do you have planned this day?"

"Well… I was asked to play the pianoforte for the family and guests last night."

"I should not be shocked but I must confess that I am. It has been months since you've touched an instrument."

"Not only that, Miss Alicia has asked that I instruct her … continue her education she'd started years ago. She wished to begin last night but we decided it would be better to make a fresh start of it this morning. She is a most eager student." And Kitty had always been an excellent teacher. "We haven't ventured far from our pre-London days, have we?"

"She will have one of the very best teachers. I have heard Miss Maddingly say such about you many times." Kate also held the same belief. She was a most knowledgeable instructor with infinite patience.

"You are kind to say so." Kitty stepped away from the open luggage and brought her cup of chocolate to her lips to sip before returning to her task.

"I have no doubt that you impressed her greatly." Kate felt the various items in each pocket of her apron, hoping she had not forgotten anything.

"You may not have thought so after hearing me play. I find it abundantly clear it has been months since I have practiced." No matter the glowing reception the family displayed, Kate understood that Kitty had not felt good about her performance. "I must admit I was not at my best."

"I shall never believe it. Your skill is far superior to most." That was Kate's humble opinion. She had heard a Season's worth of young ladies on parade. Mastering the pianoforte was the most common accomplishment for any young lady but no one's skill at the keyboard seemed to measure up to Kitty's.

"I could do better, of course," Kitty admitted. "If I wish to practice I will need to make time for it—even if that means waking early. I expect Alicia will occupy the keyboard a great deal and I can hardly insist she yield for my sake."

"Is that why you've retrieved your sheet music?" With a nod, Kate indicated the small pile on the counterpane—Kitty's prized pieces. "Have they no music for their instrument at all?"

"There are drawers full... I will look through them in the following days. I think it best to start with the pieces with which I am familiar. It appears that no one in residence plays. If I discover something of interest, I will need time to practice anything new. As to that" —Kitty paused and glanced up at Kate— "Lady James has expressed an interest in hearing you sing." She returned her attention to searching through her sheet music. "I am looking for arrangements for the two of us." Kitty flipped through the pages as if she knew exactly for what she searched. "A Mozart piece? What do you think?"

"How can you ask that I *begin* with Mozart when I haven't sung for months?" Kate ventured with caution. She did not like the sound of this. "I will need weeks of practice to work up to the task of a full aria."

"I'm afraid to tell you that your presence has been requested after dinner tonight." Had Kitty thought to place her in the same dreadful plight that she, herself, experienced the night before? Performing for an audience without the benefit of practice?

"Kitty?" How would Kate be able to manage that? Just think of her poor vocal cords! "I could sound like a screeching chicken, squawking out notes, or even worse I could sound like a frog!"

"I'm afraid Lady James is desperate for some diversion." Kitty looked up from the pages before her.

Then it occurred to Kate... "You told them I sing?" Why would Kitty do such a thing?

"Her ladyship has inquired if I had such talent." Kitty shrugged. "I do believe I can hum a recognizable tune but I would hardly pass myself off as a tolerable singer, especially when you are on the premises. Your voice is fine. I cannot think of a reason you should not sing for them. It needn't be anything elaborate. Some folk song, perhaps? One of those we sang at school."

"I suppose that could be managed." If a request had been made, Kate would comply. "Why the rush? To perform without preparation would be intolerable."

"We may work on the simple tunes but we must make headway on the more difficult pieces. Not for Lady James' sake but for your own." Kitty sounded most serious … as if *she* were a headmistress. "I am certain you do not wish to lose your ability to sing or damage your voice, and I know you enjoy it."

"Yes, I do," Kate said on a sigh. "And it has been overly long since I've done so. The thing that is truly a bother is that I need to dress for the performance … and have I mentioned that I have not sung a note for months?"

"Only several times," Kitty pointed out. "This, we should remedy by afternoon's practice. We need some preparation. You as the vocalist and me as the accompanist. We do not wish you to hit any flat notes."

"Nor would I wish to." Kitty would be mortified to do such a thing before an audience, any audience whether they be a roomful of students or a few distant family members.

"I do wish to caution you … where there might be some matter of concern …"

The suspicious glance leveled in Kitty's direction warned her to proceed with care. "It has to do with one of the gentlemen guests … Lord Stephen, he is the nephew of Lord James."

Kate narrowed her eyes and stared at her friend, wary of what would come next.

"He is not exactly sure but his lordship suspects he may have made your acquaintance in London."

"What?" That got Kate's attention.

"Lord Stephen *Emerson*," Kitty stated his name clearly. "Have you made his acquaintance?"

Kate tried to recall him. "I do not believe I have." The name was familiar, however. It was the very same she'd discovered disfiguring *Gulliver's Travels*.

"He came to the very conclusion as well," Kitty replied. "Had you previously met it could have been a catastrophe."

What a relief! Their circumstances could have taken an unfortunate turn if they had been previously introduced. Kate needed to be grateful to her hosts. "I have changed my mind. I would be more than willing—delighted to sing for them."

"Excellent. Shall we plan to practice? How is three this afternoon sound?"

"I will make it so, Kitty." If that one unfortunate, non-related circumstance had happened in London, it might have changed their stay at Grimshaw Court. Even if that meant Kate needed to give up a little of her freedom, she would make the concession. "In the music room, at three, I will be there." She exited the bedchamber with a smile and headed up to the schoolroom where she expected to find Miss Fawcett and her three charges ready to employ their pencils to sketch.

The morning was very productive for Kitty. She finished her remaining toast and chocolate on her tray and headed straight for the music room with the sheet music she would need for the day —those she wished to practice and Kate's pieces.

Kitty enjoyed the great quiet of the music room. Only she and the pianoforte shared the grand space. On a table sat the several stacks she and Miss Alicia had sorted through last night and judged the appropriateness for one, both, or neither of them.

There was no doubt that day was going to be very busy.

How did she ever think this trip would be a leisurely stay in the country when she had so much to do? Kitty sat at the keyboard and warmed up her fingers. She worked on scales, then chords. She placed her first piece on the music stand and began slowly.

Later last night, after playing for the guests, she recalled the *other* pieces she knew by memory and noted their names. Those would need to be reviewed as well.

Next needed to be the music Kate might wish to sing. There were many and it would not do if Kitty were to make a mistake during Kate's performance. Which of the pieces her friend might choose would be a quick decision, depending on what she might favor at that moment. Kitty would need to be prepared.

After an hour of dedicated practice, her confidence at the keyboard had been well-satisfied and she was pleased with her efforts. Miss Alicia entered, with her she had a small booklet and some sheets of music.

"I do not know if these are at all helpful but ... here are my old lessons." She set a booklet and several sheets of loose paper before Kitty. Since it had been some years since Miss Alicia's last instruction, Kitty thought it might be best to begin as if her new student had never sat at the instrument. In this case, prior experience could not be but a bonus.

Kitty demonstrated the hands and finger stretches before facing the keyboard. All during which Miss Alicia giggled. Yes, the exercises seemed silly but when one is idle for a length of time and those small muscles are not engaged, one's playing, one's music would suffer.

Then Kitty instructed Miss Alicia on optimal sitting, upper limbs, and hand positions. When the time came to play the first notes the excitement from the new student was palpable. She began with one hand but was soon using both hands, playing an octave apart, key by key, moving to the right. Then she repeated, this time to her left and returning to middle C. Miss Alicia had very good focus and dexterity.

"This is quite enjoyable," Miss Alicia commented.

"Just wait until you begin to play something recognizable." From experience, Kitty knew it always encouraged a student.

"How easily I remember all my old music," Miss Alicia sighed with a bit of nostalgia.

Kitty felt she needed to touch on Miss Alicia's old lesson books before the end of their session. They went over the notes scrawled on the wide margins from the prior music teacher. The few years that had passed only did Miss Alicia good as the improvements Kitty suggested were easily adapted and none of the previous small mistakes were repeated.

After an hour of instruction, Kitty moved from Miss Alicia's side and announced. "I will leave you to practice. Mind that you do not overdo."

"Is there such a thing?" Miss Alicia, still filled with the enthusiasm she had when she sat, seemed ready to continue for another hour.

"Of course, you are anxious now but should you spend too much time there you will not wish to touch the instrument for days or weeks … if ever. Then all your practice and lessons will be for naught."

"Oh, no." Miss Alicia stared at the instrument as if she could not believe she could harbor such an opinion.

"Even I must temper my practice sessions." It would not take much for Kitty to sit at the keyboard and play for hours on end. "I will allow you some time on your own. I, too, admit that I need to step away for a time," Kitty confessed. "I will sit with the work basket for a time and return with renewed interest. I am to accompany Kate—*Miss Matthews'* performance this evening. Since leaving the school, neither of us has performed."

"But you were in Town for the Season, were you not?" Miss Alicia inquired, sounding quite shy. "I thought that was the prime reason for attending, it was a perfect stage for a young lady to showcase one's talents."

"There were others who were more eager," Kitty confessed. "We chose not to."

"I see," was all Miss Alicia said and did not press for an explanation.

"I will leave you now." Kitty drew her chair away. "I will be in the sitting room if you should need me."

"Thank you, Cousin Kitty." Alicia smiled and turned back to the keyboard.

Kitty quit the room, leaving her student to happily practice. She wondered, as she left, if she first needed some fresh air but ultimately decided that sitting at this moment would be preferable.

Lady James came 'round the corner into the corridor, nearly colliding with Kitty.

"Goodness me!" her hand clutched her throat in fright.

"I am terribly sorry, my lady. I had no idea you were—" As she turned into the room, Kitty watched Mr. Drayton stand from his seated position.

"Lady—Miss Kitty." He greeted her with a slight bow.

"I beg your pardon!" Lady James had widened her eyes when she nearly ran into Kitty and glanced back into the room at Mr. Drayton. "I'm afraid I must be off," said her ladyship. "I'll have a fresh pot of tea and cups sent in for you." She immediately swept down the corridor, not allowing her accidental meeting with Kitty to impede her progress.

"I am sorry if I've interrupted." Kitty glanced from her lady-ship's retreating form to the standing Mr. Drayton.

"No, not at all. We were ... we *simply* were ..." he sounded rather sheepish. "*Listening ...*"

Eavesdropping? The two of them?

Kitty's attention dropped to the tea tray on the low table. Two cups. They must have been here for some time and sharing quite a comfortable coze before she came along. She wasn't certain the sound from the music room would reach the sitting room. However, if one were very, very quiet, it might be possible to hear the pianoforte.

"Would you care to be seated?" Mr. Drayton motioned to the furniture.

"Thank you, sir." Kitty picked up the work basket that was set aside in the corner and took a seat.

"I overheard Lady James tell you she would call for a fresh tea tray. Allow me to set this aside." He carefully placed the used china cups upon the tray. It was really not his place to do such but he was all consideration to do so.

"Why are you not with your friend—Lord Stephen?" Kitty removed the cover, small scissors, and searched for the needle.

"I prefer not to partake in shooting parties," Mr. Drayton replied. Somehow Kitty could see that type of activity might have been contrary to his kind nature. No doubt they would see the outcome of Lord James and Lord Stephen's efforts on the dinner table this evening, but the guests would hardly consider themselves starving if they were to fail in their efforts.

"And what other occupations do you have in store this glorious morning?" He kept his head down, busy with the task of clearing the area before them for the new tea tray.

"Mending from the work basket may not be exciting perhaps but it is a worthwhile occupation."

"I agree. There is always a need for a bit of charity work, is there not?" Mr. Drayton nodded. "Kindness can never be overrated. Miss Alicia is quite fortunate you have the time and talent to instruct her."

"I am only too happy to do so." Kitty smiled up from her sewing. "I must confess that I am keeping watch for four-hand pieces of music so that we may play together."

"Do you expect her to progress that rapidly?" Mr. Drayton's encouraging gaze warmed Kitty.

"I would like to think so but I expect I will need to alter the arrangements." She glanced up at him and continued, "I do try my best to find ways to encourage the students. I think she would find it amusing if we were to play together."

"Music for four hands?" He understood perfectly. "Oh, yes! I do see your point."

The tea tray arrived, set before them and the old one whisked away.

"We will need to wait a few minutes for the tea to steep if you don't mind." He said this as if from experience or had he had it from Lady James?

"This morning I have told my friend Kate that her ladyship has asked that she sing for us."

"She *is* willing to do so, isn't she?" Mr. Drayton gazed at Kitty wide-eyed. Had that been a bit of interest on his part? Did he wish it as well as their hostess?

Kitty was not as forthcoming with her answer as Kate had been. The answer was Yes ... eventually, but Mr. Drayton did not need to know how much coaxing had to be done to gain that reply.

"I've retrieved some music we had once performed together. I do not expect she will be ready to sing it tonight, but we shall begin to reacquaint ourselves with the piece."

"You were not allowed much time on your own last night, were you?" Mr. Drayton seemed to understand her position.

"No, I was not. It really could have all gone quite wrong for me." She did not care to recall that uneasy feeling of last evening. "I must admit... I have never been so ill-prepared."

"Lady James was rather insistent that you play—and she was not disappointed. She quite liked your performance—we all did." Mr. Drayton smiled and the praise warmed her. "You were brilliant—really outstanding."

"You are very kind, Mr. Drayton." Kitty graced him with a smile. She kept hold of the fabric and gaze focused on her sewing.

"But you must understand that creating music is integral for every young lady to feel whole... Without it, how can she feel truly accomplished?"

"To each his or her own. There are areas of interest that may mean nothing to one and to another may be of the utmost importance." He moved on from sounding polite to sounding quite serious. "Nothing illustrates the character of a young person than to see her, or him, make decisions under difficult circumstances. That is when you see someone's true character."

She lifted her gaze to meet his. Kitty had thought this man was of modest means but now she considered him one who had enlightened thoughts and principles. He appeared as his friend Lord Stephen had previously described, 'not ostentatious.' He also had said that Mr. Drayton, 'did not speak ill of anyone and held optimistic views of the world around him.'

"I am quite unoccupied, my hands are idle," Mr. Drayton, already settled, his attention fully upon her, politely asked, "I would like to make myself useful. Do you mind if I pour?"

"If you wish." Kitty gave him a little smile, glancing up from her hands. "Thank you very much."

Indeed, Mr. Drayton was not just a man to pursue a life in the church, as Lord Stephen had told her because he was not so devout to the bible but his fair and equitable nature would make him friend to the people around him. He did not think himself better than any other nor did he belittle himself. Kitty found him kind and very agreeable. Actually, she quite liked him.

Kate and her art students began in the schoolroom some hours before but had relocated to the 'chicken house.' The reason? To sketch birds because Mrs. Robin was not to be found. And as Candy explained to Kate, *chickens*—hens, *were birds.*

She then found herself, properly introduced, to the hens: Penny, Re*peck*a, and *Hen*nah. The other hens, for there were at least another four or five who all had names, scratched the dirt and pecked at the ground.

Kate did not know how the girls managed to draw and talk so much—at the same time. There was far more talking than drawing going on and the talking was directed mostly at her. She then decided that while instructing, she could not concentrate to sketch properly.

After an hour, Miss Fawcett insisted it was time for the girls to return to the schoolroom. The three kindly thanked Kate for her time and left. She returned to her bedchamber to swap her sketch-book for *Gulliver's Travels* and headed down to the ground floor.

At last, her much-anticipated trip to the main library. She asked a footman who led her down the corridor, through a heavy door, and into a room that did not disappoint. When Miss Fawcett said there would be something she would find she liked, it was not a comment made in jest.

In the vast space along with the shelves and shelves of books that lined the walls with several additional free-standing book-cases that went up and up and up… Kate could only stand there in awe. Never had she imagined anything so grand.

Visiting similar places while in London, various homes of the aristocracy, she would steal a look at their libraries. They were usually male dominated rooms and she recalled that oftentimes there was the lingering scent of tobacco and drink from the previous inhabitants. Those small, cramped rooms paled in comparison to this.

Neither strong spirits or foul smell dwelled here in Lord James' library. Here, she smelled… Kate closed her eyes and inhaled slowly … nothing but the slightly musty scent of old books waiting to meet her and welcome her as an old acquaintance. All she wanted to do was sink into one of the worn, comfortable-looking, soft leather-covered chairs and lose herself in a book. For many, many hours if she were to have her way.

First, she needed to find that missing volume. Wherever was she to begin amongst the hundreds, perhaps thousands of books? She hadn't expected to face a task of this measure … one person could not do this alone. It would take … perhaps not forever but a very long time.

Kate stared at a jacket that draped across the back of a chair next to a table that held a fairly tall stack of books.

Was someone else here? To whom did that jacket belong?

A very loud sneeze echoed around the room followed by a masculine voice booming down from above, "Hallo, there!"

Kate glanced about. She stepped back as he descended from one of the library ladders. Her spine stiffened and her fingers tightened around the book she held. She hadn't expected she would come across anyone here.

The wavy-haired man in his shirtsleeves and waistcoat before her had an armful of books and before he reached the final rung he hopped off, landing neatly, and almost soundlessly onto the floor. He set the books he held on the table between them, where the chair with the jacket—*his* jacket, rested, then cleared his throat.

"Who might you be?" He was tall and the loose hanging, casually tied neckcloth looked to be the dress of a simple country man. "Ah …" He eyed her from toe to head and answered his own query. "You are not a servant—though you wear a work apron. Ah—I have it!" He punctuated his revelation with his index finger in the air. "You are Lady Catherine's companion. You prefer to be called *Kate*, is that right?"

"Yes. I am her companion." Kate was at a disadvantage. She did not know his name but she could have guessed who he was— one of the gentlemen guests for sure.

"I beg your pardon." He must have sensed her discomfort at his undress for he quickly retrieved his jacket and slipped his arms through the sleeves, adjusting the garment over his shoulders. "I'm not quite—well, I wasn't expecting visitors."

"Nor had I expected to come across anyone," Kate returned. She did feel a bit shabby with her apron thrown over her unadorned day dress. It was not the thing at all. She should have realized it was possible, and very probable, that she might have run into one of the family members.

"Nevertheless I am pleased to make your acquaintance." He inclined his head slightly and graced her with a well-practiced smile. " How do you do, Miss ... *Kate*?"

Kate could not help but notice what held his attention. He focused squarely on what she held—specifically, on the book in her hands.

Seven

"And who might you be, sir?" the young lady's companion inquired. Miss Kate did not appear to be timid in the least or quelled by his presence or proximity.

"Lord James' nephew, Lord Stephen." His name could not have been unknown to her. Lady Catherine must have mentioned him.

"*Stephen Emerson?*" She repeated in an extremely suspicious manner.

"Yes, that's right." He took his time and studied her closely. "What is it you have there if you don't mind me asking?"

"This?" She glanced at the book she held protectively. Then opening the front cover wide enough for them both to see, she revealed the inscription. "Is this penmanship yours?"

He had written his name in that book many years past. It was the best he could manage at the time, taking four lines to spell: *Steph-en Emers-on.*

"Is this *your* book or does it belong to Lord James?"

"My uncle did not purchase that volume if that's what you're asking. It was in the library when the house was acquired." Stephen had no notion why she should need to know.

"So you took it upon yourself to *claim* the book by inking your name inside?"

"It was my favorite as a boy …"

"I can't see that excuses this type of action—even though you were *only* a boy."

"I can offer no acceptable apology for my younger self." He need not offer a defense, not to her. "I had thought I might like to reread it. After all, it has been many years, and it holds such fond memories."

"I shall gladly hand it over to you when I have finished." She kept tight hold with no indication that she might relinquish the book.

He had thought she would hand it to him straightaway.

"Er … where did you find that?" Stephen had been looking for that very book. The worn paneled calfskin and gilt decoration on the cover had caught his immediate attention.

"The governess, Miss Fawcett, has asked me to return this to the library."

It was no wonder he could not find it. But *where* had Miss Fawcett come across the book?

"Actually, she has requested the second volume if I should see it," Miss Kate informed him. "You wouldn't happen to know where this might reside, would you?"

No, he did not. Stephen could not prevent his gaze from swinging to his right and she, very cleverly, he thought, looked in the same direction as if he were giving its location a surreptitious glance. "That particular story has occupied many bookshelves over the years. Miss Fawcett did not happen to tell you where she found that volume, did she?"

"I'm afraid she did not." Miss Kate's gaze passed across the bookshelves in the room and Stephen could see, mirrored in her expression, the very same dilemma he faced.

"I might as well confess that one of my primary tasks during this visit was to locate them. But as you can see there are many places where the other might be now."

"Have you had any success, sir?"

"Unfortunately, I have not." It was a disheartening, but true, assessment of his progress. Stephen believed retrieving them would be easy. He thought he remembered exactly where they were. He had been wrong.

"I see that you have acquired quite a stack." She glanced at the pile of books he had set on the table next to him. "Are these all of interest to you?"

"I thought I might like to have a look at them." He set a protective hand on the top copy. "I have a fondness for stories regarding distant lands."

"Just as in *Gulliver's Travels*." Her eyes went wide and she, too, turned her head to scan the spines just as he had before pulling them from the shelf. "Look at them all. They list countries from all over the world ... such distant lands!"

"Exactly ... well, not *exactly* the same as *Gulliver's Travels*." He leaned down onto the table not far from her. When he gazed upon her he saw a bit of himself. The part that wished to climb aboard a vessel and set sail away from England. He wanted to meet people from different cultures ... to hear, learn, and speak different languages. He wanted to learn how they were similar and how they were different from him. "Except these are true tales from real people who have traveled there."

"That does sound wonderful." Her bright smile and the shine of excitement in her eyes was the first expression from another person he'd seen that came close to his own. No one understood his longing for adventure and he had the feeling that she just might.

"What type of books do you enjoy?" If Stephen were not careful, he might be losing the stack he'd only just collected.

"My interests vary and my possessions are limited." Her voice softened as if she were ashamed to admit it. "But someday... I wish to have an *enormous* book room ... such as this ... keep every book I've loved after reading it and have all the books I ever wish to read."

"That sounds wonderful." He smiled. "Will you collect these books during your travels?"

"Oh... I do wish I could. I would love to travel ... sail to the other end of the world." Her eyes were wide and a smile filled with joy, hope, and longing spread across her lips. "Just to see what is there!"

He could feel her excitement ... it was near-contagious and Stephen needed to calm himself. He stepped back from the stack of books on the table and took a slow deep breath.

"Your presence has reminded me of my original goal—to find *Gulliver's Travels*. Now, it is only the remaining volume since you are in possession of the first." He moved farther away from her, the physical distance from her seemed to help him regain his focus. "I find I am continually distracted by other books."

"May I aid you, then? Would it not make finding it all the easier with the two of us searching?" She slipped the volume she held into one of her apron pockets and stared at him. Her hands and fingers, now empty, moved in a small, intricate tangle, displaying her unsettled mood. "I was requested to do so."

"It does seem the most efficient way to proceed, I must agree." Stephen really should not refuse the offer of a second pair of eyes. "Do you mind?"

"I have a few hours until I am needed elsewhere." She glanced up from her hands. Had she discovered a confidence with a single purpose set before her? "I had planned to find it. I expect it will be far better if we do so together, as you suggest. You have already begun, have you not? Merely inform me where you have already searched and where you would like me to proceed."

He took a moment to remove his jacket he had recently

donned and draped it along the back of the chair where it had previously rested. He did have a plan but it was hardly well thought out.

"I began my search in my old hiding places. There, there, and there." Stephen pointed out each location on different sides of the room at varying levels. He coughed at the dust rising from his shirtsleeves at the sudden movement of his arms.

"Since I'm on the west side of the room, why don't you begin on the east side and we'll work our way to the center."

"That sounds reasonable." She nodded and reached into her pocket and brought out a cloth that filled her hand. "Each bookcase has very many shelves."

"That it does. Allow me to position the ladder for you. I found that one" —He gestured to the ladder he'd been using behind him with the jerk of his head— "Quite cumbersome. It could use some oil." He walked to the far end of the room where the ladder she would need stood against the tall bookcases. "If your curiosity is anywhere near mine, you will find at least one book per shelf that interests you."

"That sounds dangerous," she replied. "I cannot afford the distraction."

Stephen glanced in her direction before taking hold of the ladder. He noticed she looked a bit concerned about the notion of discovering more books than one could read. Holding the side rail with both hands, he gave the ladder a good tug, Then another, then another several until he centered it along the first bookcase. "There you go." He brushed off the palms of his hands.

"I see what you mean by *stubborn*." Now adorned in a mobcap with her apron, she appeared more prepared than he had been to sort through the dust-covered volumes. "I don't think I could have moved it."

"No need for you to make such an attempt." Motioning to the ladder as if making an introduction, he disgusted himself with the

amount of dust that came from his sleeve, and he backed away ...
slowly. "I found the treads solid enough. They may feel a bit
rickety but I can assure you they are quite sound."

"Thank you, sir." She smiled, took hold of the handrail, and
placed her foot on the first step.

"Do let me know if there is something you need." He gave her
a shallow bow, trying to raise as little dust as possible.

Stephen turned away and he realized just how much his once
clean shirtsleeves were covered in the stuff. He headed back to his
side of the room and reached up, swiping at the top of his head,
disturbing the blanket of fine debris that had settled on his hair
and sending a cloud billowing around him.

Heavens. Perhaps tomorrow he would take the precautions
Miss Kate had to maintain the cleanliness of his clothing.

After taking a final glance that his fellow-search partner,
Stephen climbed his ladder, returning to the shelf he'd been
searching. His nose began to itch. He gasped ... and inhaled—
held his breath—

His mouth opened and out came an enormous sneeze and he
brought his hand to his mouth to staunch the deafening sound.

"Oh—I do beg your pardon," he managed. Which was
followed by another two that followed in quick succession and
caused him to teeter atop the ladder. He tightened his hold,
keeping himself steady.

"Are you quite all right, my lord?" Miss Kate's small voice
came from across the room.

Opening his eyes, Stephen's gaze landed upon his jacket ...
where in his breast coat pocket lay his folded handkerchief.

He tilted his head back and took a deep breath, trying to keep
from sneezing again.

"Here, sir," Miss Kate's soft voice came from below. "You'd
best take this." She held up a—to his estimation—very ladylike-
sized handkerchief. When he did not respond, she replied, "I'd

give you my dust cloth but I've already used it and it could not do you any good." She indicated the fabric she held at a distance in her left hand.

"Thank you, miss." Stephen, who could not refute the necessity of a handkerchief, no matter what size, took the clean lacy bit of material and applied it to his nose.

"You need to step away from the pianoforte, Miss Alicia." Kitty urged her new, diligent student onto the terrace with a little push to her back. "Come along outside and let us get some air. Isn't this afternoon *glorious?*"

"Oh, yes!" Miss Alicia opened her eyes wide and drew in a great breath, stretching her arm. "The sky is beautiful … the air smells fresher … the—"

Kitty laughed, shook her head, and continued, making her way to the path. Miss Alicia could not have been sillier.

"Whatever are you laughing about?" Alicia's red curls bobbed around her head. She truly was blessed to have such a profusion of healthy hair.

"I so look forward to my next lesson, Kitty." Miss Alicia swung around to address Kitty with great enthusiasm. "When shall it be? This afternoon? Tomorrow morning?"

"Truly, it really is too soon to have another lesson." Kitty chuckled. "Perhaps in another day or two. All you need is to continue your practice. I think you are making excellent progress."

"Do you really think so?" Miss Alicia exuded such joy … nearly as much as Kitty felt herself.

"I do. Your finger strokes are stronger. Your wrists are less stiff, more relaxed. It truly is a remarkable accomplishment with so little time." Miss Alicia had put much effort into her new endeavor. "Do you know who else is interested in your progress?"

"My mother?"

"Well, yes she is." Kitty thought back when she had caught the two uninvited audience members having their tea and enjoying the private concert from the comfort of the sitting room. "I was speaking of Mr. Drayton."

"Cousin Stephen's friend?" Alicia knew who he was, of course, but the mention of his name took her aback. By the slight tilt of her head and her expression, the notion seemed to surprise her.

"Yes, he was quite taken with your enthusiasm and has remarked on your improvements." It surprised Kitty that he could put names to them.

"Do you mean to tell me he was *listening?*" Alicia stopped and realized with a gasp. "Without our knowledge?"

"That is no worse than your mother listening."

"But *she* is my mother." Miss Alicia faced Kitty to stress her concern.

"He seemed quite taken with your playing. I had thought he was rather enjoying himself." And perhaps it was more than that. Could Mr. Drayton have more than a passing interest in her?

"Are you certain?" Miss Alicia's expression turned quite sour.

"Why do you make that face?" Was it true that she did not care for Mr. Drayton?

"This is the face of disbelief, Cousin." Miss Alicia shrugged. "I made his acquaintance many years ago. He has never shown an iota of interest in my quarter. I can't think he would now. Oh, I do wish it were not true."

"You do not wish to gain the attention of Mr. Drayton? Perhaps it is not you but your music that has enchanted him." Kitty suggested and giggled. She could behave as silly as Alicia.

"Oh, that's a Banbury story." Alicia wasn't having any of it. "I enjoy my playing—it is hardly worth much to anyone else."

"Come now, Miss Alicia, I cannot dawdle all afternoon." Kitty nudged the redhead beauty. "I do not wish to keep Miss Kate waiting to practice."

"Let us return at once, then!" Miss Alicia raced ahead without warning.

"There is no need to run." Kitty could not grasp Alicia's arm in time to slow her. "I do wish to see the folly before we return. I have not seen its morning shadows."

"Very well… I did not realize you were so fond of our little rotunda." Alicia stared at Kitty who had grown up in a school for girls and limited knowledge of the goings-on outside her little world. "It is not as exciting as an actual ruin, nor do we have a hermit who lives there."

"A hermit! I am not acquainted with follies … not many of them, anyway." Kitty had decided she would like to see more and would not mind seeing this particular one a bit closer. She had woven several tales regarding how it should look upon closer inspection and what mysteries it might keep. All fanciful, no doubt but she had her dreams—perhaps insignificant to others who held something far grander.

"I do wish to hear Miss Kate sing. Will she mind if *others* listen while she is unawares?"

"I cannot think she would like it very much. About as much as you care for being overheard before you are ready to play in public." Kitty peeked at Alicia … knowing the excitement the young lady felt and the trepidation of an ill-prepared performer. "However, if you wish to listen, send for a tea tray and park yourself in the sitting room, that is what I understand is done. If you cannot hear properly, you could linger in the corridor outside the music room, just as Mr. Drayton had."

"You will not tell your companion that I am listening, will you?" Alicia bit her lower lip as she contemplated her small bit of chicanery.

"No, I shall not." Kitty smiled, knowing she was the very soul of discretion. "You needn't worry, Miss Alicia, I am someone you can depend upon to keep a secret."

She'd kept watch of the time. Kate descended the ladder, knowing she must leave for the music room soon. Before leaving, Kate had meant to set this interesting book she'd only just found on the shelf upon the table and come back to it later. However, she could not resist reading just one page but then … one page became two and two became—

"What are you finding so interesting?" Lord Stephen had somehow appeared at her side, seemingly out of nowhere.

"Oh—" Kate looked up from the book. "I was just— I only wished to see a page or two—" She closed the book, marking the page with a finger, while she turned the spine in his direction for him to read. "It's a travel book … Japan."

"Japan?" His eyes widened, showing interest. "Travel to Japan is difficult but not impossible."

"Yes, I know." That's why this book interested her. It seemed to appeal to him as well.

"At one time, not so very long ago, they closed their borders to foreigners. You are ambitious, aren't you?"

"I do not exactly know *where* the country is though," she admitted.

"It is farther east than India, which is a common destination for us British as are China and the Ottoman Empire … but Japan…" He smiled and motioned to her. "Let's look at the globe, shall we?"

Kate followed him round to just beyond the large desk that stood before a bank of tall windows. A large floor globe, mounted on a brass ring, sat in a carved wooden stand, making identification of the land masses easy by rotating the globe around for viewing.

"We are here." He placed his index finger on Britain then moved it across the channel. "Here is the Continent." Lord Stephen's finger moved farther east and he paused at each as he pointed out— "Turkey... India... China..."

"Oh, China is *very* far away from Britain."

"And across this bit of water is Japan." His finger moved from the small, longish island to China's right.

"That is not so far from China." Kate gazed wide-eyed at the globe and wondered how different it would be to live there. Besides dressing differently and speaking a different language, how would she find the people?

"No, it isn't. But it isn't the distance that prevents visitors. It's the government—" He looked off to one side— "The ruler... Who knows?"

Was it possible even for me? Why did Kate always have lofty, challenging goals?

The mantle clock chimed the hour and Kate straightened, moving from the globe and Lord Stephen.

"Oh, it's three," Kate said, regretting very much that the time had flown by so quickly. "I must leave."

"Ah, yes." He stepped away from her. "Well... I do appreciate your help this afternoon."

"I will resume my place when I am able."

"That would be splendid. There are so many, many shelves that remain." Lord Stephen glanced at her ... looked at the book she still held.

"You wouldn't by chance be leaving *that*, would you?"

"I shall, if you like." Kate handed the book to him. She had no use of it at present.

"Thank you. I would like to have a look at it while you're gone." He set it next to his two piles he'd accumulated. "Do you know where the music room is?"

"I will ask a footman," Kate replied.

"No need. Allow me, if you will. I could use a bit of a walk."

"Thank you."

He brushed off his hands before retrieving his jacket, slipping it on, and stepping away from his books. Kate headed out the door first and glanced about the corridor, waiting for her escort.

"The music room is on the other side of the house." He indicated where they would be heading with a high-arcing motion of his arm that they would need to travel far.

"I beg your pardon but I am in a hurry—I am afraid that I am already late."

"Let us be off at once!" Lord Stephen led the way. He did so without the benefit of chit-chat and in all swiftness. They walked for a good three or four minutes. It was a good thing he offered to guide her for she did not see a footman the entire way. How would she ever have found the place?

The notes of a masterfully played pianoforte grew louder as they neared. He motioned for her to enter first when they had arrived. Kate stepped inside. Kitty stopped playing and turned from the keyboard.

"There you are, Kate!" It hardly sounded like Kitty's warm welcome and she quickly changed her tone and stood when she saw Lord Stephen. "My lord? What are you doing here?"

"Lady Kitty" —Lord Stephen made a shallow bow— "Miss Kate needed an escort to the music room and I happened to be available to be of some service."

Kitty looked from his lordship to Kate. She was sure not to allow her expression to betray what she was thinking.

"Thank you, Lord Stephen." Kate nodded to him.

"Your servant, Miss Kate." He inclined his head before taking his leave and said, "I look forward to your performance this evening."

"I'm wondering how that will go myself ..." she murmured, watching him leave.

"How did you manage to meet him?" Kitty waited until Lord

Stephen had gone and far enough away so as not to overhear them.

"Do you find it unusual?" Kate cannot imagine why her friend would take exception to their acquaintance.

"I do since you are known to avoid those who reside here."

"He— I— We unexpectedly met in Lord James' book room. Apparently we are both searching for the same book and decided that it would be much more expedient if we were to cooperate and perform a coordinated, systematic search together."

"Well, that's all right." Kitty peered at Kate with some interest. "Did you find it?"

"There are loads of books, Kitty." Kate tried to contain her excitement. "There are ever so many interesting ones too."

"Are there? Any that might interest me?"

"Not so far but—I've never seen so many books in one place in all my life, Kitty. I will keep watch for any poetry."

"Thank you." Kitty pulled out a sheet of paper, her notes. "I have some pieces I thought might suffice for this evening. Nothing too difficult, I think."

"I suppose." Kate cleared her throat. She would be singing before an audience tonight. It was almost impossible to believe.

"Shall we begin?" Kitty sat at the keyboard and played a chord. "Warm ups. Slowly and not at full volume."

Kate nodded.

"Whatever is comfortable." Kitty played an arpeggio. "I will take your lead."

Kate nodded again and she began to sing. Barely a minute had passed before Miss Alicia poked her head into the room.

"Was that my cousin Stephen I saw leaving?"

"Yes, he guided Miss Kate here from your father's book room."

"My, the house is growing smaller all the time. I normally do not see my cousin until dinner."

"Really, how odd?"

"Males and females do not normally inhabit the same areas of the house. However, the book room ..." Miss Alicia had some thoughts regarding that space that she did not care to share.

"They are looking for *Gulliver's Travels*," Kitty informed her.

"The second volume," Kate clarified. "You wouldn't happen to have seen that about would you?"

"Oh, no! Not I." Miss Alicia laughed. "I shall leave you to your *practice*. I beg your pardon for interrupting." Then she left but not before a distinct wink directed at Kitty.

"What is that all about?" Kate glanced at Kitty trying to discern the meaning of what she had witnessed.

"It's nothing," Kitty shrugged. With a quick stretch of her fingers, she started where she had left off. "Never mind the off-notes, just continue."

"*Off*-notes. I noticed that... I wasn't certain if it was me or the pianoforte." Kate knew she was out of practice but ... really.

"It's not you. The instrument hasn't been tuned in quite some time and the poor thing has been played ... never so much in years as it has these last few days."

Kate began again, slowly and continued. She listened to Kitty's suggestions and after a bit they took a break where they discussed what they would perform that evening. They decided on four short pieces. They were varied in tone and tempo, enjoyable for the listener.

> *Early one morning,*
> *Just as the sun was rising,*
> *I heard a young maid sing,*
> *In the valley below ...*

Kate sustained the note—she abruptly stopped when Lady James, followed by Miss Alicia, entered. Her ladyship appeared very serious.

"Lady James" —Kitty stood from the keyboard— "Is there something amiss?"

"I am sorry to interrupt." Lady James was uncharacteristically serious and addressed Kitty without a smile. "We've just received a letter from your uncle, Lord Bradford."

That gained both Kitty and Kate's attention.

What had happened? Why had her uncle written? Kate's mouth went unexpectedly dry and she found it difficult even to swallow.

"Lord Bradford has informed us that Mr. Waddle from Rush, Stonewall, and Waddle is on his way to Grimshaw Court."

"*Mr. Wad-dle?*" Kitty repeated and tried not to appear alarmed. She glanced at Kate for some sign of how she should react.

Kate, familiar with the solicitors, and Mr. Waddle in particular for he was Kate's guardian ... her *other* guardian. Kitty might have seen him at the Academy but she would have no knowledge of his identity—who he was to Kate.

Mr. Waddle, solicitor and friend to her father, called on Kate at least twice a year doing his duty, making certain Kate was getting on well, had what she needed, and did not misbehave.

"Did his lordship indicate the reason for Mr. Waddle's visit?" Kitty inquired very politely.

"I'm not certain the gentleman needs to state a reason," Lady James replied. "He wishes to assure himself of your well-being, I am sure."

Lady James was most certainly correct and the solicitor was doing his due diligence by paying Kate a social call. After all, it had been months since she had last seen him.

"I expect you are correct," Kitty said, echoing Kate's very thoughts.

"We shall have plenty of time to enjoy our amusements. He is most welcome to join us, do you not think?" Kate commented, knowing exactly who Mr. Waddle was and what revelations his arrival would bring.

"He will make us an odd number at the dinner table," her

ladyship replied, sounding more concerned for the seating arrangement of the dining room. It would come as a shock if after Kate's identity came to light that anyone's appetite remained.

"As to that, I am only too happy to join you if needed." Kate could not think of a larger sacrifice to be asked of her but such were the circumstances.

Lady James forced a smile. "Of course he is most welcome. He may be a stranger to us but he is not a stranger to you, is that not right, Lady Catherine?"

"Exactly." Kitty nodded, appearing as agreeable as possible, and Kate thought she did an excellent job of remaining calm.

"I expect you will be pleased to see the gentleman again," Miss Alicia said to Kitty.

"It is always pleasant to renew an acquaintance," Kitty replied. "It has been quite some time."

"And I expect we shall enjoy our evening excessively since we have your music to divert us," Miss Alicia added, "even with the addition of his presence."

"Good, you are to sing for us tonight am I correct, Miss Kate?" her ladyship inquired before leaving.

"Yes, my lady," Kate answered with a nod.

"Very well, if Mr. Waddle arrives before dinner and decides to sit with us, you will be welcome to the table as well." Lady James was obviously deep in thought. "I need to have a word with Cook since there is a possibility of an additional guest and... I must arrange a room for him at once." She glanced up at them as if remembering she was among others. "If you will excuse me, ladies."

Her ladyship quit the room but Miss Alicia remained.

"Would you mind asking for a tea tray, Miss Alicia?" Kitty needed to be private with Kate. "I'm afraid Miss Kate's voice is a bit scratchy—*croaky* from disuse and her throat could benefit from some warm liquid."

"I am sorry to hear of your trouble." Miss Alicia gazed at Kate with the most compassionate expression, imagining her discomfort. "I would be more than happy to see to it."

"And if there is some honey about, it would be quite excellent," Kitty added.

"Of course. I will do so at once." With that, Miss Alicia left.

Kate glanced at Kitty in the following silence. She was unsure what was going to happen that evening but it would prove anything but dull.

Eight

Kitty once again played the accompaniment to Kate's folk song until she felt the Emerson ladies were well away from the music room. To prolong the musical interlude before they would be free to speak, Kate hummed along and when they reached the chorus, she sang softly:

Oh, don't deceive me,
Oh, never leave me,
How could you use
A poor maiden so?

"This cannot be good, Kate. Not good at all." Kitty continued to play, hoping the notes of the pianoforte would successfully mask their soft conversation. She expected that her friend knew all about this Mr. Waddle to whom Lady James referred.

"Did you say I was *croaky?* The sound that a *frog* makes?" Kate complained. "I know it has been some time since I have—"

"Kate, please! I only said that so she would leave us." Kitty had stopped playing and faced her. "I feel your alarm. What is it? Who is Mr. Waddle? You two are acquainted, I take it. All will be revealed when he arrives! He will expose us and we shall be thrown out of the house!"

"He and I are well-acquainted. Mr. Waddle" —Kate drew in a breath to bolster her courage while she confessed to her friend— "has visited me on a number of occasions at school. I am certain you must have seen him. Even I did not fully understand what his visits meant or his position in my life for he is one of my guardians, alongside my uncle Lord Bradford."

"You have *two* guardians?"

"He takes care of the legalities while Lord and Lady Bradford see to my position in society."

"And that was why we traveled to London." Kitty's expression altered to that of realization.

"They—*she—Lady Bradford* was trying to marry me off." Kate felt embarrassed but announced this bit quite stoically. "If she had been successful, I would no longer have been their responsibility, out from under their influence … but under the control of a husband. I cannot like that."

"Nor would I." Kitty could not fully understand how things were between Kate and her aunt. It had been quite obvious that they did not get on. "That is why you were sent away."

"When I did not make a match, her ladyship washed her hands of me. I apologize that you are to suffer my fate."

"That is worse than I imagined." Kitty uttered in amazement. "It is no wonder you had had enough of your aunt and London. How could you not wish to relinquish your role as Lady Catherine?"

"Thank you for understanding, Kitty." Kate could barely meet her friend's gaze. "I could not regret more that I have brought you into the catastrophe I have created. This is a circumstance of my own making, I dare not implicate that you had anything of its creation. It makes me feel wretched. You have only been an unwilling participant and should not be blamed. Actually, you were against the scheme from the beginning, never wanted to go along with it."

"That is true," Kitty admitted. It must have felt good for her to finally speak the words aloud.

"You only did so because you had no choice. You could not have spoken out in front of Lady James when we arrived." And that was why Kate had acted as she had. It really was unconscionable of her.

"Yes, that is correct."

"I will not have the blame set on your plate." Kate could not bear having her dear friend come to any harm because of her own impulsive nature.

"Thank you, Kate." But Kitty had participated by remaining quiet.

"You may be guilty by association, I am sorry to say."

Kitty sighed. It was one of those forlorn affairs that spoke of the matter that taking no action was in itself choosing an action. "I expect it will not matter as long as we are together in this … both outcasts. If we have one another we will contrive."

"I believe it will be better that I confess to them than have Mr. Waddle expose me … us." Kate lifted her chin which made her feel a bit more confident. "I will tell them all that I was the one who suggested this charade and I was the one who made you go through with it."

"The family might think you quite disagreeable. Perhaps they may refuse to speak to you again."

"I must remind you, Kitty, the Emersons are only family by marriage and not by blood. It is probable that I will never cross their paths again." Unlike the great certainty of coming face-to-face with her aunt and uncle Bradford. "I will address the Emersons, and their guests, at my first opportunity."

Kitty could ask for nothing more.

The tea tray soon arrived closely followed by Miss Alicia. Upon the tray sat three teacups.

"I hope you do not mind if I join you." She glanced at them rather shyly, hopeful that they would accept her.

"We would be delighted with your company, Miss Alicia." Kitty said.

"Oh, that is *splendid!*" She moved quickly around to take the center seat, between the two, where she could be in the center of a nice, comfortable coze. Miss Alicia gazed at her two companions with bright-eyes and filled with excitement, enthusiasm, and all expectation of happiness. "And we can speak of music ... pianofortes and singing and talk about everything that will happen this evening, shall we?"

Waiting in the front parlor until all the dinner guests had arrived, Stephen tucked the small handkerchief he'd received earlier into the inside breast pocket of his jacket and turned to face Toby.

"What's that you say?" Traces of orange blossoms lingered from its owner. He rubbed the tips of his fingers together as if that would help dissipate the fragrance, making it undetectable to his friend.

"I said, *she* is here." Toby whispered to Stephen but faced the opposite direction.

The *she* Stephen had in mind was Miss Kate but when he turned to the open doors, there stood Lady Catherine. Of course, that was who Toby meant. She was the celebrated talent in residence and mentor to Alicia. There was no doubt his friend held her in high regard.

This evening she appeared in an equally drab-colored gown as she did the last—this one had a flimsy layer of skirt with little white spots. Did she not have something more ... cheerful? It was well-appointed and equally well-made but it did little to put forth a young lady. In the manner she held her hands, still yet tense enough to brandish her knuckles white, she seemed to Stephen, who could only claim to be a passing acquaintance, to be nervous, uncomfortable, dare he say … uneasy.

Was it because she was to play the pianoforte for them later? She had played for them just last evening with great success. She was to accompany Miss Kate as she sang this evening. Perhaps she was nervous *for* her friend.

He did not know exactly what caused the disturbance but something *was* amiss.

"Did you tell Lord Stephen and Mr. Drayton about our new guest?" Lady James' trill seemed to rise above all the other voices in the room, gaining everyone's attention.

"Who?" Lord James remarked, surprised at hearing this. "I do not recall any such thing, my lady."

"My lord!" his wife chided him in scolding tones. "Will you never remember anything?"

"I clearly recall those things that matter," he said quite frankly. "I have no reason to recall *everything*. There is no need—you will tell me if it is of true importance."

"Who do you think I am … a house steward?" Lady James was not pleased at all.

"You do so well at managing all the household comings and goings… I would rather leave such arrangements to you, my dear."

"But you were to inform your nephew and his friend of our new visitor."

This bit of news from Lady James had caught Stephen's attention.

"Honestly, if Mr. Waddle would care to occupy himself with fishing or shooting, I am certain news of his arrival would have heralded such celebration!"

"*Does* he have an interest in sport?" His lordship's eyes went wide, displaying extreme interest.

"I cannot say. Lord Bradford's letter was addressed to you, did you not see it mentioned when you read it?"

"No, I do not recall Bradford saying as much." Lord James shook his head. "More's the pity."

"Lord Stephen, Mr. Drayton, if you will allow me." Lady James ignored her husband and continued, addressing the young men, "We are expecting Mr. Waddle to join us today" —she glanced around and gestured with her hand— "I am not certain when this gentleman is to arrive. I had hoped to welcome him before dinner but … as you can see he is not present. I do hope he arrives before it grows dark."

"And who is *Mr. Waddle*?" Stephen inquired.

"Mr. Waddle is a solicitor of Rush, Stonewall, and Waddle in London and co-guardian of Lady Catherine."

Stephen's glance at said lady revealed her to fidget in agitation even more at the mention of the solicitor's name. It was no wonder she appeared uneasy … one of her guardians was to join them. She, indeed, would need to be on her best behavior.

Perhaps she anticipated some sort of disciplinary action with Mr. Waddle's arrival? Stephen could scarcely believe it of this well-mannered, agreeable young lady.

The dinner bell rang and much the same as the evening before, the three gentlemen in the drawing room escorted the three ladies down the corridor to the dining room.

"I don't see a place for our newcomer, Mr. Waddle," Lord James commented. "Where is he to sit?"

"He is not here in time for dinner, my lord!" Lady James addressed him rather harshly. "I thought we had already gone through that."

"Oh, yes. That's right." Lord James approached his seat at the head of the table. "No matter if he comes late. There is plenty for him no matter when he arrives, I'm sure."

"Oh, let's do sit, my lord," Lady James urged and they all sat in their positions of the previous evening.

Already, Stephen could not help but feel boredom of dinner seeping in. It was all very a polite, sedate affair—might as well take a tray in one's room, or a cold cotillion served in the library would do. His mind strayed. He wondered if Miss Kate had tiptoed off to search the shelves while the rest of them gathered around this table partaking in polite conversation enjoying the soup course.

Stephen enjoyed spending time with her ... which was unusual for him. But then again, Miss Kate had been a rare lady. She was unlike any female he'd met before. He could imagine her refreshing outlook might make her interesting company and could understand why Lady Kitty would have her as a companion—life would not be boring.

Stephen managed to finish his dinner without incident. Lord and Lady James excused themselves while the remaining two couples would move on to the evening promenade, the ladies would switch escorts from the previous day. Stephen would walk with his cousin Alicia while Toby would have his chance to stroll with Lady Catherine.

Stephen motioned to Toby that he and Lady Kitty should proceed as he was experiencing momentary breathing difficulties. He pressed his lips together and brought the back of his hand to his upper lip ... to fend off a...

"Are you quite all right, Stephen?" Alicia inquired with genuine concern.

The fresh evening air, with its hints of floral—grassy—outdoorish smells, gave Stephen a tickle in his nose that he was going to— going to— He quickly inhaled twice—reaching into his jacket pocket for his linen—before giving a great sneeze.

"I do beg your pardon, Cousin! It is the dust from the library. I cannot seem to rid myself of its effect." He wiped his nose.

"Goodness," Alicia recoiled, pulling her hand from his elbow to distance herself. "What a *dainty* pocket square you have."

It wasn't until Stephen detected the scent of orange blossom that he realized it was not his linen he produced but Miss Kate's borrowed handkerchief.

He folded it, glancing at the diminutive size and lacy edges and explained, "Yes, for my smaller efforts."

"*That* was a small sneeze?" Alicia sounded amazed. "Oh my— I cannot imagine—"

"We should not be speaking about this. It is far too coarse a topic for young ladies."

"Very well," she agreed but carefully watched him as he tucked away the handkerchief in his breast pocket before offering her his arm to continue down the path.

"We should do our best to catch up to the others else they will think we've abandoned them." He stepped forward with purpose, causing his cousin to scurry along by his side. When the others, Toby and Lady Kitty, came into sight, Stephen slowed.

"Gracious!" Alicia pressed her hand to her abdomen, catching her breath.

"You do not wish to be left behind, do you?"

"I do not expect they will go far." Alicia remarked in half-scold, half-humor followed by a small chuckle. "They will pause to view the rotunda. We would meet them there."

"I take it you are fond of our new visitor, Lady Kitty?" Stephen had noticed, as Toby pointed out, the change in Alicia. She had appeared altered, much uplifted and brighter.

"I think Kitty is ever so kind and vastly talented, do you not think so? I cannot tell you how much it pleases me that she is to spend a great deal of time with us."

"*Will* it be a great deal of time?" Stephen had not thought of the new visitor's length of stay at Grimshaw, only how much joy she must have brought to his cousin. "How fortunate for you. I think you may have found yourself a new friend."

"I would like to think so," Alicia replied shyly, casting her gaze away. "It remains to be seen how well she thinks of me. I find her quite agreeable and a most patient instructor." She glanced up at him. "I cannot be the best student she has had, although I am trying."

"If not the best, then the most diligent." Stephen could see that Toby had been correct. His cousin was completely enamored of Lady Kitty.

"Truth be told, my lord," she began. "I am not really acquainted with anyone my own age—and I do *believe* her to be about my age. My closest sibling, Cynthia will soon be leaving the schoolroom. The few years between us do not matter but I feel decades older than she."

"Then a friendship with Lady Kitty it must be." Stephen could not see anything for it!

"I am hopeful that Mama and Papa can see that their daughters' education of the arts are lacking. We sorely need instruction in music, drawing, and dancing."

Stephen had never imagined he would have discussions regarding those topics. This was the type of thing parents should arrange for their young, *unwed* daughters … if they ever wished to see them married.

"How are we ever to attract a gentleman … a husband if we cannot dance? We must have a few accomplishments, do you not agree? How will a man ever notice us, much less admire us?" Alicia clasped her hands before her and stared at them. "Miss Kitty has Town Bronze. She has been to London—she is much to be admired."

"As to that … a few months spent in London does not mean she has mastered the art of attracting a gentleman. I believe she spent her girlhood years at an all-girls' school. That is not what I consider worldly." Stephen stepped from his cousin, holding her at arm's length as if to take a purely objective aspect. "If I were to judge you, for instance, on appearance alone, there would be no contest to any of the females in London. You are quite unexceptional and would set a trend no one, try as they might, could follow!"

"Do not say so, Lord Stephen!" The scarlet blush that suffused Alicia's cheeks nearly matched that of her hair. It was not a thing she could hide behind her hands. "But to be truly accomplished and to gain the admiration of a gentleman could be all I could wish for. I suppose I could learn to write poetry. I could recite it to—"

"I beg you—no." Stephen dreaded the thought of any young lady attempting to mesmerize any gentlemen with rhyming words.

"Oh, I see." Alicia sighed as if he had dashed all her hopes. "If only I could sing as well as Miss Kate. I have no notion if my voice is at all pleasant."

"Who? Oh—Lady Kitty's companion, Miss Kate." Stephen's quick glance at his cousin, and his subsequent reaction at hearing Kate's name gave him pause.

"I heard her sing this afternoon. Not a song … but I heard her singing voice during some vocal exercises." Alicia gazed at him through her thick lashes. Seemingly a bit guilty, he thought but did not understand why. "I thought she was quite good. Do you not recall that she is to sing for us this evening?" She tugged a bit on his arm as if he needed to be brought to his senses.

"I do, yes." There wasn't much he did not recall about the miss. He did remember that she needed to leave by three that afternoon to practice. *That* young lady had occupied more of his thoughts than he cared to admit.

Stephen expected that he was a bit smitten with his new acquaintance. It had been years since he'd felt anything near this for a female. He found her interesting and refreshing, unlike that of any young lady with whom he had previously been acquainted.

In time, perhaps sometime during the next few weeks, near the end of his stay, his infatuation with her would fade. He could not ignore that she intrigued him, and moreover, she made him think. *Imagine. Hope.*

Alicia smiled at him, silently urging him to move forward. It was apparent that Miss Kate had brought a diversion to his stay just as she had to the others. Stephen found that the realization brought a spring in his step and an easy smile that would not fade.

Lady James had sent for Kate after Kitty and Miss Alicia left for their post-dinner promenade escorted by Lord Stephen and Mr. Drayton. When they returned from their stroll, the group would gather for the next activity which would be in the music room. With the absence of appetite, Kate had pushed aside her dinner and dressed, headed in that direction, dreading what she needed to do.

While she waited, Kate paced before the long windows that overlooked the south side of the house. She had dressed in her pale yellow gown Kitty had helped her choose for her public debut. She needed to dress appropriately for her station and not overshadow Kitty—*Lady Catherine* ... although after she made her confession it would not matter.

Kate heard the guests on the terrace. They would soon be making their way along the corridor and on their way to the music room, chatting amongst themselves. She couldn't recall feeling so anxious in her entire life. She'd told several small, insignificant lies over the years at the Academy and Miss Maddingly had always dealt a fair and appropriate punishment for her misdeeds, but this time, Kate feared the consequence would not be the same.

The guests strolled into the music room and began to fill the seats. Kitty stepped toward Kate who stood next to the pianoforte.

"It was a very good thing you did not come to us before dinner and make your confession—who you are—who we are—

you would have spoiled everyone's appetite," Kitty whispered. "As it was I do not think I managed more than a few bites."

"We must go on as normal, Kitty," Kate encouraged her. "Now that everyone has come together for the entertainment, it will be my best opportunity to confess … to tell them."

"I suppose you must." Kitty appeared as guilty as Kate felt.

"Yes. But we do not know when he is to arrive but if he has stated he will arrive today, then this day it will be. I have never known Mr. Waddle to err with these types of things. I have every confidence he will be here." Kate motioned to the pianoforte. "You are to perform first, I believe. Do be seated and begin your warmups while the others settle. At least they may enjoy your portion of this evening's entertainment, for they will not care for mine."

Kate stepped back, making room for Kitty to sit at the keyboard. She could easily see for herself how much her hands shook.

"I do not know if I *can* play." Kitty intertwined her trembling fingers and closed her eyes. Kate would not doubt it was in prayer.

"Never fear, you will be fine once you begin." Kate stepped back, taking a seat behind her friend.

Kitty began to play and the audience fell instantly quiet. Their expressions were that of pure joy. Kate would be lying if she denied feeling guilty for what she was about to do to the Emersons. She would erase every good feeling and at the same time give them the complete disgust of her.

How could she do this? Kate had truly enjoyed herself these last few days. They were the best since leaving the Academy. Nothing in London equaled the joy she had found here.

Kate felt quite wretched. Would she never learn? Would this be enough of a lesson for her not to allow her impetuous nature get the better of her? She had no one to blame but herself.

Suddenly, Kate realized it was silent. Kitty had finished. It was her turn. With a nod, Kitty indicated to Kate that she should face forward and address the onlookers.

This was not going to be what they expected to hear but the audience would be riveted. Kate faced them ... all of the Emersons and Mr. Drayton. All attention was focused upon her.

They laughed softly ... the silence had gone on too long. She was feeling nervous...

"Do not be shy, Miss Kate," Miss Alicia urged in kindness.

"It is just that—" Kate had rehearsed this speech a hundred times. Now that the time was here, she didn't know exactly what to say. "Ladies and Gentlemen," Kate began, ready to face *her* music. "I beg your pardon but—"

"If you will excuse the interruption." A footman standing at the open music room doors distracted her. The seated guests, upon observing, that Kate's attention had been diverted, turned in their seats to also stare.

"Mr. Hugh Waddle," the footman announced.

That's when a gentleman stepped forward into the music room and bowed.

Nine

The solicitor … he had arrived. *Except …*

"Pardon me." The newcomer bowed again.

This gentleman was not the Mr. Waddle with whom Kate was acquainted. Appearing every bit a town gentleman, he wore sturdy, well-constructed traveling clothes, nothing out of the ordinary to display ostentation but smart and sensible.

Lord James left his seat, nearing the newcomer, studying him through narrowed eyes. "You look a bit too young to be Lady Catherine's guardian, nearly the same age as she is, I'd say."

"Sir, my father is the senior partner at Rush, Stonewall, and Waddle. I am Hugh Waddle *the Younger* and prefer my name to be pronounced *Wah-dell.*"

Oh. It was all Kate could do not to raise her eyebrows in reaction to the pompous declaration.

Whatever he wished to call himself, he was not known to Kate —*nor she to him.*

She had never set eyes on this gentleman before. He very much resembled his father in his facial features—around the mouth and eyes, his stance, and his no-nonsense manner.

"My letter of introduction, sir." The young man held out a

sealed letter. "As it will explain, my father shares the responsibility of guardianship with Lady Catherine Jessup's uncle Lord
Bradford."

"I see," Lord James murmured and accepted the missive,
broke the seal, and unfolded the paper to peruse its contents.
Then his attention moved from the letter to the man.

"My father had meant to come himself, but unexpected events
prevented him from making the journey. He sends me with his
regards. I am to ensure her ladyship has arrived in good order
and keep him informed regarding her continuing well-being." He
made a shallow bow.

The young Mr. Waddle—*er* ... Wad*dell* was punctual, just like
his father, Kate thought.

"Welcome to Grimshaw Court, Mr. Waddell," Lord James
offered the newcomer his hand and shook it heartily. "Since you do
not have the acquaintance of your father's ward, you must allow
me to make Lady Catherine known to you." He gestured toward
the pianoforte. "Lady Catherine, may I present Mr. Waddell?"

Kate elbowed Kitty gently, who made a graceful curtsy. "How
do you do, Mr. Waddell?"

"How do you do, Lady Catherine?" Mr. Waddell inclined his
head. "My father has told me quite a bit about you."

The words frightened Kate a bit. How much *could* he know? A
verbal description of them would not differentiate Kate from
Kitty. He would have to have been acquainted with one or the
other to distinguish their identities.

Lord James motioned to his left. "My wife, Lady James. My
daughter, Miss Emerson."

The ladies made their curtsies, Mr. Waddell nodded. "Lady
James, Miss Emerson, how do you do?"

"My nephew, Lord Stephen Emerson and his friend Mr.
Drayton."

"Lord Stephen," Mr. Waddell greeted each with a nod. "Mr.
Drayton, how do you do?"

"And there is Miss Kate, Uncle James," was Lord Stephen's gentle reminder.

"Ah ... oh, yes. An oversight, I assure you ... Mr. Waddell, may I present Lady Catherine's companion Miss Matthews?"

"How do you do, Mr. Waddell?" Kate sunk into a very satisfied, complicit curtsey. Her surge of relief gave her the confidence to look upon the newcomer without fear of recognition. That she had no need to make a confession, Kate realized she had gained a great advantage. The charade she and Kitty had been enacting could continue.

"How do you do, Miss Matthews?" he replied mildly, not truly noticing her ... not as anyone of importance.

"We knew to expect you, sir. It is only we had no idea when you were to arrive." Lady James sounded more embarrassed than apologetic.

"Please forgive my late arrival, my father was rather insistent that I should arrive today." Mr. Waddell replied with some discomfort. His attention had yet to move from Kitty.

Kate was not certain whether it was the manner in which he stared that bothered her or the amount of time his attention remained upon her friend. Had the description of Lady Catherine his father gave altered from the flesh and blood Kitty who now stood before him?

"I shall see that you are shown to your room." Lady James motioned to the footman who had brought the visitor. "You are welcome to join us after you have settled."

Mr. Waddell made a slight bow of thanks, acknowledging her ladyship's offer.

"There is no need to think you will miss out, sir. We plan to have many musical evenings during the next fortnight, do we not, ladies?" Lord James turned to Kate and Kitty for an answer.

"Yes, my lord," they choroused with a smile.

"Thank you, my lady." Mr. Waddell bowed. "I look forward to joining the gathering later. Now, if you will excuse me."

There was a collective sigh in the room when the new visitor left.

"Where were we?" Lord James glanced about and motioned that everyone should return to their seats.

"Miss Kate was about to sing for us." Miss Alicia reminded her father.

"Oh, yes. Yes, indeed." He nodded to Kate and eased into his chair. "Do, please, continue."

"Eh ... I was about to say ..." Kate was trying to find her words ... now she was to alter course completely by transforming into the songstress. "I hope you are not expecting too much ... Kitty—Miss Kitty—and I have not had much time to practice ... we have decided to perform some selections from the years of performances at the girls' school we attended."

"All is well, my friends," Miss Alicia said to encourage them. "We have had a bit of an upset, but I'm certain you two will do fine. All of us are anxious to hear your offerings."

Kate smiled with joy and immense relief. She turned her head to meet Kitty's gaze and nodded for her to start the music.

Kitty retook her seat at the pianoforte and ran her fingers up the keyboard in a bright arpeggio. "Kate?"

With a glance, Kate signaled to Kitty that she was ready. Kitty played the short introduction, and Kate drew in a breath and sang. She felt glorious knowing the reports to her guardian of Lady Catherine would be glowing—especially with Kitty playing the role.

Kitty always had better manners than Kate. Her temperament, mild, and she could never be described as difficult or impulsive. Mr. Waddell would use words to describe his father's ward as cheerful, helpful, amiable, polite, and good-natured.

The two of them, their identities, were safe. Kate could go on here at Grimshaw Court as if nothing had changed.

The next morning, Kitty stood at the threshold of the breakfast room. There, Miss Alicia sat at the large table with the early light of the sun providing glorious illumination.

"Good morning." Alicia's smile was a perfect start to the day. "Did you sleep well?"

"Oh, yes," Kitty replied. "I was quite exhausted after we had finished."

"You cannot be blamed." Alicia held the cup and saucer off the table, preparing to sip her chocolate. "You played non-stop for at least an hour last night. Miss Kate did sing for us … but again, you had no choice but to accompany her."

Kitty smiled, coming to a stop at the sideboard to find a bite to eat for herself. "I will not be burdened for long once you are able to play."

"Me?" Alicia's tea cup dipped precariously, slipping from her fingers. She recovered without spilling a drop. "I can-not—" Her face flushed to a deep crimson. "Do you mean before *others?*"

"It will happen sooner than you think." Kitty concentrated on the buttered eggs and bacon rashers she served herself.

"I hardly think that possible. I am not yet near-accomplished to attempt such a thing." Alicia blinked, regaining her composure, and sipped from her cup, returning it to its saucer and setting both to the table with only a slight tremor. "You were correct about Kate's voice. It is quite fine, indeed. And what of our songstress? Will she not share breakfast with us?"

"She was gone by the time I arose." Kitty was not Kate's keeper. It would not surprise Kitty if half the time Kate became distracted by some other task that suddenly emerged than the one she initially had set her mind to undertake. "She knows the location of the breakfast room, and if she is hungry, she will arrive."

"I suppose we are destined to breakfast alone," Alicia replied, sounding disappointed.

"But we shall both have uninterrupted time to practice," Kitty reminded her. "Where is everyone?"

"The gentlemen have gone shooting, and Mama is having a tray in her room." As soon as Alicia had answered they noticed Mr. Drayton and Mr. Waddell at the doorway and they stood.

"Good morning, ladies …" Mr. Drayton greeted and bowed, as did Mr. Waddell.

Kitty and Alicia dipped a shallow curtsy and inclined their heads.

"I beg that we do not disturb you. Will you not be seated?" Mr. Waddell must have known the ladies' show of formality was for his benefit.

"Would you care for breakfast?" Alicia, playing the hostess, inquired.

"We have done so earlier, thank you," Mr. Drayton answered for the two. "Just returning from seeing Lord James and Stephen off."

"Will you not sit and have a cup of coffee or tea?" Alicia glanced toward the sideboard where both could be found.

Mr. Waddell exchanged glances with Mr. Drayton, whose small smile relayed his consent. "Thank you, we shall."

Kitty and Alicia retook their seats while the two gentlemen retrieved their hot drinks and sat across from the ladies at the table … but not before Alicia smiled and exchanged glances with Kitty. She thought her hostess was enjoying the company of the *gentlemen* very much.

"I am certain my father was quite disappointed when you did not join his hunting party."

"I have not come to the country to pursue sport. I am here merely to *observe*." Mr. Waddell said the last pointedly, Kitty had no doubt his answer was in someway in reference to her. He never did comment on his preference to join the shooting party. "I am here in a purely supervisory capacity."

"If you are referring to me, sir, I do not need supervision. What trouble might I possibly cause?" Kitty could not imagine she would be the source of any trouble and felt rather insulted. "I plan to sit with Miss Alicia for a music lesson... I do not understand what harm that might do unless I am accused of assaulting the keyboard."

"A music lesson?" Mr. Waddell seemed taken aback and said, "I cannot see how you could cause mischief with that endeavor."

"*Mischief?*" Miss Alicia sounded slightly alarmed at the accusation. "I hope that is not a slight of *my* musical abilities nor Kitty's."

"I cannot accuse either of you of that. Your playing is a delight, my lady. I cannot wait to hear more this evening." His expression as if he'd shocked himself. "You *will* be playing again, will you not?"

"Only if I can continue to practice." Kitty could not be expected to play new music as the days went on. There were only so many pieces one could play by memory and play well enough before others so as not to embarrass oneself. Were they to be relied upon to entertain the entire household for the duration? "I hope it will not be a disappointment if some selections are repeated, Mr. Waddell."

"I don't expect any of us will mind, Miss Kitty." Mr. Drayton had proven to be Alicia's staunch supporter and apparently Kitty's as well. His gentle smile must have meant to reassure her of his sincerity. "It is a delight to hear you play, which we all anticipate with pleasure."

His words caused Alicia to blush yet again. She must have grown accustomed to the occurrence, for her face did not redden quite as dark, nor had it lingered for quite as long. "You missed the promenade last night, Mr. Waddell." A momentary pause was all it took for her to regain her composure. "We had just returned before gathering in the music room when you arrived."

"I am sorry to hear that." Mr. Waddell said over the rim of his cup. There was something odd about the manner in which he gazed at Alicia. "Mr. Drayton was telling me about your *evening promenades* and of the folly."

"Did you not show it to him when the two of you wandered about the estate?" Alicia inquired with a tilt of her head.

"No, I thought I would leave that pleasure to you," Mr. Drayton replied with a distinct brightness in his eyes.

"That was very kind of you, sir. I am proud of our little architectural novelty." She smiled very prettily at him.

"I must admit I am rather interested to see it for myself." Mr. Waddell raised his cup in cheers.

"Allow me to assure you it is an activity we often do—oh!" Alicia gasped with inspiration. "Let us take Mr. Waddell out to view the folly now, shall we?"

"And what of your music practice?" For Alicia to delay her lesson for the sake of Mr. Waddell... Kitty thought that was something quite unexpected.

Stephen returned from shooting with Lord James and cleaned up, changing into appropriate clothing to continue his search of the library. Forgoing his jacket, he did not dress in a comfortable banyon or the informal garb of a country gentleman.

This afternoon he added an apron, a pair of sleeve protectors, both borrowed from a footman, a swath of linen fastened around his neck, covering his cravat. A second hung loosely under his chin to be pulled up over his nose and mouth to keep away the dust. He had not known before yesterday how much breathing the stuff bothered him. He found Miss Kate sitting in a chair, out of the way with her head down, a book held very close to her face. He nearly overlooked her presence altogether. It seemed to him to be quite odd.

"I say ... are you sleeping?" Stephen whispered very softly and carefully so as not to disturb her. He would hardly expect to find Miss Kate slumbering, but the book was held much too close for her to be reading. He had no wish to wake her and peered closer at the figure curled in the armchair with an open book to her face.

He neared, keeping as quiet as possible, and reached his hand out toward the spine to gently pull it away from her face with the tip of his index finger.

"Oh—" She startled, eyes wide and she straightened in the chair.

Stephen recoiled, drawing his hand ... arm away and stepping back at her loud gasp. Her eyes opened wide at the disturbance.

"I beg your pardon! I had not meant to—" She blinked and must have realized where she was and who was near. "I was so very tired. We were up very late last night—"

"There is nothing wrong with that, Miss Kate," Stephen tried to assure her. "There is no need for excuses. You graced us with your singing, and we would be most fortunate if you would plan to do so again. It is understandable that you might feel—"

"—And I had to rise very early this morning." She held the book against her chest and stood, still blinking, trying to clear her eyes. "Thank you for your kind praise." She stared at him. "You look like an amateur highwayman."

"*Amateur*?" He did not care for the idea of representing an amateur anything.

"Well ... you are not a *real* highwayman, are you?" It was not said as if she were frightened but in a manner of disbelief.

"No. I'm not." He smiled, then pulled the linen covering his face up over his chin to his nose with his thumb and forefinger, covering his mouth and said through the fabric, "I am merely following your example."

"I see." She glanced at his newly-donned accouterment, lingering at each momentarily. "Better wrapped up than sneezing all afternoon, I expect."

"Exactly." He removed the fabric from his face with a tug to his mask. He would wear the linen when he had to but did not care much for the constriction. "The maids do come through here but don't clean much above Uncle James' height." Stephen glanced about with a discerning eye toward the state of the upper shelving. "Which reminds me..." He pressed his hand against his breast pocket. "I thought I had your handkerchief here." Still unable to find it, he patted along his sides, checking for the object. It should have been easy to identify ... a small, folded piece of ...

"Not to worry," she said. "I have others."

"I will, at some point, return your handkerchief." He nodded, making his promise. "Will you not don your mobcap and let us resume our search?"

"Very well." She closed her book, set it on the table and reached into the pocket of her apron for her cap.

He strolled with her to the center of the room where they would part, heading for their respective search areas. "What were you doing this morning that had you up and about so early?"

"The younger Emerson sisters, their governess Miss Fawcett, and I were sketching birds." She pulled the cap over her hair, settling it just above her ears.

"Chickens?" Stephen reached out to remove a small, curled white feather from the strap of her apron. "I would have never known."

"Mrs. Robin, our previous subject, was not to be found this morning. Candy suggested we find new subjects and suggested the hens near the kitchen yard. Chickens *are* birds."

"Yes, I am aware of that." The smile he offered was not exactly smug, but he could not help but tease her just a little.

"The girls have named them and have their favorites among the flock." Miss Kate pulled a length of linen, her dust rag, from another pocket and allowed it to unfold.

"Oh, I don't know if that's wise." He would not wish to encourage endearing oneself to the poultry because, in the end, the fowl were considered livestock. As such, an asset of the estate to be utilized in any manner to benefit the running of the property … and livestock's end was not usually a happy one.

"The girls like the chickens because they are loud and scatter when you chase them."

"I can see that is one of the benefits of chickens." Stephen understood the girls. Any child would enjoy that type of thing. "But I must say that piglets do the same and are much louder. It is great fun. I should caution you not to become familiar with any farm animal, especially to name them… No, it is not in one's best interest to become overly-friendly. You see, heartache is bound to follow."

"*Heartache*?" Miss Kate faced him.

Stephen drew his linen up over his nose once again, leaving only his eyes exposed. He felt as if he were hiding—there was the embarrassment of having to tell her such a blunt thing, and the implied sadness in the tone of his words, he indicated, would cause her not to inquire further.

Have a care… He had not wished to shock her.

For all her intelligence and bold demeanor he sensed an innocence about her. He studied her face and questioning expression. Miss Kate's steady gaze met his direct one. How could he tell her that living in the country it was quite ordinary that livestock ended up on one's dinner table?

"Your advice is noted," she said in a calm manner. "Shall we resume our search for the book?"

Ten

After their morning walk, Kitty and Alicia headed for the music room for a lesson and the practice for which they both longed. There was some talk between the gentlemen regarding fishing. Although Kitty did not know for certain, she assumed that when they disappeared, they had gone to find their morning's occupation.

That evening, the guests would once again come together. After the Emerson family and their guests had finished dinner, Lord and Lady James remained in the dining room while the others headed toward the back of the house for their evening promenade. It was the first time Kate had graced the dinner table. She always proved to add gaiety to any gathering, but she could not like this disruption to her usual routine. However, the alternative of discovery was far more catastrophic than Kitty would have cared for ... dare she say, even *ruinous* to their immediate future?

So Kate joined the other guests, pushing aside her personal endeavors and considered herself content to be included in their daily pursuits. She could confess to herself that she was, very much, of a single mind, and she had her own goal of wishing to do as she pleased in sight.

Kate, she had told herself, would not complain. She would portray a polite, agreeable, amiable miss as both she and Kitty had been taught. They had years of schooling on how a young lady should behave in polite society.

It was only that it was much more in Kitty's nature to be agreeable. Kate had … *difficulties* … in that quarter. Currently, she was trying to overcome her decidedly selfish tendencies. She would have liked to believe she might be better than this, but apparently she was not.

Kate had to admit that sitting at a dining room table for a proper dinner was better than eating from a tray in one's bedchamber. She remained calm, put on a pleasant smile, and *attempted* to enjoy herself.

As the ladies were making themselves ready to leave the table, the gentlemen moved to follow. It was then that Kate recalled Kitty telling her of the evening promenades that took place after dinner. Kate waited at the back and allowed those who knew better to lead the way out of the dining room.

Mr. Drayton stepped onto the terrace and drew in a deep breath. "I must admit I am glad of your arrival, Mr. Waddell. The addition of a few more guests, I do include your presence as well, Miss Kate, make our small group quite jolly."

"I am sorry if you no longer find my company entertaining." Lord Stephen chuckled. Kitty was certain Mr. Drayton's words were not meant to insult.

"Do not despair, Stephen. You are not to blame," Mr. Drayton assured his friend. "You are not at all tiresome, but considering the longevity of our friendship, you must know to find new visitors while rusticating in such an isolated, rural setting is quite unexpected."

"Agreed, Toby. It is a pleasant surprise." Lord Stephen offered Kitty his arm. "Shall we proceed?"

"I feel as if I am leading a parade!" Kitty glanced over her shoulder at the others following.

"A parade to the folly?" Kate inquired with some enthusiasm while taking Mr. Drayton's arm.

"*Of* the folly, Miss Kate," Mr. Waddell corrected. "I had the pleasure of viewing the structure this morning with Lady Catherine and Miss Emerson."

"You did not see the long shadows of the rotunda columns then, Mr. Waddell," Miss Alicia kindly pointed out. "In the evening, when the sun is lower, the shadows stretch far to the east. It is very beautiful."

"We still have some time yet before we reach the viewing area." Lord Stephen said in a loud voice, allowing it to carry to Mr. Waddell some feet behind him. "Miss Kate—" he said even louder "—I have a recommendation for you if you need something to read after *Gulliver's Travels*."

"You're reading *Gulliver's Travels*?" Mr. Waddell turned to the lady on his arm. "It was one of my favorites as a boy. Are you enjoying it?"

"Yes, I think it very exciting," Kate remarked in her polite voice. "I just finished the first volume yesterday. Lord Stephen and I are currently searching for the second."

"Without much luck, I take it." Mr. Waddell chuckled.

"It *is* a large library," Lord Stephen stated in Kate's defense, and rightly so. The room was enormous and the books too numerous to be counted.

"Would you two care to begin our promenade or carry on a conversation? You could very well continue your discussion as we walk if you would only—" Mr. Drayton interrupted. "If you will allow me to—"

"And over the course of the years, someone has rearranged the books." Her *polite* tone was falling away. "Perhaps more than once or twice."

"Why do you not—" Mr. Drayton motioned to his friend, then to the couple behind him.

"They had no ordering system in the first place." Lord Stephen kept turning, facing to the rear, to speak to Kate over the heads of and between Mr. Drayton and Miss Alicia, making forward progression difficult. "I still have every confidence we will find it, Miss Kate. Allow me to offer you *Robinson Crusoe* until we unearth the second volume."

"And perhaps you, Miss Kate, could—" Mr. Drayton made some hand gestures, indicating there should be some rearranging within their group. Perhaps she should move forward and Lord Stephen could more easily …

"Oh, yes, *Robinson Crusoe* is a splendid story," Mr. Waddell agreed most heartily. "It is about a man from York who has been shipwrecked off the coast of America and he is rescued by pirates."

"Pirates!" Kate, who had either not heard or ignored Mr. Drayton, sounded quite excited by the idea and the entire group came to a halt.

"My lord, you are going to stumble and fall!" Kitty warned. The path was not smooth and the footing precarious and his attention was not directed forward as it should have been.

"Here—allow me—" Mr. Drayton took it upon himself to place the couples in the most comfortable arrangement. He held out his hand to Kitty, who hesitantly placed hers into his after Lord Stephen nodded his approval. "If you would only exchange escorts, Miss Kate, Mr. Waddell … Lady Kitty could continue *their* conversation." He then guided Alicia to Mr. Waddell's side.

"Whatever are they talking about? What is it they're searching for?" Miss Alicia whispered to Mr. Waddell.

"They are discussing books!" Kitty remarked tersely to Alicia.

"A story called *Robinson Crusoe*, Miss Emerson," Mr. Waddell replied eagerly. He must have felt quite elated that he could add to the conversation.

How kind Mr. Drayton was to notice that pairing.

Miss Alicia and Mr. Waddell may have some interest developing between them. Others may have thought him insufferable but her eyes never glazed over.

"If you two could walk together" —Then reaching behind him he led Kate forward and had her stand next to Lord Stephen — "I am sure you could continue your conversation unencumbered … however … the rest of us still seem to be a bit too close."

There were soft chuckles and muffled giggles as people shuffled this way and that. Everyone found that moving about, swapping partners amusing.

"Perhaps that is not the most efficacious order." Mr. Drayton's brows furrowed and, with a tilt of his head, he reconsidered. "The rest of us should follow you two, so as not to distract you from your conversation you began at dinner," he amended, urging Mr. Waddell and Alicia to move on as the first couple moved forward, undeterred by Kate and Lord Stephen's continual discussion of books.

"There … how is that?" Mr. Drayton, who stood between the first and the third couple, considered the result of his efforts with several slow nods of satisfaction.

"And that will leave me to offer you my arm, my lady. If you do not mind the unworthiness of your escort." He held out his arm to Kitty and smiled.

"There is nothing of that sort to concern you, sir," she said with all sincerity. "You have done all of us a great service and managed the entire thing quite well, Mr. Drayton! Now we can all be comfortable." Kitty returned his smile and took his arm. Her palm touched the back of his hand.

"It only took a slight rearrangement of— of—" He stared into her eyes and … and … Mr. Drayton seemed to forget what he was about to say.

"Oh, *do* go on, will you, Toby?" Lord Stephen complained from his position from the back of the group. "You're holding up the rest of us."

Stephen was quite pleased to move to the back to escort Miss Kate. He did not much mind that Toby stood in the middle of the path as if he were a donkey refusing to move. It was only that Stephen did not care for his conversation with Miss Kate to be overheard by the others.

"I am very glad you are turning your attention to *Robinson Crusoe*."

"It is only on your and Mr. Waddell's recommendation. However ... I hardly have a choice, do I? Poor *Gulliver's Travels* is not to be found," Miss Kate lamented. "Its final volume is quite out of reach—and I do not mean to infer that it sits on an upper shelf where we are not aware of its existence."

"Yes, yes ... quite amusing," replied Stephen. "Not to worry, I am certain we shall find the volume soon enough."

"I hope so." Miss Kate sounded somewhat dejected. "What of *Robinson Crusoe?* How many volumes are there and are you aware of their location?" She exhaled. From pent up frustration or disgust, Stephen did not know.

"There are three in total. I have just completed reading the first volume and will begin the second this evening," he said, hoping the news would reassure her. "And the last volume is in my possession."

"That is good to know." She seemed satisfied with his answer.

"I do not wish to tell you too much of the story, lest I spoil it for you. I imagine you would like to discover it on your own." He glanced down at her, checking to see if he had made a mistake on his assumption. "I know I would."

She returned his inquisitive gaze with a smile. "You would be correct, my lord. I would prefer to read about Mr. Crusoe's predicaments for myself."

"Will you not tell Miss Kate that the tale takes place on a

distant land, living like savages, and—" Mr. Waddell continued with great excitement.

"I think *we* have said far too much already," Stephen hoped his discouraging glance would silence the man.

"Yes … yes, of course," he replied, nodding, and turned to face forward once again. To Stephen's delight, Cousin Alicia immediately engaged him in conversation.

"Do you think I might have the book this evening, my lord?" Miss Kate's manner was very secretive. "I would like to begin the story" —she leaned closer to whisper— "after the musical portion has concluded."

"Ah… I must confess, I would like nothing better." They spoke softly. Nothing illicit, it was only to place the book in her possession. "I shall retrieve it once our evening has concluded and we all disperse. I shall meet you in the library." Stephen would request extra candles set in *her* corner, the one where he'd found her sleeping.

"That sounds lovely. I shall look forward to that very much." Miss Kate's smile appeared genuine. Until now he had only been privy to her displays of practicality and determination. To see her indulge in an expression of joy was refreshing.

Cousin Alicia's laughter permeated the air, causing everyone to quiet. It was high pitched and delightful, the most distinctive Stephen had ever heard. It tinkled, as clear as a bell. Miss Kate and Lady Kitty's jovial expressions were far more measured. He wondered if this was because of their upbringing at a girls' school. He couldn't imagine a hall filled with girls who laughed like his cousin. It would be *maddening*, he was certain. Female students needed to learn restraint and temper their emotions and their voices. That was what Society expected of a well-behaved young lady of a certain standing, was it not?

They had just rounded the base of the tall hedge, and the group approached the old oak tree. Alicia's laughter ceased and

Mr. Waddell's sharp turn of his head to face south caught Stephen's attention. Here was the folly's vantage point.

"Oh … *the folly*," Mr. Waddell said, spotting it. "The rotunda looks much larger than I remember."

"It only appears larger because of the shadow it casts," Alicia confirmed.

"Can we move closer?" He leaned in that direction, and Alicia restrained him, preventing him from stepping off the path.

"I have been informed that it is farther away than it appears," Mr. Drayton replied, cautioning the new visitor. "We have been discussing a trip there these last few days. Miss Alicia said—"

"I shall plan our picnic, gentlemen," Alicia replied. "Kindly stop putting your oar in and allow me to handle the arrangements, if you please."

"Will you, Miss Emerson?" Mr. Waddell gazed warmly at her.

"We must stop merely talking about it and make the arrangements. Perhaps it will be tomorrow," she said enthusiastically.

"I do not think that very likely," Kitty told her in a calm, soft tone.

It seemed to Stephen that Lady Kitty was correct, such plans could not be set into motion so quickly.

"If we wish merely to travel to the folly—I'm certain all we need do is speak to Lord James, who could put forth the request to the stable master to arrange the transportation," Lady Kitty continued. "If we wish to enjoy a picnic there …" She glanced at Kate before resting her gaze upon Alicia. "There is much more to be done … not to mention the food preparation itself."

Lord Stephen nodded, confirming her assumption.

"That is true. We have no notion of what the kitchens have on hand or what can be obtained in so short a time," Alicia concluded. "I shall inform you all when it will be and of the final arrangements."

"That sounds splendid, Miss Emerson!" Mr. Waddell appeared

well-pleased with the announcement. "You have made me feel more welcome than I can say."

"I do hope I can rely on some help from your quarter, for I have never attempted such a thing before," Alicia leaned toward Kitty to whisper.

"Not to worry, Alicia," Lady Kitty replied to his cousin. "I am accustomed to making preparations for many and have done so at school more times than I can count. I would be happy to help assist you."

Alicia straightened and smiled, exuding confidence, appearing in high alt.

That evening, Kate had enjoyed listening to Kitty's performance and she, as always, cherished the opportunity to sing along with her friend's accompaniment. None of the music was new, but the audience enjoyed hearing a repeat performance nonetheless.

Was it wrong of Kate to wish for the end so soon? The high-light might have been when she stepped before the others to sing. It was not so this night. What she truly looked forward to was the time *after* the music … when she could gain possession of the new book and begin reading.

When she had finished singing, Kate made a small curtsy then waited for Kitty to stand next to her when they would bow together. After that, everyone would go their separate ways.

She watched Lord Stephen quickly slip out of the room. How stealthy he was, it appeared that no one had noticed his depar-ture. Kate knew exactly where he was to go and what he was about to do. She could not wait until she stole away to the library herself. She was certain that no one would notice her absence. Kate stood quietly and did her best to blend into the wall. Lord James excused himself. Where he was headed, Kate did not know.

The two remaining couples smiled and laughed. Lady James suggested they should remove to the parlor to play cards. She ushered them out of the music room stating she would keep them company, sitting nearby with her knitting.

After everyone had left, Kate made her way to the library. She couldn't help but imagine herself ensconced in her favorite, most comfortable chair. It would be sheer perfection of there were a small fire in the usually empty hearth on this cool evening.

When Kate emerged into the entrance hall, where the main staircase sat in the middle of the house, she knew the library was only on the other end of the central corridor.

While walking through the entrance hall, Kate noticed a figure on the terrace to her left. She slowed for only a few moments until she saw it was Lord James. The smoke of his pipe swirled about him as he strolled back and forth on the terrace. He did not seem to be taking in his surroundings and stared ahead, deep in thought.

She would step into the book-filled room in less than two minutes. She also wondered if Lord Stephen would be waiting for her, book in hand, or if she need wait for him. The unsettling thought that he did not know the exact location of the book he'd finished reading crossed her mind. Perhaps someone had moved it. Perhaps it was now lost as the second volume of *Gulliver's Travels*. There were many unknowns … Kate could feel a knot tighten in her stomach.

She need not worry nor wait long for an answer. The atmosphere upon entering the library was different from what she had expected. A golden aura eliminated from the hearth toward the interior of the room on the other side, from where her favorite chair stood. It was not too hot, but deliciously warm. Next to the chair was a pair of lit candles, providing excellent illumination. How cozy this all was!

"I hope this meets with your approval," Lord Stephen said.

She turned her head and saw him standing off to her side. He

observed her, waited to see her reaction. Her expression of amazement must have amused him.

Her approval? Did he not arrange this setting for himself? Lord
Stephen could not have done this for her. He could not have …

"I believe *this* is the last item to complete your evening." He
held out a book and Kate smiled. It was exactly what she
wished.

"Thank you." She took the book from him and felt a mixture of
pure joy and relief that she had not been disappointed. He was
here, and he had brought the book.

"I hope you don't mind, but I can understand you have no
wish to be disturbed while you read. I feel very much the same …
not wishing to be bothered, but I have taken the liberty of asking
for a tea tray."

"I don't know what to say, my lord. This is very kind of you.
Very kind." Truth be told, it was not common for Kate to experience such kindness, not shown to her by others. Such things were
possible at the Academy when the students did for themselves,
but for someone to think of *her*, in her current circumstance, was
unexpected.

"I am glad this pleases you." He smiled and did not make any
motion to indicate that he would be joining her.

"You plan to remain, do you not? All this" —she motioned to
the setting he had arranged— "Is not only for my benefit … it
cannot be. Will you not be seated and share the solitude you've
created?"

"No, indeed. I had not thought to… I had no expectations that
I would join you. I had *hoped*… You do not mind?"

"Why should I mind? This is your house … your uncle's
house."

"Thank you," he said and smiled. "Are you certain?"

"How could you not?" She stepped toward her chair and he
followed, pausing when he reached the matching chair flanking
the hearth.

From the inside of his jacket, he pulled a slim volume and held it up for her to see.

"*Robinson Crusoe?*" she asked, and he nodded.

"Volume 2," he added with a knowing tilt of his head. Lord Stephen motioned for her to be seated and once they settled, both facing the fire. The candles were perfectly placed between them, sending light in both their directions.

"Shall we begin?" Kate opened the cover.

Stephen
Emerson

She glanced over the top of her book and caught his gaze staring back at her over the top of his.

"For shame, sir. You have defaced another book."

"I was only ten," he replied. "It took me two years before I found these hidden amongst the piles and piles in this vast chamber."

Kate's attention returned to the page, and she studied the size and slant of the letters created by a juvenile hand. "And your penmanship does not seem to have much improved." Her words were spoken in jest.

He glanced from the pages of his novel to her again, a slow tentative smile spread across his face. "My only defense is that I cared more for reading than I did writing. I suppose I felt I had to make my mark in those few stories I cared for. It was a way to distinguish the ones I wished to retain ... or wished my uncle would ... in case he had it in mind to empty the lot for whatever reason."

"I have often dreamed of having my own library ... a book room ... for I wish to fill it with books, from floor to ceiling ... ones I have read and wish to reread, ones that I am currently reading, and ones I have yet to read."

"Goodness ... I imagine it would be an enormous room—and that room would need to be attached to a house and household to support it, I expect."

"Yes, I'm afraid so," she confessed. Her hopes and wishes were just as grand as she imagined her book room would be. "The house need not be so large, I think."

"It might be odd to have a library that was larger than the rest of the house," he remarked.

A footman entered with the tea tray and set it on a nearby table. With a glance he checked the status of the fire and that the occupants were properly warm and appeared comfortable.

"Would you mind?" Lord Stephen indicated the newly arrived tea set with a nod to the footman.

"Not at all, sir." The footman saw to filling the cups and placed them within reach before leaving the two to their privacy.

"Do tell me more about your house," Lord Stephen prompted, turning his full attention to her.

"I believe I will need a morning room, where we will take all our meals, a music room, for the pianoforte, and a kitchen, of course, along with a few bedrooms. They need not be large, just enough for a small staff."

"Will you employ a maid whose primary job it will be to dust all the books?" he asked thoughtfully. "I have learned just how much dust accumulates. I had no idea before now."

"Nor I," Kate admitted. "I believe you have the right of it."

"Why so few reception rooms? Most houses have several parlors, a sitting room, a dining room or two, and many bedchambers to house their guests."

"I don't plan to have any guests." Kate lowered the book, resting it in her lap, and used her index finger to mark her place.

"None at all?" Lord Stephen's attention moved from his beloved book to focus on her.

"No. I plan to spend all my time with my books." Kate had only recently realized how many servants she needed to employ. They would all live under the same roof and she would care for them as well.

"But what about Lady Kitty? You do intend to keep up your singing?"

"Kitty and I shall be together." Kate expected she and Kitty would spend time ... musical afternoons and evenings when they would work on their pieces just as they had done at school. They would perform for themselves and for their own enjoyment.

"And what of your travels? You have such an interest in the Orient. I thought you wanted to visit other countries."

Kate placed the book on the small table next to her before reaching for her tea. "I *would* like to do that, but I cannot see how I would ever manage. There is much planning and—" It was not the funds, for she had plenty, but he could not know that. It was making the arrangements themselves. She would need to find someone *experienced* ... a knowledgeable traveler who could lead her on the expedition.

"I shall help you plan—make suggestions. This is only *pretend*, is it not?" he offered. "And if so ... perhaps then I might be included in your party."

Kate never thought of Lord Stephen as a traveling companion. He had not traveled, but he, as she had, wished to do so. "Well ... if this is only *pretend* ... *only our made up stories and dreams. My house and travels.* I suppose we can talk about making whatever plans we wish." After all, there was no harm in it ... it was only *talk*.

Eleven

The group of young people fell into an easy routine as they passed the next few days while they waited to hear of the picnic.

In the mornings, Lord James and Lord Stephen went off together to shoot, both Mr. Waddell and Mr. Drayton removed to a small, nearby pond for private instruction. Mr. Drayton was kind enough to take Mr. Waddell under his wing, introducing the city-raised young man to the joys of fishing. He had never before had the chance to stay in the country for any length of time to take up the sport.

It was not long before, all four gentlemen headed for the river. Mr. Waddell seemed to gain an appreciation for the sport and participated with his limited skills. He actually seemed to enjoy himself and the company of the other gentlemen who were happy to welcome the newcomer into their party.

Alicia and Kitty had to push aside their music practice and lessons over the course of the next few days, while they were immersed in plans for the long awaited picnic at the folly. Miss Alicia had been making such improvements that it would have been soon possible for her to be ready to make her debut, with a short, simple piece, of course. *All that*, for the picnic's sake, had to be delayed. There simply was not enough time for any proper practice and her attention could not help but wander from her sheet music, making the entire undertaking impossible.

The majority of the time was spent with Cook. More than anyone, she understood what they had, what was needed, and what was possible. Soon, the day of the picnic had finally been decided. Kitty and Alicia were delighted indeed that their plans could move forward as they had hoped.

She informed them of the particular details which would determine its scheduling, though gathering the food and its preparation would be the most difficult effort. The preparation and the packing of their nuncheon would not only be paramount but it would enhance, or detract, from the outing itself.

Mr. Waddell himself added a certain amount of tension among the others and set in Alicia some urgency to schedule the picnic. With so many guests about, they all needed something to antici- pate and plenty of activities to keep them busy for a long stay in the country. For empty days, ones filled with idleness, would prove to be *very* long stays indeed.

Kate ate in the breakfast room early enough every morning to sit with the gentleman at the table, and wished them good fishing when they left. She was not involved with the picnic plans which was just as well for she could spend the next several hours with the Emerson girls for art lessons.

The topic of the upcoming picnic was much discussed in the schoolroom as well. What would be found at the folly? Exotic plants? Some unusual animals? The soundness of the structure? Perhaps the back was a pile of crumbling brick rubble.

All three girls, and the governess, had been there several times but Cindy maintained that Candy could not properly recall the details for she was far too young to remember.

Miss Fawcett intervened, ending the disagreement. Kate rather enjoyed listening to the girls squabble. The on-going quarrel reminded her of living at the all-girls' school where there were frequent and equally juvenile disagreements among the students. Apparently, despite the lack of a large group of young females was not needed to instigate such an uprising, two or three could do so quite adequately.

By the time the afternoon arrived, Kate found herself with idle time on her hands. With Kitty and Alicia completely occupied by picnic related tasks, there were more than enough hours before dinner to return to the library for her ongoing search of *Gulliver's Travels*.

Perhaps *this* would be the day she would find the missing volume!

Kate's evenings, while she was in the company of others, was always a bit of a trial. It took a great deal of effort for her to mind her manners—temper her emotions, and keep her opinions to herself. She had to remember that speaking out did no good at all and it would place Kitty in an unfavorable position.

After dinner proved the most challenging for Kate. While accompanying the others during the long promenades to view the folly it was difficult to remain quiet. She found Mr. Drayton and Mr. Waddell stiff and formal. The promenade was far more enjoyable if Lord Stephen happened to escort her.

There was some sort of musical entertainment each night, in which she always participated. Lady James was anxious to hear something played upon the pianoforte or raise their voices in song … with or without accompaniment. It was only a matter of time until Alicia joined Kate and Kitty for the *a capella* portion. Kitty thought there was still some work to be done on their harmonies and would not dare ask them to perform before they were ready.

The best part of the evening was after all the *group* activities were at an end and Kate could retreat to the library to enjoy her book. *Robinson Crusoe* was a fine distraction for Kate and knowing that volumes two and three were readily available was a comfort. But as much as she thought she might wish to spend time alone, Kate had to admit that she also looked forward to sharing the library with Lord Stephen as well.

Sitting before the fire and reading felt quite calming, Kate reflected on the various issues they'd talked about that day—that afternoon, that evening. Simply sitting there, having him near, was satisfying enough.

The guests did not need to wait long until the day of the picnic. When the day finally arrived, it started off swimmingly.

Kitty peered out of her bedchamber window to the frantic scene below. The unmistakable, gleeful cries of Cindy, Sandy, and Candy, carrying their day bags, preparing to board the wagonette seemed louder than any three little girls could possibly create. Miss Fawcett directed them to the transport and encouraged them to climb in while the pair of horses stood calmly, and the driver patiently waited, not being bothered in the least by the small, rambunctious passengers.

The furniture, food, and servants must have been delivered to the folly first just as Alicia had planned, with her sisters and their governess traveling next. Upon its return, the six guests who remained at the house would make the final journey.

"We need to prepare to leave in about two hours," Kitty said over her shoulder while still gazing out the window watching the confusion below.

"I am ready to leave at any time, Kitty." Kate stood behind her friend with her tattered straw hat and day bag in hand.

"You cannot wear *that*," Kitty remarked, shocked at the state of her friend's apparel. She did not wish to say that Kate was *shab-bily-dressed* but this was not a schoolgirl outing.

"Whyever not?" Kate stared down at herself, straightening her apron.

"You must be more ... more ... *presentable,*" Kitty explained. "We are to keep company with the gentlemen."

"But this is clean and *serviceable.* I will be attending the children and we are to sketch the trees, flowers, and any animals we should see."

"That may well be, but you are not their governess nor are you responsible for them. You must consider that you are to be in the company of the *adult* guests as well." Kitty did not wish to sound harsh. "It is true that neither Lord nor Lady James will be in attendance. However ..." How was Kitty to put this forth kindly? "The picnic was planned not only for our amusement but for Lord Stephen, Mr. Drayton, and Mr. Waddell."

"*Kit-ty,*" Kate groaned in frustration. The disdain in her voice could not be missed.

"I thought your blue muslin with the small white flowers would be nice," Kitty suggested, trying to sound encouraging. She could tell by her friend's expression and stance that she might be compliant but not necessarily accepting of her suggestion. "And I did choose a bonnet for you. I did not think you would mind."

"*You go too far*—I will not wear that broad-brimmed, *fashionable* monstrosity Lady Bradford purchased for me."

Kitty glanced away, feeling uncomfortable. She did not truly believe Kate would mind if Kitty had *helped herself* to the 'monstrosity' of a bonnet she detested.

"All those fussy, horrid flower buds—" The hat was not at all to Kate's taste and she never wore it.

"They are better suited as embellishments," Kitty said and wondered about her friend's reaction.

"Why ... yes, they would be, Kitty." Kate brightened and quickly put her outburst behind her.

"That is why I clipped all but a few off and sewed them to Alicia's bodice," Kitty confessed. "And had retained the bonnet for my own use." She glanced away, feeling as if she might have overstepped her boundaries. "I hope you do not mind."

"You did not!" Kate's eyes went wide in disbelief. "I do not care what you do with it in the least!"

"I knew you did not care for the hat and poor Miss Alicia … she has not had a new frock in ages. It was quite nice to help her freshen one of her old ones a bit." Again Kitty directed her gaze away, not because she had acted without asking Kate's permission but the circumstances which both of them knew only too well.

"We completed the alterations yesterday and stitched the buds onto the bodice and sleeves of her green-sprigged muslin dress. It looks very nice and Alicia is so very pleased." Kitty smiled, and Kate would smile too if she knew what would become of the hat.

"I am happy to hear of the improvements to Miss Alicia's dress." If only Kate truly understood how much it meant to Alicia.

"The unembellished bonnet itself looks quite nice."

"I hope you do not think *I* would wish to wear it." Kate's scowl returned.

"We must all wear bonnets for it is very sunny today—" When Kate stared hopeful at the bonnet in her hand Kitty was quick to remark, "But not *that* one."

"What? You refuse me my comfortable bonnet and you have taken my new hat and remade it into a dress … What shall I wear then?"

"I have already remade your favorite straw bonnet with a ribbon to match your dress." Kitty had hoped her offer would be warmly received. Blue *was* her favorite color.

"My close fitting poke bonnet?" Kate narrowed her eyes with suspicion.

"Yes, that's the one. I know you like it because its brim is just wide enough to keep the sun out of your eyes but does not block your surrounding vision."

"Where is it? Oh, do let me see." Kate, who eschewed all items deemed *fashionable* was all of a sudden quite enthusiastic to see her own remade accessory.

Kitty brought out the remade bonnet and Kate welcomed it with delight.

"It is *brilliant!*" Kate held it high and spun about, the ribbons fluttered through the air and wrapped around her arms. "It will go very well with the dress, will it not?"

"I thought it might." It pleased Kitty that both her friends could be happy with their ensembles. For herself, she had decided on her primrose-sprigged day dress. Her bonnet, Kate's unwanted bonnet—after the removal of the rosebuds, was now on the plain side and Kitty had embellished it with a yellow ribbon to tie under her chin.

"Alicia informs me that half-boots might be the best choice for footwear as we are to spend a great deal of time outdoors walking and climbing."

"Some sensible shoes ... I am glad of that," Kate remarked and set her bonnet aside. She slipped off her apron, removed her work dress, and stepped into the blue muslin. Pulling the sleeves on, Kate held the shoulders in place. "Do fasten the back, will you?"

"Of course." Kitty went to work, tying the tapes and tucking them in place.

Kate stepped before the full length glass, making last minute adjustments, certain everything was in place.

Noises from outside lured Kitty to the window once more. Below was the wagonette, returned from its journey, waiting for its final passengers to board.

"Come, Kate. We must leave now." How had time passed so quickly? Kitty reached for her bonnet, gloves, and parasol on her way to the door then wondered if a shawl might be necessary ... hardly ... the sun was to be shining all day long.

The six of them piled into the transport. It was far too crowded, sitting cheek to jowl to one's neighbor was too much. Kate could not like it.

Kitty and Miss Alicia could not contain their blushes as their knees and lower limbs came in brief contact with Mr. Drayton and Mr. Waddell. There were many shy and shocked glances exchanged among the four of them and Kate could only think that Lord Stephen had the right of it when he sat at the end of one of the benches and dangled his leg over the edge to remove himself from the crowded conditions.

The conversation, laughter, and gaiety of the passengers made the journey feel as if time passed very quickly. Soon the vehicle slowed noticeably.

"Did ya want ta stop 'ere, Miss Emerson?" the driver called out over his shoulder.

"Yes—YES! Do stop," Miss Alicia returned, waving her small gloved hand. "Now that we've gone halfway, we should move about some, do you not think?" She glanced around for a consensus.

"Yes, that sounds like a splendid idea," Mr. Drayton moved down the bench after Lord Stephen had hopped off.

Kate wished she could have made so nimble a move. His lordship was out of the confines of the transport and free to stretch his limbs in any fashion he wished. Those who disembarked made similar movements and ambled about, not straying far.

"Do look there—" Miss Alicia pointed with her collapsed parasol. "It is Grimshaw."

"Ah, yes. This is the south-facing aspect, is it not?" Mr. Waddell gazed into the distance alongside Mr. Drayton who nodded, agreeing that they were indeed observing the south side of the manor. The many large, high mullioned windows and symmetrical towers were the predominant features of the red-brick Tudor style house. It was old and must have been considered attractive in its day.

They discussed the familiar landmarks they relied upon while taking their evening promenades appeared completely different from this vantage point. After some twenty minutes of strolling about, Miss Alicia murmured something to Lord Stephen.

"Quite right, Cousin," he replied, holding out his hand as an offer of help into the transport. "Shall we all board and continue our journey?"

Whereas the gentleman aided Kitty and Miss Alicia, seeing them safely aboard, Kate refused when Mr. Waddell held out his hand to her.

"I would rather walk the remainder of the way, thank you." Kate actually took a few steps back.

"Really?" Mr. Waddell appeared shocked. "It could prove to be a very long distance."

"It is quite far, Miss Kate," Miss Alicia informed her—them all.

"I do not care in the least." Kate could not imagine circumstances so dire that she would beg the driver to stop and allow her to climb aboard.

"That sounds splendid to me," Lord Stephen remarked. "I shall walk as well."

"If you do not mind the crowd of an added person …" Mr. Drayton maintained. "I will walk alongside my friend Stephen."

"The road is very wide, Mr. Drayton, unlike the wagonette," Kate mused. "I believe there is room for all here." She motioned to the open road with the sweep of her arm. The gentlemen laughed heartily.

"I am not used to walking any great distance." Mr. Waddell bowed his head, excusing himself. "I believe I will ride with the ladies."

"We'll not complain," Miss Alicia said through a giggle then glanced at Kitty.

"You are most welcome to join us, Mr. Waddell." Kitty smiled, settling herself on the bench now able to make herself comfortable, and making room for Mr. Waddell should he wish to sit beside her. Both Kitty and Miss Alicia sat more comfortably with the absence of three fewer people. They could wear their bonnets without fear that their brims would catch and their hats flung from their heads.

Miss Alicia instructed the driver to be off. Kitty and Miss Alicia waved to them as the wagonette pulled away. Truth be told, they were not moving *that* much faster than those who walked.

Kate's short-brimmed poke bonnet acted like blinders, helping her focus straight ahead. The sound of footfalls on either side of Kate reminded her she was not alone, or as alone as she would have liked.

Some minutes later, Kate could see something appear in the distance. It was a small structure and around it, there was some movement.

"Miss Kate! Miss Kate!" The three youngest Emerson girls called out. They ran to the side of the dirt road, ignoring those in the wagonette, jumping and waving for her attention.

"They all know one another, do they?" Mr. Drayton remarked to Lord Stephen.

"Girls! Girls!" Kate ran ahead, her arms held wide to welcome them. As good as it had felt to stretch her legs, it felt wonderful to surge forward to greet the trio. There was all sorts of chattering and squeals just as she had been accustomed to hearing. "You are here! How nice to see all of you!"

The girls stilled when they saw the two men approaching, and their eyes grew wide open with uncertainty. *Strangers.* The men were strangers to the girls and they were right to be cautious. With the exception of their father, and a few footmen, the sisters were not exposed to many males.

"I see that these gentlemen are not known to you," Kate mimicked the same wary motion to that of her young friends. She then altered her behavior a bit, hoping to sound encouraging. "Will you allow me to make the introductions?"

Miss Alicia, who was not shy of the two men, and had known Lord Stephen all her life. He, over the subsequent school years, had brought with him Mr. Drayton to visit on several occasions and had a previous acquaintance with him as well. She felt quite comfortable in their company. Her calm demeanor would prove to be a soothing presence to her sisters.

"Would you, Miss Kate?" Miss Fawcett who stepped closer to their group lent an air of comfort and support for her charges. "If you will allow me to be introduced first as to provide an example?"

"Of course," Kate replied and addressed the girls. "Proper introductions are usually performed by a third party who is known to all. A gentleman is usually introduced to a lady—unless he is of very high rank, such as an earl or a duke. In this case, Lord Stephen is the highest ranking member among us, but he is a member of your family so we are not so formal." Kate turned to the governess. "Miss Fawcett, may I present Lord Stephen Emerson and his friend Mr. Drayton? Then Miss Fawcett says …"

"How do you do, Lord Stephen? Mr. Drayton?"

"And then she curtsies." Kate nodded to Miss Fawcett who did the pretty.

"How do you do, Miss Fawcett?" Lord Stephen and Mr. Drayton chorused and both bowed.

"In your case," Kate whispered to the girls, "The younger persons are introduced to the older."

"But I don't know how to *cur-cee*," whispered Candy.

"You must try. There will be time enough to learn and practice," Kate returned. "It is a skill that is performed many times in a young ladies' life. I daresay you will master it soon enough. Go on, then."

Candy nodded and Kate could see the girl working up her courage to attempt this enormous undertaking.

"Lord Stephen, may I make you known to your young cousins ... Miss Cynthia, Miss Sandra, and Miss Candice."

"But my name is *Candy*," the youngest corrected, slightly shaking her strawberry blonde head.

"Yes," Kate replied and explained further, "But this is a proper introduction and you must give your proper name."

"I knew that," Cindy replied and made a very respectable curtsy. "How do you do, Lord Stephen?"

"How do you do, Lord Stephen? Mr. Drayton?" Sandy replied and mimicked Cindy's gesture and bowed her head.

"We were not introduced to Mr. Drayton yet." Candy scowled, made no mention of being delighted to make anyone's acquaintance. She bent her knees, bobbing down a few inches, losing her balance, and nearly tipping over.

"Watch out there—" Mr. Drayton reached out a hand to steady her. "Do be careful, young miss."

"I cannot believe that we have been at Grimshaw Court for more than a week and not yet made the acquaintance of my young cousins." Lord Stephen chuckled, seemingly quite amused at the antics of the girls.

"We are kept in the nursery and away from the guests, sir," Sandy informed him.

"Ah... I see." Lord Stephen leaned toward his friend and uttered under his breath, "I believe this is the *longest* introduction I have ever experienced."

Tired of the exercise of formalities, Cindy, Sandy, and Candy could no longer remain still and were soon hopping and spinning around Kate as if she were a maypole. She did nothing to dissuade them, her actions might have even encouraged them.

"I believe our introductions are at an end, gentleman. I hope it was to your satisfaction," Kate, as the maypole herself, stretching to the tips of her toes, laughed, and danced away.

Had anyone seen a dancing maypole before?

"It takes many bricks to lay the foundation for social comportment," Miss Fawcett said with great wisdom ... or experience of what type of behavior she could expect from her charges.

"Well... I must suppose ..." Mr. Drayton replied, somewhat nonplussed. "I believe you are correct."

"Miss Kate, have you no restraint?" Miss Fawcett came forward, chiding in a tone well-known to Kate, not dissimilar to that of her old headmistress. Only Miss Fawcett's countenance held a smile unlike that of Miss Maddingly. "I suppose we must all enjoy this day and realize that it is not to be spent only for learning."

"Quite right, Miss Fawcett," Kate replied cheerfully between steps. "Will you not join us?" She held out her hand to the governess who, with a widening-smile reached to take hold, made her way between maypole-revelers, and joined in the hop-step dancing.

The dancers, led by Kate and her meager ballet skills, soon escaped the confines of the maypole and proceeded toward the folly in *glissades,* not-so grand *jetés,* and various *pirouettes.* The structure was no longer to be admired from a distance. It appeared a very substantial rotunda, from this aspect, appeared entirely different from the familiar view that faced the house.

It faced south with strong sunlight, warming the stone columns and encouraging the vines and climbing roses to spread around the structure and grow upward toward the sun. It made for a lovely sight.

"There they are! There they are!" Candy called out, pointing toward the lake. "Look at the ducks!"

All this was exciting—so much to see—so much they could do ... and there was only one short afternoon. Kate wished she could take a few minutes to sketch the columns but her limited time would not be enough to draw the sight before her. There were too many people around, too many interruptions.

"Come now, girls!" Kate called out. "Let's get a move on— today we shall have such a grand kick-up!"

Twelve

~

'*A grand kick-up*'... It was such an odd phrase for a female ... and one that Stephen *had* heard uttered before. Rather recently, but exactly *where* and *when* that was, he could not readily recall.

As Miss Kate and his three young cousins had scattered to the winds upon the final guests' arrival in the wagonette, he stepped toward the vehicle to assist the ladies only to find that Toby and Waddell had already done so.

Stephen's attention wandered toward his small cousins running hither and thither along the edge of the pond. The girls, all dressed in a similar-like type of frocks were beautiful, swirling about with their varying shades of red hair moving in the gentle breeze. The governess who trailed behind them followed her three charges at a respectable distance to keep her watch over them near the water's edge.

"How long are you going to stand there watching your young cousins frolicking about?" Toby elbowed him with a nudge. "I'm gasping for a cup of tea ... or some other cooling liquid might be preferable."

With an unexpected snort of amusement, not in reference to his friend's parched state but his assessment of what Toby thought Stephen had been doing. He hadn't been watching his cousins at all. He'd been contemplating ... thinking about ... *Miss Kate.*

The two men then wandered toward the rotunda, stepped under the domed ceiling, and out of the direct sunlight. Toby sighed in obvious relief at the immediate cooling effect.

"You must be thirsty after walking all so far, my lord." Alicia greeted them once they reached the rotunda, handing each gentleman a glass.

"Thank you, Cousin." Stephen accepted the lemonade.

"Very kind of you, Miss Emerson." Toby nodded, then very inelegantly proceeded to drink.

"Goodness, Mr. Drayton," Alicia remarked at the sight of his empty glass. "Let us refill your glass, shall we?" She gently slid her hands around his coat sleeve and drew him toward the punch bowl.

"That would be appreciated, thank you." Toby allowed Alicia to reclaim his empty glass and she held it out to the footman.

"Do put some ice in, will you, Joseph? Mr. Drayton is feeling particularly warm," Alicia instructed and the footman placed a few frozen chips in the glass before adding lemonade.

"You are most kind," Toby said with a nod to Alicia and then Joseph. He accepted the cool beverage and held it to his lips, swallowing with only a slight squint—a reaction to the tartness rather than the temperature was Stephen's guess. "Delicious. I thank you."

"You have not had a chance to see the house sitting atop the small hill, Mr. Drayton," Alicia commented, then to Stephen, she remarked, "I know you have no wish to take in the view. 'Seen it a thousand times,' is your sentiment if I am not correct."

"You are, but it is a view well worth seeing if you have not seen it before," Stephen said to Toby.

"Well, then... I think I shall allow you to present it to me, Miss

Emerson." He smiled and offered her his arm. The glass Toby had twice emptied was handed to the footman.

"If you will excuse us, my lord." Alicia smiled at Toby, leading him away. Stephen thought they appeared rather cozy despite his friend's previous comment that her Titian locks 'had put him off.' Perhaps they did not matter so much now that he grew to know her a bit better.

The two strolled toward the north side of the rotunda where Lady Kitty and Waddell stood, mesmerized by the sight of the house. From what Stephen could hear, they were pointing out familiar landmarks. The conversation and laughter increased once the second couple joined them.

"It is rather a splendid view, I must say," Mr. Waddell replied. "Life in the country has much to recommend it."

"I think Kate would like to sketch this ... if she were here." Lady Kitty's words must have been uttered with a shake of her head. It was her tone more that indicated such, for Stephen did not look in their direction.

"Where has she gotten off to?" Stephen wondered if had Toby paid any attention to their arrival beyond the lengthy intro-duction?

"I'm afraid my sisters have lured Miss Kate away."

"Frolicking by the pond last I saw," Toby informed them.

Yes, they were having *'a grand kick-up'* ... as Miss Kate had phrased it. Stephen leaned against the column of the rotunda, brought the lemonade glass to his lips, and stared off toward the pond. He couldn't see them now. Were they still there or had they found something else of interest and wandered farther off?

Those words, *her* words still haunted him. He *had* heard that phrase before. Then he remembered ... he was sitting in a dark-ened corner trying his best to shut out the surrounding noise, not unlike the voice and clammer of his current surroundings.

Ah ... the Club ... his brother's Club in London a few months back. Stephen sat in a chair, doing his best not to be noticed because Greg had *insisted* they escape the townhouse.

"It will do you good, Stephen," he'd said. "It would do us *both* good."

And so the two went to White's, Greg was a member and Stephen was allowed entry as a guest. Greg ended up sitting with Lord Something-or-Other while Stephen sank into a chair in a corner with his book.

"The girl's a hoyden!" his lordship proclaimed. "Never seen the like before. She's a nuisance I say. Lady Bradford's pushed to her wit's end! She has no clue what to do with her ... wants to send the chit away—far, far away."

"Good God, Bradford, did she say that—really?" Greg sounded quite taken aback. Stephen thought his brother was rather stalwart about such things.

Bradford? *Bradford?* Was that not the uncle of Lady Catherine?

"Then the gel prods her ladyship by saying, *'Come on, already! I won't mind, it'll be a grand kick-up!'* "

Of course this was Lady Catherine's uncle but ... the hoyden he spoke of could not be Lady Kitty. Stephen glanced at her, standing with Alicia and the two men in quiet conversation. She was the least likely to go charging about saying such a thing.

On the other hand ... Stephen caught sight of Miss Kate now dashing about, squealing with his young cousins. Did he not hear her say the exact thing earlier?

"I have never seen such an outrageous, undisciplined gel in my life. She has no regard for anything or anyone and does exactly as she pleases," his lordship had blustered in outrage.

Stephen could not believe Miss Kitty was capable of behaving as he had described.

"She has the most absurd ideas about what is acceptable behavior. I expect it is because she was not raised by her mother." Lord Bradford continued his lament, "Lady Bradford had shipped her off to a Girls' Academy and I suppose it was not the best environment for her. She lacks the nature of a refined, young lady even after spending all those years at the girls' school. Honestly, Greg, did she learn nothing?"

"She might have grown up that way in any case," came the reply. "Who is to say?"

"I must say that now I harbor a few regrets," Lord Bradford mused. "She was not raised as my own children were—at the time of my brother's death. I was young, just married myself."

Stephen understood that Kate did not really behave as a sensible young lady ought. She wanted to travel the globe and have adventures. Did that make her *outrageous?*

Actually… Stephen thought the unorthodox Lady Catherine had the qualities of Kate and did not much resemble Kitty in the least. She appeared to have all the characteristics of what he would expect of a daughter of an earl—well-mannered, polite, and demure. Attributes that would have been taught at a girls' school and that she had in abundance and perhaps Kate had none. He had observed Kitty to be more than merely accomplished in music and showed exemplary qualities such as encouraging his cousin in her pianoforte lessons, capable in many areas: management, common sense, loyalty … they were also qualities one would wish in a personal servant.

Might there have been a mix up along the way?

So … who was who? Stephen's gaze swung toward Kate. The rambunctious one who hopped about with the girls, a behavior which more resembled Lord Bradford's hoyden niece.

If Lady Catherine had displayed the most disagreeable and unladylike tendencies, a behavior his lordship and Lady Bradford proved to be such an embarrassment that it was not to be borne. No one could use those words to describe Kitty.

"Just increase her dowry and unload her on the first man to make an offer," Greg had suggested.

"If only I could." Lord Bradford tossed back the remaining liquor and shook his head. "That's just the problem—it's not the lack of interest or the blunt … she won't have any of them. *Demmed* nuisance, I say. Drat the girl."

"*Gad*, she *is* difficult, ain't she?" Greg gazed into the fire thoughtfully.

"Exactly." Bradford motioned with his empty glass to a club footman eager for a refill.

In that instance, the club footman had inquired if Stephen would care for something to drink. He hadn't, but it was then he caught a glimpse of Lord Bradford's worried brow and sour expression. Now his words made sense. However, none of what Bradford said seemed to indicate he was speaking about Kitty. Kitty had the most agreeable character, why would her uncle … *her* uncle … unless he was *not* her uncle, or rather … *she* was not his niece.

Stephen wondered …

Gazing toward the pond where his young cousins had finally settled, his gaze swung toward the familiar-looking brunette young lady in a quite feminine-looking day dress. Gone were the serviceable apron and plain work frock but it was the same female. He wondered why she had taken the step to alter her appearance this day.

Could it be possible that Kate, and not Kitty, was Lady Catherine?

He could imagine *someone* having the opinion that Kate was *disagreeable, disruptive, and wild* … but it would not be him. Stephen would instead describe her as *inquisitive, energetic, and adventurous.*

The more he thought about it, the more Stephen was convinced that somehow … *somehow*—the two had exchanged places. Lady Kitty was not a *lady* at all but the companion to Miss Kate, the real Lady Catherine. As to *why* they should do so … he did not know.

It all would make perfect sense *if* their roles had been reversed …

Stephen smiled. *If* indeed.

After the antics of the dance had died down, Kate brought the girls around to the edge of the pond to seek out an appropriate subject for them to sketch. It was to everyone's benefit that each girl had their own ideas about what interested them. That way, there would be no conflict of *what* image was best or *who* was the better artist. Kate had removed her bonnet and strolled from one sketch pad to the other, offering suggestions and words of encouragement. It pleased her to see how much they enjoyed themselves. There was no bickering over where each should sit.

As it turned out, Miss Fawcett had been very modest about her own skill. With a bit more practice, Kate was certain the governess would be a more than suitable instructor. The governess confessed that she had neglected her love of art and she vowed to seek out her forgotten watercolor set.

Kate enjoyed watching the girls. On the rock near the pond's edge was the perfect place for Candy to observe the ducks. A small stool was used for Sandy. Its strategic placement 'not too close nor too far,' was optimal for the upward stalks of grasses, and she was particularly fond of the rushes that poked out from the water's surface. Cindy, who had found a place away from her sisters to work on a landscape and …

Kate squinted at … What was Lord Stephen doing peering over Cindy's shoulder?

His hat remained on his head to keep the sun off his face but he had removed his jacket and strolled around in his braces and shirtsleeves that he had rolled up to his elbows. His lordship paused to gaze over Cindy's shoulder. The two cousins never looked at one another but exchanged some words before he wandered some distance away.

Lord Stephen pulled something small out of his pocket and lowered himself to sit near the water's edge. He removed his hat and placed it next to him before glancing down at his palm, at what he held in it, then up at the pond. No, he did not look at the pond but past it.

Kate was curious to know exactly what he was doing. What had he said to Cindy? What had she said to him? And what did he have in his hand? She strolled in his direction to find answers to her questions.

"Why are you not with your friends, Lord Stephen?" Kate still couldn't make out what he held and when she approached he wrapped his fingers around the object, hiding it.

"I thought I would stroll over here and see what occupied my young cousins. Tell me, Miss Kate, do you see some budding artistic talent among them?"

"I am hardly one to spot a prodigy. That said, the subjects they sketch are all recognizable, all I truly care about is that they are enjoying their endeavors and happy with their progress."

"And are they?"

"They seem to be, but it is still early days yet." Kate glanced to her right where the three girls were occupied. "Why are you not with the others in the rotunda?"

"I did not wish to intrude. They appear quite content, do they not?" Lord Stephen gave the small group a glance without much further consideration. It seemed as if he had not cared what they did or that they had not included him.

"What do you have there?" She indicated his hand with the lift of her chin.

"This?" He loosened his fingers and in the palm of his hand he held a ball … at least Kate thought it was a ball. "It's a globe. A very small globe. I've had it since I was a boy because … because …"

"You've always wished to travel and see far off-lands," she finished for him.

"Yes. It's in a box. It's also round but a box all the same. Come closer and see for yourself." He straightened his arm, holding it out to her. It was a very small globe, colored blue and green with black lettering. He lifted the orb and she peered inside that was marked with the constellations of the night sky.

"It's beautiful." Kate settled on the ground next to him. "And why are you looking at it now?"

"Cindy ..."

"Who is sketching a landscape," Kate added.

"She told me she thought that when she looked across to the other side of the pond ... it almost seemed to her as if it were not England but another place."

"Really?" Kate looked from the globe to his lordship then across the water where his attention remained. Had Cindy hit upon something?

"Look there ..." He pointed across the water and stared. "You see how you can almost make out the shore? I was just imagining that I was sitting here looking across to France. The shortest crossing point is about 20 miles. I've been told one can see across the Channel on a clear day such as this."

Kate gazed across the span, looking in the same direction as he. She tried to imagine what she would feel seeing such a site. *Is this a view that would welcome her if she crossed the Channel?*

"You know I've always wanted ..." Kate stared, trying to imagine she was gazing at the French coast. She smiled, feeling a rush of excitement at the thought. It was the unknown. Then it occurred to her ... "I've never been on a boat before. What if travel by water makes me feel ill?" She'd heard of those who wretched while moving across the water. "I'll never be able to visit India or China."

"You cannot know that if you have never tried. You might attempt a short trip first," he suggested. "A small boat to discover if you find water travel tolerable."

"That's a very good idea." Kate wanted to learn this as soon as possible. "Perhaps we can find a rowboat and—"

"You are not suggesting we do so now?" He sounded a bit

shocked. Kate may have spoken a bit abruptly. " Uncle James must have one about but I do not know for certain. We may need to delay until we first speak to him."

"Well … perhaps." Kate thought the idea sounded somewhat daunting. She wished she had bought her spyglass. "I do wonder what lies on the other side of this pond."

"Hmm …" was his reply, and not so much a decisive reply than a thoughtful comment. "I must admit I was wondering that myself."

"You don't know?" Kate could not imagine that with all the time he'd spent here—during all those past years, all the school breaks—and he had never ventured past this pond. "What boy does not wander the land around him to discover what awaits?"

"One who is occupied with an intriguing tale in hand and a comfortable spot to read it." He gazed at her through lazy eyes.

"I thought you wished for adventure and—"

"I had but I did not think it truly achievable until very recently …" he said softly as if revealing a secret. "There is no need for a boat if you wish to explore the other side. We could walk. I cannot say how far it is… I cannot say that it is part of the Grimshaw estate."

"Does it matter?" If it was someplace they should avoid, could they not turn back?

"Not really, but it would be best to know." He stood, closed the globe in its box and returned it to his pocket before holding his hand out, helping Kate to her feet. "Let us speak to Alicia first, shall we? We should hear what other activities she has arranged for the afternoon."

Kitty stood next to one of the tables with Alicia and the two gentlemen. The day for the picnic could not have been more pleasant. All hats and gloves were removed as the guests readied themselves for their light afternoon meal. Linen-covered tables were set up in the shade of the rotunda for the comfort of those who did not wish to chance the sun's rays. Next to it was a table with those dishes that needed to remain cool.

"A triumph!" Mr. Waddell proclaimed.

"This could not have been more magnificent!" Mr. Drayton went over and beyond mere praise. "The setting, the provisions, the day itself—"

"I am afraid I cannot take credit for our summer's day, sir," Alicia told him.

Kitty found the repetitious praise tiresome and she could only half-listen to their words. What interested her far more was the manner in which they conversed with her. Both gentlemen were bright-eyed and ardent in their sincerity.

However, Kitty could say the same in which they spoke to her. Her music had touched them, she could see that, and other than her experience in London this last Season, she had no prior inter-action with men. She really could not make sense of their behavior.

Kitty felt that Mr. Waddell *had* to remain interested and very formal toward her. For Mr. Drayton, whose aspirations were to be a vicar, it must have been in his nature to behave with such warmth and kindness.

"All this was not only my doing. Miss Kitty was instrumental in the planning," they were Alicia's words. "I conferred with her at every step I was merely providing guidance since she did not know the workings at Grimshaw."

The gentlemen swung their gazes to Kitty.

"I stand corrected," Mr. Waddell replied with added respect to Kitty, bowing his head.

"As must I." Mr. Drayton offered her a smile, which she returned. "Although, I believe you may share in accepting credit for such a grand achievement. Every comfort has been attended to."

"I am used to making preparations for a large number, you see," Kitty admitted. She had no wish to do so but felt she should say something.

"Oh, look! My cousin and Miss Kate have returned!" Alicia greeted them. "We were just about to have something to eat. Will you join us?"

Lord Stephen glanced at Kate before answering "Of course, Cousin."

"Good. If you will help yourself ..." She led them to the table that held the light meal she had arranged.

"Alicia," Lord Stephen motioned for Kate to precede him. "I was wondering if you could enlighten me about the land surrounding the pond."

"*This* pond?" Her voice rose high as if she were quite surprised to discover its existence.

"Yes. Do you know what lies on the other side? Is that part of the estate?" He took hold of the plate his cousin handed him, clearly more interested in the landscape than the food.

"I have no idea, Stephen. I think you might ask Father." She shook her head with a scowl. "Why are you asking these nonsensical questions?"

"I'm afraid we will need to delay our expedition," he replied, glancing at Kate who appeared uncharacteristically quiet.

"What?" There was nothing wrong with Alicia's hearing. "Were you thinking of leaving us? Tramping all the way over there? Nonsense! You cannot—not after I have arranged this entire afternoon for us," she scolded him. "You can take your *adventure* on your own time. Do sit and be sociable, will you?" She leaned toward him and uttered in a softer voice, "We have guests."

"We shall join you shortly," Lord Stephen excused his cousin with a nod, and Alicia returned to the others.

He turned to Kate after his cousin's departure. "It is time we do the pretty, Miss Kate, despite our wishes. They must be delayed."

"I find that is often the way, my lord," Kate said rather stiffly. He may not have understood that particular tone she held but Kitty knew of it all too well.

"You must own that our nuncheon looks rather good, does it not?"

"Are you suggesting that a full stomach is preferable to satisfying our sense of adventure?"

"Not at all," he replied. "It is merely something to keep us occupied until we can make an attempt." He asked for a few slices of cold meat to be placed on his plate. "There is nothing for it, we must speak to Lord James before making the expedition across the pond."

Expedition across the pond? Kitty was at a loss as to what this meant. But Kate knew. She turned her head away from him. No doubt to mask her frustration at having to wait.

"The Salmagundi looks excellent, why don't you try that?" he suggested.

"What is this?" Kate asked the footman, indicating the next serving dish. It was her way of rebelling.

"Fowl, miss," the footman answered.

"What type of *fowl*?" Kate seemed unnecessarily concerned about the very common chicken basket. "Can you be more specific?"

"Chicken," the footman answered.

Kate's head snapped in his lordship's direction. "He doesn't mean ..."

"Well, Miss Kate, it is difficult to say *which* chickens these might be, I expect," began Lord Stephen. "However, a hen who can no longer lay eggs has little use other than ... let's just say that the Emersons cannot afford to have pets."

"Oh." Kate glanced from him down to the contents in the

serving dish before her, then into the face of the footman who waited for her to decide if he should place items from that dish onto her plate. "No, thank you." The queasy expression slipping over Kate's visage was a familiar one Kitty recognized, but she did not understand why. "I shall have the Salmagundi, thank you."

Kate and Lord Stephen joined the other guests at the tables. The three men sat at one and the three ladies at the other. Kate sat next to Kitty and Alicia.

"The only thing we are missing for our picnic is a pianoforte!" Mr. Waddell declared.

"Oh—to have music at our picnic!" Mr. Drayton sighed. "I could not imagine anything grander!"

"I am sorry to disappoint you, sirs, we do not have one that can be easily transported," Alicia informed them with a sigh. "However, Mama is having ours tuned as we speak and I can't imagine that tonight's music will sound anything but quite exceptional!"

Thirteen

Kate thought the picnic the day before had been great fun. There was plenty of time spent outdoors and sketching … but not for Kate who had merely observed the others take part in an activity in which she had dearly wished to participate. In the end, she had missed an opportunity for any artistic expression and lost an entire day searching for *Gulliver's Travels*. Today, she was determined to devote much time in the library, resuming the effort.

After rising, she began doing what was expected, making her best attempt to be companionable by taking her morning meal in the breakfast room with whoever was present. Entering the room, she saw Kitty and Alicia sitting together in conversation.

"Good morning, Miss Kate. Will you join us?" Alicia sat close next to Kitty, the pair of them together looked lovely. The first in a light green muslin, complementing her red hair, and Kitty in primrose with floral embellishments down the front.

"I would be delighted, Miss Alicia, thank you," Kate returned. She helped herself to a cup of tea, some toast, and jam. Returning to the table, she sat across from them. "Has Kitty shown you the piece for four hands she's found?"

"Yes, Kitty says we're to begin this afternoon," Alicia replied and tapped the sheet music on the table between them. "I can hardly wait to begin."

"I am glad to see you have something to look forward to now that you no longer have to spend time planning the picnic." Kate gasped. "I beg your pardon… I do not believe I thanked you for the picnic yesterday. It was quite splendid." There was no pretense needed there. Kate appreciated all her efforts sincerely. "I think I spent more time with your sisters than with you. I enjoyed myself immensely."

"*Ah, me* … they did consume a great deal of your time. I do apologize." Alicia glanced down solemnly.

"*Fustian!* They are eager to learn and there is nothing wrong with that." Kate was pulled from sister to sister, from one sketchpad to another for hours. Miss Fawcett, who would normally be their teacher, needed not so much guidance as some practice. Kate simply had to accept that this was not the afternoon she would make any sketches of her own.

"Their pictures were very nice. I find them quite talented, and I am not saying that because they are my sisters."

Since the day was spent outdoors at the picnic, the evening promenade had been abandoned. A small art exhibition the girls and Miss Fawcett had set up in the library where the Emerson family, friends, and guests were invited to view the sketches after dinner.

"You are quite right. They *are* talented," Kate maintained. Eagerness to pursue something of interest always made one a more attentive student. "It does not hurt to find a subject that is of interest."

"I expect so." Alicia gazed wide-eyed at Kitty who was suddenly overcome by a fit of giggles.

Kitty? Kate had never seen her friend behave in such a silly manner.

Alicia seemed as if she was not about to allow Kitty to lead her down the path of foolishness. Her countenance remained serious and she cleared her throat before turning to Kate to comment, "I see your plans are to return to your search for *that* book."

"I do wish to find it," Kate admitted. The apron over her work dress told of her intentions. "Other than music—did you have plans for today?" She thought it peculiar how the two kept glancing at one another as if they were involved in some sort of mischief.

"Well… Kitty and I had been discussing" —A rose flush washed across Alicia's cheeks followed by a grand smile that spread to her lips and narrowed her eyes— "Creating fishing lures for the gentlemen."

"Fishing lures?" Kate wasn't certain she'd heard correctly.

"I believe they would love it above all things!" Alicia turned to Kitty. "Your stitching is so superior, how could you not create a tempting, realistic lure?"

"I doubt *sewing skill* has much to do with it," Kitty replied very even-tempered. "I imagine a collection of feathers, fur, and other materials would create a creditable likeness."

"I believe that is how it is done. We've bits of fabric we could use for color, tail hair from the horses as sturdy twine that should do to mimic grasshoppers and beetles."

"Bugs?" Kate blurted out, slightly repulsed.

"I beg your pardon, Miss Kate. This is hardly a topic for the breakfast table." The color in Alicia's face rose again … even deepening, perhaps.

"We were discussing *hand-tied flies,*" Kitty informed Kate. "Do you think they would care for them?"

"I suppose …" Kate could not really say … couldn't even hazard a guess what men would think of being presented with fishing lures. A silly grin played across her lips. *No idea. None.*

If they truly wished to impress the gentlemen … she *knew* there was no better way than by their music. It seemed to Kate that might have become a priority.

"I shall leave you to it then." Kate stood from the table,

anxious to return to her own occupation and left the two giggling ladies to their tasks.

Kate soon left the two to their discussion of fishing lures. She headed out the door, down the corridor to the library, pulling her mobcap from her pocket as she strode down the corridor, wondering if Kitty or Alicia had a preference for Mr. Drayton or Mr. Waddell and when had that happened? Her friend had not said anything to Kate. Kitty had never shown any sort of preference for male company a month ago when they were in London. So why now?

Moments before Kate stepped foot inside, the image of Lord Stephen came to mind, that he might be within. Movement from the corner of her eye caused Kate to turn suddenly to her right. There stood Candy.

"What are you doing here?" Kate whispered, glancing around for anyone else who might be in the room.

"I can't find my sketchpad. I think I left it here last night," she said quietly.

"Isn't it with your drawing? Does Miss Fawcett have it, perhaps?"

"No, she doesn't." Candy sounded sad and the corners of her mouth quivered downwards. "I hope I haven't l-lost it."

"I expect it will turn up," Kate said, encouragingly. "I shall help you search for it. I'm certain it could not have gone far. Let us look about and see if we can find it, shall we?"

Kate's gaze skimmed the vast surface of the desk before them. She could picture every detail of Candy's sketchbook in her mind and would spot it easily. It was a fairly thin, small-bound book with a soft brown cover. It was new and should stand out amongst the ancient tomes that inhabited this room.

"I had so much fun last night, Miss Kate. Mama loved my duck drawings." Candy followed Kate as she made her way to the far side of the room, her gaze skimming over the various surfaces where the girl's sketchbook might rest.

"I think the duck family was her favorite." Kate recalled how a gentle, warm smile graced Lady James' lips while she studied that particular sketch.

"The baby ducks were so cute!" Candy's voice squealed with delight.

"And they are fun to draw, are they not?" Kate kept up their conversation easily while she moved between the chairs and small tables that had been shifted from their original positions.

"The duckling family was fun … but I like the first duck I saw the most."

"Oh, the drake. He was quite magnificent, very regal." She noticed the small stacks of books Lord Stephen had placed into orderly piles had been moved out of the way to make room for the art displays. He would not be pleased when he saw what remained, but he would surely not complain.

"Mr. Duck had a pretty green head." Candy recalled with clarity. "It's too bad I can't draw that."

"You could make a watercolor," Kate suggested.

"I don't know how."

"I'm sure if you continue your art studies with this much enthusiasm you will." Kate smiled and touched the girl's shoulder indicating they should continue on their way. Candy went first and Kate followed. "You could encourage Miss Fawcett to find her paints then she could demonstrate."

"Miss Fawcett knows how to watercolor?"

"That is what I understand."

On the way to the hearth … the one Lord Stephen had ordered lit to warm them in the evenings. They would sit companionably side by side with the pot of hot tea on the small table between them. Sadness and regret welled up that they—*she* had missed out on spending that quiet time. However, tonight … *tonight* … she so looked forward to its return.

"There it is!" Candy ran past Kate to her chair. Kate's *favorite* chair where she read each night, lying on the seat cushion was

Candy's sketchpad. The girl picked it up and held it tight against her, she scolded the inanimate object. "Don't you ever—ever get lost again!"

"Now that you've found your sketchpad, let's get you back to Miss Fawcett. I daresay she will be wondering where you've gone off to."

Candy's eyes grew round and her mouth formed a large "o" as she must have realized how much trouble she might be in. "Do let's go … before she misses me." The girl's small hand grasped Kate's apron, assuring she would follow close behind.

Out of the library, down the corridor to the main staircase, they went. Climbing the steps, Candy paused on the landing to stare out the window.

"Can we see Mrs. Robin from here?" Candy peered out the window. The girl was getting distracted. Kate knew the signs all too well.

"No, we're not high enough. We need to be in the school-room." They resumed their climb and Candy ran to the window once she reached the second floor.

"Oh … look! You see, Miss Kate? They are all in there … the chickens. *Hen*ny Penny, *Rep*ecca, *Beak*-atrice …" Candy pointed each of the hens out with a chubby index finger. "And the ones I named … Effie, Feathery, and Susan. Aren't they beautiful?"

Kate moved to the window and stood to one side to see the kitchen garden where the poultry found their morning meal. There were six hens, Kate could not refute that, but were they the *same* hens of a few days ago? She could not say. Perhaps it did not matter. As Lord Stephen had said, one hen must have been much like another … especially when all were the same breed, and appearing to Kate identical.

"Come away, Candy." Kate wanted no more comments about the chickens and urged her companion to continue. "Let us get you to the schoolroom before you are missed."

The four gentlemen headed to the chalk stream early the next morning. Not *very* early the next morning for the evening before had kept the residence at Grimshaw Court up late with all sorts of merriment.

Stephen was more than happy to lag behind his Uncle James by Toby and Waddell. To be alone with his thoughts was all he wanted. Why had he even come along on this fishing trip if solitude is what he craved. Not solitude precisely but he yearned to return to the library where he knew *she* would be but his obligations came first. He needed to be here and *here* he was.

As he lagged behind the others, Stephen's thoughts wandered to the day before ... to the picnic. Never was there a more diverting, enlightening, and more frustrating day. The *diverting* portion was being among the ladies. What man did not delight in the company of females? Always interesting, but not always in a pleasant, agreeable fashion. The *enlightening* portion was his discovery of Miss Kate's true identity.

That was something remarkable.

Once he had made that realization, he began to see all sorts of clues in their diverse behaviors which told him his conclusion that Kate and Kitty had exchanged places was probable. He spent the remaining part of the afternoon observing the two, comparing and contrasting their very different behavior, and wondering how anyone could mistake them for one another.

No one who was acquainted with them would make that mistake.

Stephen kept the ruse to himself. It was not for him to disclose the particulars to anyone—especially when he could not answer for the reasons she had initiated the exchange. Which also meant that once exposed, it would be *she* who would deal with the consequence.

Perhaps she would never be found out. Getting away with a bit of mischief was not the worst a person could do. In the grand scheme of things, her deception harmed no one.

Some might find her outrageous or irritating. Never had Stephen thought a female so intriguing, and he found it quite difficult to keep his thoughts from returning to her.

Farther up the path, before approaching the bridge crossing, Lord James handed the equipment bag to Toby. He abandoned the two men who had kept him company and waited for his nephew. His lordship kept hold of his fishing pole and made movements, which looked to Stephen, as if he practiced his casting.

When Stephen had finally met his uncle, Lord James said, "And what has you smiling, Nephew?"

"I am contemplating my hours of calm and quiet, Uncle," Stephen returned, moving his long fishing rod from one hand to the other, making room to walk close to his lordship, and to avoiding an unfortunate tangle. "You need not wait for me. I am quite satisfied to keep my own company."

"Do you wish to shun them? *Zounds*, Stephen—did you not enjoy yourself yesterday?" His uncle's gaze hardened and his tone harsh. "Never have I seen you show less gratitude for all the effort shown to you by your own family!"

"Strong words from a man who did not attend the gathering and avoided the dancing last night until the late hours." Was doing one's family duty only for *other* family members and not the head of the family?

"I did enjoy the art display." His lordship confessed with a smile. "More delightful girls I could not wish for—and I can see they are becoming quite accomplished. Was the art exhibit not fine?"

"It was most enjoyable." Stephen nodded.

"Miss Fawcett and the girls did a brilliant job."

"I think the sketches were quite good. I felt as if I were standing there myself." He thumped his fist lightly on his chest with a certain amount of pride. "I had nearly forgotten what a handsome view there must have been from the rotunda. It has been a good while since I've been there."

"It was much admired by all, sir."

"Glad to hear it, Nephew." Lord James pointed to Toby and Waddell saying, "Shall we join the others before they catch all the fish?" He proceeded forward at increasing speed, once again joining the two.

Catching *all* the fish in the stream seemed highly unlikely, but they were welcome to attempt it. Stephen set his pole aside while he removed his jacket and rolled up his shirtsleeves. He was willing to wait and allow the three eager anglers to claim their territory before he began.

To conclude his reminiscence, there was his *frustration* that should not be forgotten. It began after dinner—when he had anticipated spending time with Kate. Gone was their hours together seeking the shelves for the elusive *Gulliver's Travels*. Gone was his evening alone with her, sitting before the blazing hearth, enjoying their books, light conversation, and tea.

And this morning … he *might* share her company in a mere few hours from now. If he could wait that long. Stephen retrieved his fishing pole. He may have been staring at the water but he did not see it. Again he thought of the previous evening … and of *her*.

Last night, after dinner, he did not wish to appear too eager for her attention and ended up standing behind the others in the back of the room, admiring her. From the feminine blue frock she'd worn at the picnic, she had changed into a fine rose-colored gown. Her shiny brown hair had been pulled off her neck and bound at the back of her head, cascading in ringlets. Tendrils trailed softly along either side of her face, brushing her cheeks.

If he was not mistaken, the flowers that adorned her hair had originated from the rose vines that climbed the columns of the rotunda. It seemed odd that she would think to procure them at that time to use now, but it might be a detail a maid or companion might think to do for her lady. *Well done, Miss Kitty.*

"Toby?" Coming out of his revelry, Stephen realized he no longer stood off to the side alone.

"I believe I have utterly lost my heart. I realize I might be an unsuitable consideration, but I must try." Toby relayed in a confessional tone. "I must speak to Lord James and ask to pay my addresses."

"Lost your mind, more like." That brought Stephen's attention to his friend. He wished to marry Alicia? That was quite a change from his earlier opinion of her. "What of your studies and University? I thought it was your entire future?"

"How can I concentrate on my studies knowing she remains here at Grimshaw?" Toby took hold of Stephen's shirtsleeve. "I know she feels the same as I."

"That may well be, but—" Stephen grasped his friend's arm in urgency, hoping he could make him see reason. This was insanity! Toby had gone absolutely mad! Had he not, only days before, renounced all dealings with Titian-haired females? Now he seeked his Uncle James to ask permission to marry his cousin Alicia?

"Release me, Stephen. I must act before it is too late. I cannot leave Grimshaw Court without an attempt at securing my happiness."

"How could you have so utterly changed your mind? It was only days ago you could barely look at her."

"I did not *see* her for who she truly was. Perhaps I was *indifferent* to her at first but now— Now, after spending all day in her company yesterday that has changed and I have begun to see reason."

Stephen could see the change for himself, but he would hardly call it *reason*. Toby was a mooncalf, gazing toward Lord James standing with Waddell, waiting to have his chance to speak to his lordship. Should Stephen intervene? Make his friend see reason?

"Never did I think my days could be filled with such fun and joy! We must marry for I will be destitute without her." Toby sounded determined to seek permission to do exactly that. Stephen was convinced his opinion would make no difference.

Toby fidgeted with his fishing pole, tipping it to and fro, moving it from hand to hand, and was quite unable to remain still long enough to properly concentrate. He mumbled to himself, as if rehearsing what he would say, what he needed to say to Lord James.

A wave of uncertainty came over Stephen as he considered his friend's sudden change. Stephen had known Toby for a very long time and yet ... could never imagine him taking such a rash step ... one he felt determined was imperative for his lifelong happiness ... with Alicia of all people. Stephen then wondered how easily one's aspirations could so swiftly be swept aside to be replaced by another, entirely new, unexpected set.

Kate would have felt very bad indeed if Candy had been subjected to the wrath of Miss Fawcett for only retrieving her sketchpad. On her return to the library, Kate was eager to get back to the search. She had just finished donning the last of her protective wear when Lord Stephen entered dressed in his dust-repellent garb ready to continue the dusty search.

"I hadn't expected to see you so soon," she said. "I had heard that *all* the gentlemen were going fishing."

"Well ... yes. I was with them earlier but found it a bit crowded." He drew a protective sleeve up one of his forearms.

"*Crowded?* Outside? By the river?" What a bunch of stuff and nonsense!

"It was not so much a *river* where we fish ... a stream, more like," he explained, donning the second sleeve. Kate had no idea where the men went for their sport. "I suppose I was just not feeling the thing."

"It was fortunate you did not remain. Your blue devils might have frightened the fish, who knows?"

"*Who knows,* indeed." He smiled at her and in that smile she saw … something. He seemed different somehow. Was it the way in which he glanced at her? The manner in which he spoke to her? Certainly it was of no import.

"We should get back to it—*I* should get back to my section." All of a sudden she felt unsettled. Kate took hold of the handrail on the ladder and turned back to him. "You know what?"

"What's that?" he replied.

"I think today is the day," she told him in confidence. Kate felt as if something substantial, something important was to happen.

"*The* day?" he echoed, sounding puzzled.

"The day we'll find the book." Kate smiled.

"I do hope so." With a nod, Stephen proceeded to his end of the room and Kate headed off to hers.

She climbed up the ladder, reaching to the very top shelf.

After more than an hour had passed, Kate stopped to straighten and shrug her shoulders. As she glanced across the library, at where Lord Stephen stood … not so very far away now. It occurred to her just how close their ladders had grown. It would not be long until they would meet at the center of the room —and without finding the book they both so fervently wished.

Kate's early realization that *today would be the day* began to fade. *What if today was* not *the day they would find the final volume?*

Goodness … she had felt such optimism about their search. Now Kate felt increasingly downhearted. She began to scan the spines, starting left to right, book by book. How many times had she done this? How many *hundreds* of titles had she read over the course of the last few days?

There was some determination—*nay,* stubbornness on her part. She *would* keep focused, alert, and not allow the monotony and boredom to deaden her senses. More than anything, she wanted to find that book.

With a pre-emptive swipe of her dust cloth on the first shelf of a new section, Kate prepared the books sitting upon the upper-most shelf. But—there—*there*—she saw ... she read: *Gulliver's Travels.*

It was the same reddish leather spine with the same gold-leaf lettered font displaying the title and below it, the number '2.' It was the second volume.

"It's here! I've found it!" Kate cried out in delight. "Lord Stephen! It is here!" Goodness—she was excited! "I found it! I have—" Nothing could have been more—but when Kate pulled at the top of the spine to draw the slim volume free from its neigh-bors. "*What?*" Only then had she discovered she held the outside of the book. The insides, its contents, were missing.

Lord Stephen called out something—the words were unintelli-gible—at least Kate did not know what he had said. His heavy, brisk footsteps grew loud as he neared.

She felt the ladder shake. "Oh—NO!" Then it wobbled beneath her.

"What is it? Is it not the book?" Lord Stephen had taken a few steps behind her and stopped. "You *have* found it?"

"Well ... it *is* the outside of the book ... but it is *only* the spine," Kate stated in as direct a manner as she could. She held the shell of the cover out to him.

"It must be ... it *still* must be in there ... perhaps behind the other books." A groan accompanied another tremor of the ladder when he took an additional rung to see for himself. "Let's have the lot out, shall we? Perhaps it's been pushed to the back."

Kate took hold of several books at a time, handing them down to empty the shelf. Only a few remained and she could touch them with the tips of her fingers.

"I can't reach the rest of them." She swiped her hand to the back and came up empty handed. "I cannot see any farther."

"If you will allow me to have a rummage around." Stephen motioned her away and he placed his foot on the next rung to move up the ladder. "Do allow me ..."

"If you will *please*—" Kate pressed back into the vertical handrail, there was nowhere for her to go. "There is simply not enough room for *both of us*—" She groaned in discomfort as she descended the very same ladder he was ascending. Parts of their anatomy came into contact in a manner ... *quite improper, indecent* ... also quite *not* altogether unpleasant. In addition to exchanging places, he had placed the book spine into her hand once again.

The sound of the rickety contraption made her feel uneasy and it—not exactly buckled under their combined weight ... but it had shuttered with their unorthodox movements. Surely this was not meant to hold two people, not to mention two disgruntled people exchanging places from top to bottom and bottom to top.

"I need more light," he called to her as he struggled to look deep into the shelf.

"Let me find a candle." Kate moved to the desk, depositing the empty book cover on its surface and spotted several candles, burned low in their holders. She lit one and carried it back, tending the flame so it would not extinguish. She was careful when climbing the ladder and handed the light to him.

In a quick motion, Lord Stephen brought the light source to the shelf and pushed the books to the side and peered behind them, in the back of the shelf, searching for the contents of the spine she'd found. "I don't see it ... I don't think it's here."

"But where could it have gone?" Kate found this whole business so very vexing. They were so close to finding— The knot of emotion collected in her throat at the disappointment.

"I'm sorry ..." There was no reason for him to apologize.

It was not in any way his fault, of course, but this made her so angry!

"This is—is *intolerable!*" Kate had had enough ... she didn't know what was different *this* time but ... she could no longer tolerate this ... *disappointment*. "I— I—" She groaned and out emerged a pent-up groan. She snatched the mobcap off her head and threw it on the ground as hard as she could manage and exhaled.

"I understand your frustration completely," he said from his elevated position on the ladder.

"I beg your pardon, Lord Stephen. If you will excuse me." Kate bent to the floor, and in a sweeping motion retrieved her cap before stalking out of the library.

Fourteen

❧

Lady Catherine did have a temper.

Stephen blew out the candle and bit back a smile. It was not because the contents of the book were missing—there was nothing humorous about that. He could not deny that he was also disappointed but for her it was not to be borne.

What he had found amusing was that he had witnessed the fury of the real Lady Catherine. Perhaps she needed to remove herself from public view because she felt her mask slipping. The thought made him chuckle.

Stephen carefully descended the ladder with one hand on the rail and the other holding the extinguished candle. He could not blame her for becoming angry at *almost* finding the book for which they had been searching. They had spent many mornings, afternoons, evenings looking for it … *it* had occupied nearly every spare moment of their time.

Stephen had always known the book lay somewhere in that room. It must have been quite frustrating for her. Kate had no such knowledge. He replaced the candlestick on the desk and picked up the empty cover, studying the outside, imagining what she must have been feeling when she had laid eyes upon the words of the spine.

She had come so very close to finding it, touching the volume itself was, however small, the ultimate prize. It was just at her fingertips, within her reach! It would be the end of her searching, she could sit and spend a few hours immersing herself in Jonathan Swift's tale.

Stephen moved to the window and caught sight of movement in the distance. It was Kate. She strode down the path with some purpose. A few minutes later, she disappeared, obscured from sight by the overgrown shrubbery. She was most likely fueled by her anger she could not freely express before him. He hoped for her sake the walking would do her good and her calm would return quickly. Perhaps then, they could together decide how to proceed or if they would.

A pile of books sat on a small table quite out of the way. Stephen recognized them as ones he had chosen. He removed the top four and placed them beside the original stack. The two did not belong together. Stephen rounded the large desk and neared the globe … the one Kate stared at and studied when she didn't think he was watching. But he had seen her. His fingers tripped over its surface and he slowly rotated the orb on its axis.

When he first arrived, Stephen thought finding the pair of books was something to occupy his time while here at Grimshaw. In reminiscing about his past visits, he recalled how much he had enjoyed reading that story. Now, many years later, he thought it was easy enough to find those books and reread them during this stay. But what Stephen had discovered was more than the tales of Lemuel Gulliver.

He'd met the most interesting and adventurous young lady he had ever come across. Kate was so very different from the Society Miss who populated London searching for a husband. Kate—*Lady Catherine* had been there. How had he managed to miss making her acquaintance? Would he have thought she had any of the qualities he prescribed to her now? Or would she have come across as one of those simpering, smiling, giggling insipid young ladies? He doubted that very much.

Kate had not the least interest in marriage or finding a husband. However, if some gentleman wished to change her mind, he might find success if he swept her off to the ends of the earth, promising her a grand adventure and further travels.

It was a perfect excuse to enjoy one another's company and learn of their mutual love of books and wish to visit other lands. The man who wed her would be very lucky indeed. The manner in which Kate and he passed the time … idle talk of the places they would travel and of her building a very small house on the side of an enormous book room—that sounded ridiculous. It *had* until Stephen had discovered she was a young lady of considerable means. Then his opinion, the way he thought of her had changed.

Were the musings of Miss Kate's country house with an enormous library or worldwide travels just that—mere dreams or were they unrealized goals? *Dreams* of Lady Catherine's were most probably not so much dreams but being an heiress … a *very wealthy* heiress would make all she wished for easily possible. She outranked him and had far more wealth than he could ever attain. Kate could do as she pleased.

There were so many unexpected turns occurring at the same time. With the failure of finding *Gulliver's Travels,* Kate's identity crisis, and Toby's marriage consideration … Stephen had been left feeling very unsettled. His world had turned upside down and his hands were feeling quite full.

Kate's anger was enough to sustain her all the way to the folly. As she suspected, the walk took no more than twenty minutes. She went up the steps of the rotunda and crossed through the vacant center. Last she had been here, there were tables laden with food and conversation all around.

Now it was quiet and she was alone. Finally ... *alone.* This is what she needed ... craved.

The peace she'd found there soothed her, calming the agony of disappointment she'd had in the library. Here there were no servants, no children, no Kitty, and no Stephen Emerson—and why had she thought of *him* specifically?

A glimpse of whimsically-shaped clouds, the sight of ducks gliding along the surface of the water, and the slightest breeze causing the tips of the long grass to twist and flutter easily reminded her of the girls.

Kate had become too close to the Emersons, wrapped up in their family goings-on and plans to fill the hours of their days in the country. She had never wished for this—all she wanted was to find a bit of joy. Was it so very wrong to be selfish ... just this once?

She pulled out the small sketchbook from one of the pockets of her apron and settled on the steps, facing the lake resting her back against the column.

Kate studied the view before deciding where she should begin. She sketched rough lines for the landscape that Cindy preferred to draw. Then with the long, loose stroke of her pencil, she put in the surrounding weeds and tall grasses that Sandy spent a great deal of time contemplating. Finally, she added quick dots for later placement of the ducks of which Candy was so fond.

Some minutes later, Kate found herself squinting in the diminishing light. She glanced up from her paper, noticing some dark clouds gathering, covering the sky. Heavy raindrops began to pelt the ground, the ducks gathered and rushed away, to the edges of the pond. They found shelter under some foliage, taking cover from the approaching inclement weather.

Then there was the sound of heavy raindrops hitting the

rotunda and running off its dome. Kate laughed at the sudden, abrupt deluge. It was fortunate she had made it here when she had, else she might have found herself very wet.

Despite the rain, Kate still thought her surroundings pleasant. The rain cleansed the air and brought a crispness and a slight chill. She pulled her feet away from the edge of the step and well under the path of the downpour to keep them dry. The landscape before her was a bit grayer and hopefully the weather would soon pass and take the sudden cold with it.

The sound of laughter, a man's and a woman's, in the distance grew louder as they undoubtedly approached the folly to find shelter. Their footfalls and her squeals of playful protest increased with the rain. No doubt they were escaping the downpour just as Kate herself had. She huddled behind the column, hoping to remain unnoticed.

Who were they? The couple must have been from Grimshaw, surely. Kate dared not turn round from behind the column and chance being seen. She did not wish to make her presence known … embarrassed that she would be intruding in their privacy.

Holding her sketchpad close to her chest and her pencil clutched in her hand, Kate hugged her legs, keeping as much as she could behind the column. The female giggling was high pitched and playful … *this* could only be Alicia.

But who had accompanied Alicia?

"This is most improper … we should not be alone together like this," he said. The man's voice was soft which made him difficult to identify.

"What are we to do? It is pouring rain … we will be soaked to the bone!" Laughter trailed her reply.

"True." He hadn't said enough for her to know his identity.

Kate wanted to see them—*him*. She wanted to know who *he* was. From the echo of their voices, Kate could tell they stood directly behind her, in the center of the rotunda, the farthest place they could from the edge, keeping dry.

"I never expected I would meet anyone who I would form such a sudden and strong attachment."

A long period of silence followed.

"*Hu-gh* ..." Alicia said in a soft, prolonged gasp.

Hugh Waddle? Ehm—Wad-dell?

"No, do not release my hand." Alicia's emotion-filled voice shocked Kate. How could she allow ...

"I only wished to keep you close ... to keep you out of the rain." There was a rustle of fabric as the two drew together, presumably avoiding the drips around them.

"Of course," Alicia agreed.

Kate could just imagine, how in such circumstances, Alicia blushed. And would not Mr. Waddell find that attractive, even in this dim light?

"Miss Emerson—*Alicia*... I wish to ... I ... know we have not known one another long but ..."

"Yes, Hugh?" Kate could just imagine how the color in Alicia's cheeks would darken.

"I only wish to tell you ... how *fond* I am of you."

Fond? Kate mouthed with complete distaste. *Who says that?* If he had expected to capture her heart, Mr. Wad*dell* needed to say he felt more than *fond* of her. That was his point, wasn't it?

"I cannot say I have an overly-bright future... I am currently a junior member of my father's firm but I hope someday to join my father as a partner."

Would the firm then be known as: Rush, Stonewall, Waddle, and Wad-dell?

"It sounds as if it is a most promising future," Alicia replied.

"I do not wish to sound forward because our association has not been long but I was wondering ... *ehm* ... if you would ... if you would consider becoming my wife?"

"What?" Alicia gasped in surprise.

What? Kate clapped her hand over her mouth to stifle any sounds she might make.

Alicia must not have expected this from him ... nor had Kate.

"I have never before found anyone so delightfully agreeable and immensely suited to my own temperament and whom I utterly adore."

"I am so very flattered, Mr. Waddell—*Hugh*... I cannot think what to say."

"Miss Alicia, you have quite enchanted me. I am completely charmed by you—please, you must say yes."

"Oh, *Hugh!*"

"We will live in London. I will take you to the museums and the theaters. We will take walks—long walks—in all the parks. We will attend parties!"

Another long silence punctuated the air. Kate did wish she could know what occurred between them but dare not chance discovery by peering around the column.

"I have not spoken to your father as of yet. I first wished to know your opinion on the matter."

Opinion? You flat! *How could the man speak of marriage without knowing how she felt? This interlude could end very badly.*

"I only bring this up now for your consideration because we are private—"

"Yes, we are." Alicia's soft voice diminished to silence that Kate could well-believe led to some impending intimacy she did not care to witness.

No, they were not. Kate closed her eyes, hoping that would keep her from being seen. She should not be here and she should not be hearing this. It was a matter that concerned only these two people.

"I have written to my father on behalf of Mr. Drayton. I do not have the authority to accept his suit, for he wishes to offer for Lady Catherine."

WHAT? Kate's eyes went wide and she pressed her hand more firmly over her mouth.

"I expect him to arrive this evening."

Mr. Waddle the Elder was coming to Grimshaw Court? Here? Tonight?

What she had previously delayed only a few days before would need to be revealed to all *before* her guardian arrived.

Kate's eyes closed as she realized there would be no escaping the inevitable.

Kitty stood from the chair next to her newly laid fire in the hearth situated in the corner of her bedchamber. She gazed out the window, watching the skies open and the deluge of rain fall from the dark clouds. It felt good to be inside, someplace dry and warm … and safe.

"Miss Kate! Miss Kate! Are you here?" A girl's voice called from the corridor. A small figure dashed by the doorway in a blur then returned. Candy rounded the corner to Kitty's bedchamber, briefly pausing to call into the room.

"Kate is not here, Candy," Kitty replied. "Is there something I can do for you?"

"Not here? Is she still—still … out *there*?" The girl's small voice, hesitant and filled with emotion trailed off. Tears welled in her eyes.

"Where?" Kitty had no knowledge of Kate wandering off by herself. She thought her friend was in the library searching for that book.

"Outside … and now it's raining …" By Candy's pained expression, Kitty could see there was a far more serious concern.

"What do you mean?" Kitty had the most unsettling feeling starting to grow in her stomach. "She is not … she *did* not… Alone?"

"She's gone outside… I saw her … wander off the path," Candy continued slowly.

Off the path? Kitty hated to admit it but that sounded *exactly* something Kate would do.

"She's been gone for such a long time… I think she went to the folly to sketch the ducks!"

A clamor of movement and voices came from outside. The two pressed near the window to see what was happening below. A pair of servants had put up umbrellas and quickly ran away from the house down the garden path.

"Look—there are the footmen… I am certain they will find her," Kitty reassured.

"No, they're going out for Alicia and Mr. Waddell. They don't know about Miss Kate. That she's gone too."

"Are you certain?" Kitty did not wish to falsely raise an alarm, but if Candy was correct— Kate would be left out in the storm.

"She's *still* out there and no one's looking for her!" Candy insisted.

"Let's go." Kitty took Candy by the hand and headed to the staircase. If need be, Kitty would go herself to retrieve her friend. Stepping onto the main floor, Kitty really had no idea what to do next. She heard Mr. Drayton's voice coming from the opposite end of the house, the portion of the house away from the music room and headed in that direction.

Surely he could help. Still with Candy's hand held firmly in hers, Kitty stopped just inside the library. Mr. Drayton and Lord Stephen stood at their appearance.

"Miss Kitty…" Mr. Drayton stepped forward, offering her a gentle smile that soon faded when it was not returned.

"Is something amiss?" Lord Stephen quickly added, glancing from Kitty to his young relative. "What are you doing down here, poppet?"

"Cousin Stephen—I'm w-worried," Candy said in a trembling voice.

"About what?" He did not disregard her words, instead he showed great interest.

"After it started raining, Miss Kitty and I saw the footmen go out with their umbrellas to find Alicia and her beau."

"Did they?" He glanced toward the tall windows observing the weather for himself. "I am certain your sister will be found. You need not concern yourself." Touching her shoulder, Lord Stephen offered his young cousin a comforting smile.

"But what about Miss Kate?"

"What about her?" His hand came away and he straightened.

"She is *still* out there. She left long before Alicia and she hasn't come back."

He glanced at Kitty for confirmation but she could only shrug. She had no knowledge of Kate's whereabouts. All this was from Candy's observations, and it might just be possible the girl had been correct.

Lord Stephen surged forward, leaving Kitty, Candy, and Mr. Drayton in the library. They soon followed, trailing after him.

The door to the rear terrace opened, several of the staff were on hand, ready to dry and help with the sodden couple, Alicia and Mr. Waddell, and the accompanying footmen. The couple managed to laugh about the adventure now that they had returned to the warmth and dry of the house. The footmen, in their sodden raiment, held the drenched umbrellas aside, mindful that they should not drip on the floor. Other staff approached with towels in hand came to their aid. They were informed that a tray with hot tea and a fire would be waiting in the drawing room when they had dried and changed clothing.

"Did you find anyone else?" Lord Stephen glanced about looking for the *other* missing person.

"*Sir*?" one of the footmen replied. "There was no one else, your lordship."

Lines of panic etched across Lord Stephen's face. "Fetch my box coat," he ordered, heading in the direction of the entrance hall. "Toby, remain with Kitty, if you will."

Kitty nodded, she would do exactly as she was bid. She

stepped toward Mr. Drayton, craving some comfort. He slid his arm around her and pulled her near, keeping her out of the way and safe by his side.

"See Candy returned to the nursery, if you please. Never fear, Kitty, I shall find her." Stephen took hold of his coat from the approaching footman and swung it around his shoulders, gathering it at the front before stepping outside. The rain immediately flattened his hair. Without regard to his inadequate footwear, he proceeded on the path into the jungle.

Fifteen

Venturing outdoors in one's velvet slippers onto the sodden soil was not an act of a rational man. Stephen never claimed to be rational and at the moment it was more important to locate Kate. If ruining his slippers is what it took, so be it.

He'd refused the umbrella, carrying it—returning with it seemed impractical. He ignored the heavy raindrops pelting his head and swiped away the long strand of hair now hanging before his eyes, only mildly blurring his sight. He did not need any more impediments than he had.

Stephen could imagine her seeking solitude at the rotunda after her bout of frustration in finding—not finding *Gulliver's Travels* in the library. He strolled down the narrow dirt path toward the large oak tree where he would see the rotunda in the distance. He moved in that direction, pushing through the bushes, stepping over and around the large rocks. It may not have been the exact route Kate took nor the most expeditious but he would not lose his way.

He saw only the nonstop rain with no hint of it letting up, obscuring the sight of the structure that should soon come into view. The drenching rain soaked further through his unprotected areas, his head, his hands, his lower limbs, and his feet.

He kept watch for her as he passed by the trees and shrubs. Perhaps she had taken the notion to huddle beneath. Stephen did not know what he would do if he did not find her... He called out for her a few times and realized he would not be heard over the pounding rain. The best he could do was continue forward.

Kitty was glad to have Mr. Drayton near. She wasn't certain what she would have done without him to lend her strength and steady her nerves. He was of great comfort. He told her everything would be all right. He told her it would not be much longer for them to wait. He told her he would not leave her side.

Miss Fawcett was sent for to collect Candy. Kitty could not have been more thankful for Candy's keen observation and promised to send word when Lord Stephen and Kate had returned.

Kitty spent some long minutes in Mr. Drayton's company before realizing she needed to make preparations for Kate's return. She *would* be returned. Shaking from exposure, wet, and cold, on her arrival to Grimshaw, Kate would need to be dried, and her clothing changed, before sitting before a fire to warm herself.

Mr. Drayton understood. He wanted to be on hand for Lord Stephen and would not leave the rear entrance of the manor.

"You stay and wait for his lordship," Kitty reassured Mr. Drayton with a touch to his arm. "I need to prepare. Do not fret, I shall return soon."

"Will you manage on your own?" he asked.

"Never fear, Mr. Drayton, I will do quite well, but I must make ready, sir." Kitty had set her mind on what needed to be done. She would not worry about *if* Kate returned but *when* she did.

"As you say," Mr. Drayton agreed but did not seem pleased that she was venturing off. "I shall send a search party for you if you are too long gone."

That made Kitty smile and with an affectionate pat of appreciation on his sleeve, she withdrew.

"Maud!" Kitty called out upon reaching the landing and hurried to her bedchamber. "Maud!"

"What is it, my lady?" The upstairs maid, hurrying to tend to the guest. "Have they found Miss Kate?"

"No, not yet but we must make ready." Kitty moved to the clothespress to pull the warmest garments she could find. She knew that hers were far warmer than Kate's for Kitty always felt a bit cold.

"Yes, ma'am," the maid awaited her orders.

"Have a footman light the hearth. I will collect some dry garments—and we'll need blankets, towels ... many towels. We'll need to dry her and lay some on the bed. We'll have her put there when she arrives." Kitty pointed to the counterpane. "And some warm—hot water, I think."

"Yes, my lady." Maud took the clothing Kitty handed her and set them to one side.

"I need to return ... belowstairs ..." Kitty murmured aimlessly. "Please wait here until I return with her."

"Yes, ma'am. I'll see to gatherin' the things right away and I'll be waitin' here."

"Thank you, Maud." Kitty wasn't certain what there was left to do. She needed to do *something* ... keep her mind from thinking the worst. Keep busy.

"Don't be frightened, my lady. Miss Kate will be found safe, don't you worry."

"I know she will be. I know ..." But Kitty was still frightened. "It shouldn't be much longer, should it?"

"Lord only knows, my lady. Lord only knows." Maud dipped a curtsy and went on her way.

After leaving Maud in her bedchamber to oversee the remainder of the preparations, Kitty returned to the back of the house where she'd left Mr. Drayton to await Kate's return. It could not be much longer, could it?

"Nothing yet," Mr. Drayton said upon Kitty returning to his side. "Is everything in order?"

"Yes, I believe I've done all I can do," she replied, her hands began to tremble and she clasped them together. Waiting for Kate's return was becoming unbearable. It felt as if hours had passed.

Kitty could feel her heart pounding with dread that seemed to be growing with every passing minute. She peered out the window, waiting for Lord Stephen's approach, hoping it would be soon, the mere act of breathing was becoming a chore.

Mr. Drayton must have sensed her unease for he gently took up Kitty's hand and rested it in the crook of his arm before covering it with his own. The action caused Kitty to jump. She had not found it unpleasant but was startled by the sudden contact. She gazed at him, into his eyes, and he offered her a smile that brought her immediate comfort.

"Do not despair, Miss Kitty, you can depend upon Stephen, he will return with your Miss Kate, never fear." His words were spoken in a soothing manner and standing next to him gave her strength to endure. "It will not be much longer. You have done what you could for your friend and to worry will do neither of you any good."

Kitty's labored breathing eased and her heart ceased its accelerated rhythm, instead the increased pounding related more to Mr. Drayton's presence. Kitty could not but feel more at ease when near him.

The fifteen-twenty minutes Stephen had been gone felt more like hours and it soon grew nearer to thirty minutes—then an imagined hour or two had passed—he did not know for time had ceased to matter. Sometime later, he finally arrived.

Stephen stepped out of the rain when he entered the rotunda. There was not much light but he could see no one was there. Fear streaked through him upon realizing what this meant. He thought for certain this would be the place he'd find her.

If she were not here, he had no idea where to look next. Moving to the far end of the rotunda, the closest point to the lake, he tried to calm his mounting fear that she was truly lost.

He lowered his head and closed his eyes, not knowing what he would do, where he should search next. When opening his eyes, his fear turned into relief when he saw her small form curled into a sitting position on the step, on the outside of one of the columns.

"There you are," he crooned, not wishing to frighten her. She did not reply nor did she move. "Are you all right?"

Stephen had found her. She wore no wrap, nor did she have a bonnet. Her arms encircled her bent legs and her head rested on her knees.

He bent and gathered her into his arms. He could feel her breathing and when he settled her against his chest she shivered, shaking with cold. Stephen pulled the edges of his coat around her for protection from the rain and set out for Grimshaw.

Kate was wet, to keep her from slipping in his arms was challenging, but he held tight. He moved forward and had no thought as to how far he had gone or how much farther he needed to go. He just kept on.

Before long, he needed to resettle her ... but he would not allow her to slip from his arms. He hoped the heat generated from his exertion and proximity would warm her. One step after

another he continued, looking for the large oak tree as a
landmark.

Stephen had spotted the oak in the distance and he headed in
that direction. By the time they had reached the main path, near
the tree, her breathing had deepened. Kate had grown sufficiently
warm but it could not last for long. His arms ached and his legs
were about to give way. By the time they had reached the house, it
would be all Stephen could do not to collapse.

"There he is." Mr. Drayton alerted the staff who stood ready to
care for the wet arrivals. "I don't see Miss—"

Kitty had grasped hold of Mr. Drayton's arm and both stared
out the window. Upon his approach, his lordship's gait was
unusual, labored until Kitty realized that he was burdened with
the weight of Kate in his arms. His coat wrapped around her ...
around them.

"He wouldn't come back without her... Stephen wouldn't
have left her—nor returned without her." Mr. Drayton waved the
footmen to the door. "He's got her—under his coat."

A footman pulled the door open. A great deal of water rolled
off the garment and onto the floor when Lord Stephen's coat came
away from his shoulders, revealing the bulk underneath ... the
precious figure in his arms.

"Oh, goodness—*Kate!*" Kitty was near tears at the sight of her
rescued friend.

Towels were briefly applied, blotting the excess moisture, as
much as could be removed in the few moments it took for Lord
Stephen to speak, "Lead the way, Miss Kitty—*quickly.*" He
gestured to the staircase with his head.

"Yes, the maid is waiting." Kitty ran ahead, glancing over her
shoulder with concern before climbing to the upper floor. "I've

had the fire in my bedchamber built up and there is fresh clothing for her, and blankets to wrap her in."

"Hot tea and a spot of brandy should help," Lord Stephen said as they rounded the corner, stepping into her bedchamber.

"*Cor*—" Maud swore when she set her wide-eyed stare on Kate while stepping out of the way. "If she don't look dead already ..."

"She is no such thing, Maud!" Kitty scolded. "Please!"

Lord Stephen laid Kate onto the bed with great care and moved back. "She will be fine now. I know you'll see that she's properly cared for," he said to Kitty, then sighed. "I need a change my clothes, then I'll return."

"Thank you, my lord. Thank you so much!" Kitty motioned the maid closer while he exited the room. "Help me get her out of these wet things."

"Yes, my lady." Moved forward and set to work untying the apron. Kitty pulled away the small sketchpad and opened Kate's fist, pulling the pencil clasped within free and set the items upon the nightstand before taking up a towel.

"Kate... Kate... What have you done?" Kitty whispered, helping to move her friend this way and that while drying her. "What do you think you were doing out there? And why are you not speaking?"

"She ain't talkin', she ain't. You *sure's* she's not dead?" The maid patted Kate dry on the other side.

"She's not!" Kitty maintained. "Here—let's sit her up and get these wet things off her."

The act of moving her upright caused Kate to moan ... groan ... wake.

"What's happened?" Kate eyelids cracked open. "Kitty—what am I doing here? *How* did I get here?"

"Good gracious, Kate! What are you thinking—how is it you've gone outside, so far away, by yourself?"

Kate tried to cooperate. She helped by not struggling against the removal of her wet clothing and slipping into dry garments. Kitty's scolds accompanied the entire duration, but Kate was not listening. She was too preoccupied trying to recall—recall *exactly* what it was she had heard before … before … she awoke here. It was not too much longer before Kitty placed her in front of the corner fire to warm herself.

Kitty thanked Maud and dismissed her so she and Kate could be private.

"Here—put your hands around this." Kitty held out a cup of hot tea. "It should help warm you. Lord Stephen said a dose of brandy might—"

Kate took hold of the teacup. "Kit-ty," she whispered. *That* … not her return to the house but what she had heard back at the folly was unfortunately *not* a dream. She remembered it all too well. The folly. Alicia. Hugh Waddell. Kate's voice was a bit raspy and felt a bit sore but she had to speak. "Do sit next to me. I have something to tell you."

"Of course. I am sorry for scolding you but we were so very worried." Kitty lowered onto the other chair near the small hearth to sit by her friend. "What is it?"

"What— How long has it been since…" Kate blinked, measuring the light, or lack of it, from the window. It was dark outside yet the shutters were not drawn. Surely an entire day had not passed. "What time is it?"

"What is wrong?" Kitty had sensed Kate's confusion. "Do not worry, you are safe."

"How did I…" Kate looked around at her surroundings. She was no longer at the folly … she was in Kitty's room, sitting warm by the hearth. "How did I get here?"

"Lord Stephen brought you, goose, don't you remember? Lord Stephen brought you in from the rain. He's carried you here."

"Oh, yes. Yes, of course." Kate did recall. His strong arms, the warmth of his body. It was as if it was a distant memory and not quite real to her.

"Tobias was so very kind as to stay with me while we waited for Lord Stephen to retrieve you."

"*Tobias…*" The use of his Christian name gave Kate pause.

"Yes, Mr. Drayton." Kitty tilted her head to regard her friend. "Perhaps you are not yet fully recovered?"

"I am quite well," Kate assured her. However, there was a more pressing topic she wished to address. She set her teacup on the nearby table. "I need to tell you something. It is all too shocking, and you must be strong."

Kitty clasped her hands together as if to steady herself.

"I was not alone at the folly."

"Who was there with you?" Kitty's voice was soft and hollow.

"Soon after I arrived … when the rain started, Alicia and Mr. Waddell ran under the rotunda for shelter." Kate winced. "They had no notion I was there … and I had no wish to disturb their privacy."

"Did you hear something you ought not to have heard?" Kitty fell quiet and waited.

Kate nodded. "Mr. Waddell has asked Alicia to marry him."

"That is wonderful!" Kitty who had look worried, smiled in relief. "Shall we not wish them happy?"

"He has, not as yet, spoken to Lord James. He wished to know her feelings on the matter."

"I believe she is quite fond of him." Kitty sounded shy but animated. Then she turned to one side to pose a rhetorical question, "Does she find him a suitable *parti*? I cannot say. I do hope so, do not you? It is the most wonderful news!"

"Yes, yes, it is but …" Kate had to continue. What she had to say wasn't all wonderful news. "I am telling you this because … because… Mr. Waddell believes he could speak with his father about the matter when he arrives to discuss the marriage offer for *Lady Catherine.*"

"*Lady Cath* — But you have no marriage contract to be settled."

Kitty narrowed her eyes, still trying to work out Kate's meaning. "Do you?"

"Of course not. No—but *you* are Lady Catherine."

"Me? Do you mean *my* marriage..." Kitty took hold of the sides of the chair, stunned at the news. "Who, Kate? Who wishes to marry me?"

"Mr. Drayton," Kate answered. Had Kitty no idea of his affections? "Are you in love with him?"

"*What?* No—*NO.*" Kitty's voice softened and she glanced about as if her deepest secret had been discovered. "Well, *maybe.* I am afraid we have become somewhat close. But he cannot possibly love me. He cannot."

"*Maybe?*" Kate offered an unconvincing smile. "He cares for you enough to discuss marriage with *your* guardian."

"Kate—I do not *have* a guardian." Kitty stared hard at her friend.

"I mean to say *Lady Catherine's* guardian. Mr. Waddle ... the Elder."

"Mr. Waddell's father? He knows you by sight."

Kate nodded. "I shall be found out. There is no escaping it."

"They shall throw us out of the house! We shall be destitute! Tobias will never wish to see me much less marry me." Her eyes teared up, finally realizing her—*their* predicament.

"We shall never be without a home," Kate stated without a doubt. She had an inheritance. What better time to make inquiries about her funds than in the presence of her solicitor whose imminent arrival would then be welcomed rather than dreaded. "I shall not allow that to happen."

"Tobias doesn't know who I *really* am. He will know I've lied to him ... all this time! And he is to be a vicar!" She clapped her hands over her face to hide herself—so she could not see or be seen. Her tears flowed freely down her face, between her fingers. "I cannot face him ... ever again. How can I? I just want to run away, Kate."

"Stop it!" Kate could not bear the thought of someone thinking ill of her friend. "If he truly loves you he will not blame you. He could not." Kitty was the sweetest, most wonderful person Kate had ever known.

Kitty bent her head forward, sobbing into her hands. Kate had placed them squarely into this predicament, causing her friend this pain. It was because of Kate's immature, selfish needs.

"I realize there will be no escaping it this time." Kate laid her head against her friend's shuttering shoulder. "Mr. Waddle *the Elder* is on his way and for me, that means it is only a short time before this masquerade ends."

"For you?" Kitty wept uncontrollably. "I'm afraid it will be the end for the both of us."

Sixteen

"AH-*choo!*" Stephen reached into his pocket for his linen and brought out a lacy bit of nothing. *This would not do.* He smiled at the pleasant recollection of the delicate handkerchief's owner and placed it upon his dressing table.

He imagined a *lady* would not suffer from a sneeze such as his and this decorative ornamentation was only meant to dab at a female's lone tear when it dared to streak down her cheek.

With a quick motion, Stephen made a last scrub of the towel on his head, to dry his hair, pulled it down from his head, over his face, to pick up any lingering moisture, and used it to wipe his nose.

"I say, Stephen?" Toby came through the open door. "You all right?"

Stephen peeked over the top of the crumpled towel he held to his face.

"You look dreadful. You need someone to look after you … let's get a footman in here," Toby suggested. His sensibilities must have been well-shaken, or perhaps Stephen looked a right mess.

"I don't need a footman." Stephen grumbled, feeling thoroughly uncomfortable with his present situation. He was cold and wet. His mind was at a loss in regards to where he should begin to correct his soggy state.

"What say we borrow Lord James' man? He'll know what's to be done."

"That would be splendid but I am in no condition to hunt him down... They'll be water wherever... I'll leave puddles." Stephen shrugged, feeling momentarily hopeless.

"*Now* you're concerned about the carpets after walking through the house, up the staircase, and from one end of the house to t'other?" Stepping into the corridor, Toby gained the attention of the footman stationed near the staircase and requested, "Do fetch Lord James' valet, will you?"

Toby approached Stephen and busied himself by removing his neckcloth until the arrival of the valet. "Ah—*ehm* ..." Toby fidgeted, realizing he stood in the way and his once helpful efforts were now more of a hindrance.

"Warren, sir," intoned the manservant, regarding Toby with an arched eyebrow.

"I beg your pardon." Toby released the long linen, draping the end over Stephen's shoulder. He stepped back, finding a chair where he could sit out of the way and wait for Stephen to finish dressing. "This is best left to the more proficient, is it not?"

Warren approached, taking up the linen, and wordlessly proceeded to take matters in hand.

"Sorry about the mess, Warren." Stephen, who had previously relied on the valet on a few occasions, never cared to burden him with additional work. "I've left my slippers belowstairs. I believe they cannot be saved."

"Not to worry, sir," the valet never paused in his ministrations. "I have seen to their retrieval. Their sacrifice was for a worthy cause, I hear."

"Very worthy." While standing there, Stephen began to feel anxious. He wished he were already dressed and off to check on

Kate. He should not concern himself, Kitty would have called for him if something had gone awry.

"And you have safely recovered the young lady?"

"Returned safe and sound. I shall make inquiries in due course." Stephen would do as soon as he had had a change of clothes.

"Well done, sir." During that short conversation, Warren had removed Stephen's wet clothing, dried him, and provided a freshly laundered shirt and a pair of breeches. Pulling the shirt over his head, Stephen felt much improved by the warmth of dry fabric.

The valet came and went through the dressing room several times, removing the discarded garments. During his absence, he spoke quietly to someone in the dressing room ... outside the bedchamber in the corridor, giving instructions for the care of the clothing. Finally, he returned with a fresh waistcoat and jacket.

"Thank you, Warren." Stephen ran his hand along his sleeve, quite pleased with how quickly his discomfort had turned to comfort under the valet's ministrations.

"Very good, sir." Warren eyed Stephen's coat, assuring the fit. He stepped back, seemingly satisfied with his efforts. "Will that be all, sir?"

"I believe so."

"I have just been informed that the others are gathering in the drawing room if you and Mr. Drayton wish to find them." Warren turned to address Toby and spoke in a softened tone, "Lady Catherine is presently making her way belowstairs."

Lady Cath— Stephen became instantly attentive at the mention of her name. His pointed stare directed at Toby must have alarmed the valet.

"Oh, I beg your pardon, Mr. Drayton. I had expected his lord-ship would already be familiar with your preference for the lady."

Toby shrugged and stood. He waved the valet away. "That's all right."

Warren bowed himself out of the room. When the bedchamber door closed, Toby cleared his throat.

"I've not spoken about my *intentions* to Kitty yet." His discomfort was immediate and he fidgeted, glancing about.

"I had no idea," Stephen replied. *Ah... Kitty.* Somehow, he thought this entire time that Toby was partial to Alicia.

"Chatty fellow, ain't he?" Toby commented. He cleared his throat again. "Meant to tell you myself 'bout Kitty ... have to, really, because I'm about to come up to scratch."

"So soon?" It amazed Stephen that something of such importance would not have come up for discussion earlier.

"Don't know when her daft relations might call her back to London—she would be lost to me forever! I thought it best I get things settled while we're in the country." Toby motioned that they should be on their way to join the others. "I actually thought I'd never have a chance ... her being an earl's daughter and I am... Well, I don't have the most promising future, do I?"

"Come now, Toby..." His friend was a champion among men. There was not a finer fellow than Toby. But ... Toby could not know that Kitty was not Lady Catherine.

It was inconceivable to Stephen that his friend would marry her for her money. In any case, Kitty probably did not have any and thus remained Kate's companion and was subjected to her whims, no matter how fantastical.

"I could see that if I was ever to have a chance it would be now. I saw no reason to delay—spoke about her to Lord James who referred me to Mr. Waddell, who could not sanction such an arrangement, immediately wrote to his father who replied post haste that he would leave London for Grimshaw."

"How long ago was that?" How could Stephen have been so blind as to his friend's wound by cupid's arrow? In truth, was not Stephen equally distracted by his discovery of Kate's identity?

"I asked Waddell to write to his father yesterday after we

returned from the picnic. His father's reply waited for him this morning."

"He is to come today, isn't he?" Stephen wondered if Kate knew. One look at Toby asking permission to pay his addresses to the female he thought was Lady Catherine, would be laughed at by the solicitor, and Kate's charade would be revealed. What ensued would be confusion, discontent, and broken hearts.

For Toby to marry meant he was in love with Kitty. Her diminished status would not matter to him. Kitty could not have encouraged him, knowing she would be discovered as a fraud.

"Will she be content as a vicar's wife?" Stephen wondered if Kitty could see herself in that new role.

"That is a question only she can answer." Toby drew in a breath and straightened. "Shall we see what the young ladies are up to? I would not be surprised to see an additional setting at the dinner table this evening."

Kate and Kitty stepped into the drawing room side by side much the same as when they arrived at the entrance of Grimshaw Court. Kate's hair was still damp, plaited, and pinned up before making an appearance in the front parlor. She had changed out of the wet frock and now wore Kitty's long sleeved, claret-colored velvet gown.

The garment only added to her discomfort. Kitty said the velvet constructed gown was needed for added warmth because of the chill Kate had taken. The bodice fit a bit snugger and the shoulders sat lower than Kate cared for. The ruched ribbons at the neckline, fixed with decorative fabric-covered buttons, seemed excessive and too fussy for her taste.

They had been informed that most of the family and guests had gathered there in light of today's rain, recuperating with a restorative tea and the additional warmth of the blazing fire. When they had originally arrived at Grimshaw, Kate had only briefly hesitated to take that first step into the manor that had landed her in the brambles. Now, because of it, she waited. She would continue to wait until Kitty entered first.

"Not everyone is present," Kitty whispered to Kate, adjusting the paisley-edged, cream-colored Norwich shawl she carried.

"No, but I shall wait." Kate had no doubts that the rest would arrive in due course. She had hoped to make her confession in haste and have done with it. She could expect that heated words, confusion, and explanations would be needed ... *how* could she do something like that ... *why* did she do it ... *how* could she have not considered their feelings?

"Goodness, Miss Kate, you are so very pale. Are you certain you should be out of bed?" Alicia left her seat.

"I am quite all right." Kate glanced at Kitty, hoping for a rescue from this kindness.

"You must sit near the fire and have some tea—very sweet, strong tea." Alicia stood, guiding Kate to her seat she had just vacated. "You will soon feel quite the thing, I am sure."

"Thank you, Miss Alicia, you are so very kind." Kate never felt more undeserving. She tugged at the one shoulder of the dress to draw it up. She was feeling decidedly *exposed*.

"Stop fidgeting with that," Kitty scolded in a whisper.

"I can't help it. This doesn't fit properly." Kate tugged up on the other sleeve. She hadn't realized that drawing the sleeve upward caused the fitted bit on her arm to bind.

"Its fit is adequate," Kitty assured her friend. "The gown is far more practical than anything you own."

"Kitty, does Miss Kate have a shawl?" Alicia retrieved a blanket and returned to settle it onto Kate's lap. "I do believe she has developed a chill."

"Allow me to fetch it for you," Mr. Waddell offered, rising from his seat.

"I have it here." Kitty handed the shawl draped over her arm to Mr. Waddell. Kitty then headed to retrieve tea for Kate. Upon handing her the cup and saucer, the two missing guests arrived.

Kate hated to admit she had needed the additional warmth. She drew the soft silk and wool woven fabric over her nearly-bare shoulders, now very glad Kitty had insisted she bring the shawl along *'just in case you have need of it.'*

"You see, Toby, they are all here." Lord Stephen gestured to the occupants milling about the room. "I feel quite left out."

Now that Kate understood where the lines of affections were drawn, it was easy to see the subtle warming glances between Mr. Drayton and Kitty.

"I don't know what you mean, Stephen. I feel quite adequately welcomed." Mr. Drayton moved past his friend, setting off in Kitty's direction.

Lord Stephen caught sight of Kate almost immediately upon his arrival. He waited until his friend stepped away before approaching her. He, as Alicia had, drew a chair from its place against the wall, positioning it near Kate.

"I went to check on you, only to find you had gone." He sounded relived upon seeing that she had been capable of moving about without any ill effects. Kate had a shawl around her shoulders to ward away the cold. "I cannot tell you how happy it makes me that you feel well enough to be up and around. You are well, I trust?"

"Yes, sir. I am quite well." She felt as though she needed to meet his eyes to relay her sincerity. "Kitty tells me that you were the one who brought me back from the folly. I do not know what to say except thank you, sir."

"You are most welcome," he returned. "I am perplexed as to why you were out there by yourself. Surely you were not there all that time since you'd left the library?"

"I was." She felt ashamed about the manner in which she'd behaved. It was quite childish. It felt as if that had happened a lifetime ago, not mere hours. "I could apologize for my actions, sir, but I cannot apologize for my frustration."

"I think there is no need. I, too, was quite vexed." The strain on his face was equal to what Kate felt. If only she had the maturity to manage her outbursts better. "As to the book... I honestly do not know what is to be done next."

"Do you think the book—the *inside* of the book—is lost? Has it been thrown out?" Would *he* wish to continue? She adjusted the shawl, settling it higher, nearly to her neck.

"I cannot say. I have no idea where it could be." Lord Stephen must have been equally as angry, disappointed, and frustrated as Kate. She never paused to consider that *she* was not the only person who had— had—

That *was* the issue, wasn't it? Kate had only thought of herself. She could be kind and generous to others but when it came to her own discomfort ... she could not abide it. How lowering to realize this about oneself.

The distraction of the book had been all-consuming until ... until she'd overheard Alicia and Mr. Waddell. It had to end now. There would be no more frolic and fun for her. Kate had more serious matters to address.

Life was so very difficult and perhaps it had been made more so for her because she had no parents to guide her. Kate was certain that if she had a father and a mother she would have been less selfish and more considerate. Care and kindness, the type a parent provided, could not be imitated.

"Alicia, you have had a chill," Lady James scolded her daughter. "You could have caught your death. And Miss Kate—you should not be out of bed. You might have suffered worse."

"I can't imagine worse than *death*," Alicia replied.

"I can," Kate whispered under her breath ... being entirely despised and a complete outcast was not something to which she aspired. She adjusted her wrap, pulling it tighter around her. Had it occurred to Kate that society's expectations were mere guidelines meant to give her direction and not constraints to test her will?

"I had planned to have dinner trays sent to everyone in their bedchambers—but here you all are!" Lady James said with the shake of her head.

"That is just as well, Mama, as we are to have an additional guest, I understand," Alicia announced in an offhandish manner. She knew. Mr. Waddell and Mr. Drayton knew. Kitty knew, Kate had told her. Somehow it came as a surprise that anyone in the household would not know.

"*Another* guest?" Lady James wavered between helplessness and hysteria. "Why was I not told?"

And before the new guest arrived, Kate had to speak. Everyone, with the exception of Lord James, was present. This might be the best and only opportunity to make her confession.

"Father knows, I am perplexed that he did not tell you," Alicia's flush deepened.

"This is what happens when one loses control of one's household!" Lady James exclaimed in severe tones. She gestured to Alicia, her nephew, and the four guests currently residing at Grimshaw Court who had all gathered in the drawing room despite the hostess' wishes. "One does not know how many are expected for dinner!"

"Excuse me ..." Kate began, standing, and facing the room occupants. "I beg your pardon, Lady James. If I might have everyone's attention. I hate to ruin an already dismal, dreary afternoon with worse news ... but I have something to say—a *confession* to make before... before..."

Oh, dear. Where was she to begin?

"Oh, come now, Miss Kate, there is no need for additional drama." Mr. Waddell had certainly become quite bold to speak out in this manner. "I think we have had quite enough for one day. Have we all not returned to the safety of the manor? Now we can be comfortable."

"Of course, we can," Kate replied. "And that was my very intention when I arrived, that Kitty and I should be comfortable. However, after the last few months in London, rustication in the country sounded very pleasant."

"And it is, is it not?" Alicia straightened as if preparing to be told the contrary.

"Yes, it is very enjoyable … and the new acquaintances … they are—all of you, so agreeable. I would never wish to hurt you or have you feel that I have betrayed you in any way."

"*Miss Kate* …" Mr. Waddell drew out her name as if expecting something unpleasant and *unexpected*.

"This is my doing … you must not think badly of Kitty or blame her."

"*Kitty?* What has she done?" Mr. Drayton rose immediately to defend her.

"She had to go through with it, don't you understand? I insisted she participate. It was all my doing."

"*What?*" Mr. Drayton said to Alicia who stood next to him before addressing the speaker herself. "Miss Kate, to what are you referring?"

It was best said straightaway without delay—Kate drew in a breath. "I exchanged positions with Kitty when we arrived. I am Lady Catherine Jessup and Kitty is my companion, Miss Catherine Matthews."

Alicia gasped, turned paler than her usual porcelain coloring, and reached out to steady herself.

"I am terribly sorry, my intentions were not to—" Kate attempted an apology to Alicia, Mr. Waddell who now held her hand, and the fallen Lady James who had swooned and reclined fully upon the sofa.

"Why? Why would she deceive us?" Lady James addressed those around her and the gods above, producing a handkerchief from her wrist and pressing it to her face.

"I only wanted some anonymity after spending the last few

months in London," Kate confessed. "It was all so much after having every hour of every day planned out for me. It was all I could do not to allow Lady Bradford to push me into a match." With every word she uttered, Kate felt as if she deeply wounded Lady James. "I… I meant no harm."

Lady James' high-pitched wail added a heart-wrenching, plaintiff cry that sent Kitty beyond endurance and she burst into tears.

"No, please—I cannot bear this." Kitty stood and fled from the room.

"Kitty!" Mr. Drayton stood rather abruptly from his chair, keeping hold of it and setting it on its legs, before following her out of the room. He pushed past a man just entering and mumbled, "Excuse me, sir."

"*Lawks!*" cried Mr. Waddell. His attention had shifted from the two ladies close to him to the doorway.

"What is the meaning of this? Hugh?" The elder, portly Mr. Waddle, Kate's guardian, called on his son to explain.

"Kitty— Kitty—" Tobias had come running after her.

Kitty ran out of the drawing room and did not know where to turn next. Driven by sheer embarrassment, she continued down the familiar corridor to the comfort of the music room. Tears blurred her eyes—if she could only find a remote corner where she could hide and no one would see her.

She found a corner but it was evident it was not deep nor dark enough for concealment. Tobias kept calling her name. He had followed her into the music room. Moving around the pianoforte, he scanned every inch of the room. How could he know this was where she chose to hide? And he had found her much too soon.

"Dearest... *Dearest* ..." he murmured soothingly, placing his hand upon her trembling shoulder.

"Please, Tobias ..." cried Kitty, sniffing into her handkerchief. "Do not show me any pity ... kindness ... it will unravel me."

She had no wish to talk to him nor did she want him to look at her, knowing that he must think of her as a fraud and a liar. Kitty felt so ashamed.

"It does not matter. You did nothing wrong, I know it to be true," he spoke to her softly. "It is just as Kate said, you *had* to do as you were bid."

"But it was *wrong*. *We* were wrong to attempt such a ruse. We had no idea— *I* had no idea what might happen. I never expected that I would... I would ..." How could Kitty have known Kate's aunt's sister's nephew had brought his friend along for a visit? And that she would lose her heart to him?

"Dare I believe that you might care for me as I care for you?" His smile, his honest expression lifted her spirits.

Kitty could feel her heart lighten and what she had moments ago feared left her. Tobias cared for her ... as much as she had for him. What she could not tell him as Lady Catherine, she could admit it to herself, and now, confess her admiration and affection.

"If you had known how I fretted that I might lose you. What hope could I have offering for an earl's daughter? I am a lowly younger son of a younger son. I have no prospects of a *better life*. The only opportunities I might have are the ones I create for myself. Still ... I felt I had to try."

Kitty thought him very noble. He was the kindest, most thoughtful man. She could not help but gaze at him with loving eyes.

"Now that it is revealed that you are not an earl's daughter, I feel as if I have a true chance of securing your hand!" A smile of joy and an expression of relief spread into his eyes and across his brow. "I need not beg your guardian ... you need no permission from anyone to decide your future. If I have won your heart, I only need to ask you if you will be my wife and you only need to accept."

He had the right of it. Kitty had no parents, no guardian to whom she need seek approval.

"I have nothing to offer." He took up both her hands in his. "I will need to find a clergyman who will take me under his wing and make me his curate—a vicar if I am lucky. I dare not hope to find a parish for myself ... not at first, but perhaps later. Then we could look forward to a very comfortable life indeed."

A comfortable life, how nice that sounded. Kitty could just imagine ... she and Tobias would be husband and wife. Perhaps in time, a small family would follow. They would all live in a small house near a church. *His* church.

What more could she want? Kitty gazed up into his eyes and felt her heart answer—*Yes*. It would be her dearest wish to marry him.

Seventeen

In the drawing room, Stephen's attention shifted from Kate, stationed at the opposite end of the room, to the newly arrived gentleman, Waddell's father. Had Kate delayed her announcement a moment more, the visitor would have divulged her secret and her scheme would have branded her as a liar and a charlatan.

Kate appeared very much a mature young lady, and faced her guardian in a confident and calm manner. She allowed the ivory shawl she wore to slide down her upper arms and gather along the inside of her elbows. The dark brown color of her hair, braided and coiled on her head, and deep red of her dress were a striking contrast to the paleness of her skin.

"Good day, Mr. Waddle. You appear well." Kate curtsied, paying her guardian his due respect.

"I am well, thank you, Lady Catherine, but somewhat perplexed by my surroundings." He tugged on his coat, straightening the material. Hours traveling in a coach wreaked havoc on one's garments.

The newcomer's confusion might have been exacerbated by Lord James' sudden arrival. His lordship came striding into the drawing room in such excitement, he nearly passed, and was obviously oblivious to the stranger, and exclaimed, "I have heard the elder Mr. Waddell has arrived."

"It is *Wad-dle*, sir. Hugh Waddle of Rush, Stonewall, and Waddle. I'll have none of that pompous inflection that my son adopts as our proud family name." Under his breath, he muttered, "*Sheer pretentiousness*."

The younger Waddell stepped away from the ladies and cleared his throat. Moving forward, Kate, who was the only other who was known to all, remained silent as he made the introductions between this father and the Emerson family.

"And who were those two young people I passed as I entered?" With a glance over his shoulder, Mr. Waddle indicated Alicia and Toby.

"They are not members of the family, sir," Hugh replied. "But … something … perhaps you should know …"

"I expect I shall make their acquaintance soon enough," Mr. Waddle mused, "But I remain curious."

"The gentleman is Mr. Drayton, friend of Lord Stephen. The young lady is Miss Matthews, companion of Lady Catherine," his son clarified. Hugh Waddle did not let on that anything was—or had been amiss.

"I have seen Miss Matthews previously, have I not?" Mr. Waddle's attention settled on Kate for his answer.

"I expect so, sir," Kate replied. "We attended the Academy together. You may have heard her play the pianoforte at one of the school concerts where she frequently performed."

"Yes, of course." Mr. Waddle nodded in satisfaction.

"Would you care to be shown to your room to freshen up?" Lord James posed the question not so much out of consideration but a needed delay tactic to give the rest of them time to *discuss* the arrival of the solicitor.

"That sounds fine, sir, fine. However, I have been told" —Mr. Waddle looked around the room with narrowed eyes, scrutinizing the gentlemen in attendance— "My presence had been requested because there was an inquiry regarding Lady Catherine's marriage proposal. I would like to know who wishes to marry my ward?"

There was a long silence and during its duration, many weighted glances were exchanged. Hugh Waddell must have been in shock not to have spoken to explain how Tobias Drayton had asked permission to pay his addresses to the female he thought was Lady Catherine—and it was now clear that the *true* Lady Catherine stood not six feet away from the both of them.

Stephen could read regret in her expression but didn't understand why. Was there disappointment in her eyes as well? She could not state the truth that no one wished to marry her. Her guardian had made the journey from London for naught.

"I would, sir." Stephen met Kate's gaze when she glanced in his direction. "If you and Lady Catherine agree to the match."

"What?" Kate blurted out in a voice Stephen hardly recognized.

"You, sir?" Hugh Waddell remarked, taken aback.

"Well, well…" Mr. Waddle eyed Stephen.

"How…" Kate had the most perplexed reaction. It was unexpected and quite adorable. Stephen willed himself not to show any expression. "You never—"

"May we have a few moments alone?" Stephen said softly to Mr. Waddle, hoping the man would allow them some privacy. Then he could explain himself to her—his reasons for stepping forward, attempting to lessen the scandal that might have ensued. "I'm afraid I have quite taken her by surprise. She had no notion of my intentions."

"Ah, I see," Mr. Waddle intoned, nodding his head. "It is best to seek out permission to pay addresses first. And I imagine, Lord Stephen" —The solicitor eyed him from toe to head— "With your family connections, the Marquess of Woodley is known to me, and you must know that I would have no objection."

"I— I—" Kate managed, apparently still in shock.

"You may move to the far side of the room. Right over there, young man." The solicitor nodded to his son and Lady James. "If you will be so good as to observe the couple, make certain the proprieties are observed."

"Yes, Father," Hugh replied, returning to a somber, official capacity with a business-like mien.

The vapors and hysterics Lady James' suffered moments ago vanished and she sat upright, ready to take on her new duty.

"Do give them enough time to discuss their future but do not allow them to become over-familiar, eh?" Mr. Waddle motioned to Lord James. "I believe I would like to be shown to my rooms. We can discuss matters later when I return. Lead the way if you please."

"Of course, of course." Lord James nodded and quit the room with Mr. Waddle in his wake.

Stephen turned to Kate, gazed into her eyes, smiled, and offered her his arm. *"Lady Catherine?* Will you allow me to escort you?"

Kate felt as if she were once again being forced, tricked, and cajoled into a match not of her choosing. Granted, Lord Stephen was far more amiable than any of the swains Lady Bradford had chosen. Still ... how dared Stephen announce a ridiculous marriage proposition while in the company of all these people.

This must have been *his* ruse. What was he about?

Kate returned his smile. She placed her hand upon his arm and allowed him to lead her across the room to a remote corner. His arm beneath her hand felt solid and oddly comforting. She would not have expected this gesture to affect her in this manner. Her back faced the others for only a few moments while they

strolled deep into the corner. If only there could be further opportunity to avoid the scrutiny of those in the room.

She was able to breathe again. If only momentarily, for she was
about to confront her one-time partner-in-search with whom she
had kept company during the long afternoons in the library. How
could he have admitted that he wished to marry her? He knew
how she felt about the wedded state.

"I beg your pardon," he whispered, keeping his back to the
other occupants of the room while he spoke. "Although quite
expected after your *confession* just prior to Mr. Waddle's entrance,
I found it intolerable that you should be subjected to direct scrutiny of the others. I would see you removed from their company, if
only for a few minutes."

"I thank you for your kindness, sir. I must admit that I had
never thought it would come to a full confession, nor had I
expected matters to progress quite as quickly as they had." Kate
was very lucky indeed that no one revealed her deception. Perhaps
they were too much in shock themselves to let on, to a newly
arrived stranger, the *upset* that had happened only moments before.

"I am relieved that the Emersons have had the good sense not
to mention your recent misdeed to your guardian." Once he had
finished speaking, he repositioned himself, turning Kate so that
she did not face them. The two performed the slow dance,
revolving as the earth and moon, moving in and out of view from
the others.

"As to that, the offer of marriage of which Mr. Waddle spoke
came from Toby for Miss Kitty who was, at that time, known to
him as Lady Catherine. I heard that Mr. Waddle would be joining
us from Toby not ten minutes before our arrival."

"It was quite the surprise, was it not?" Kate remarked. She had
no wish to let on exactly how much she knew and kept her
expression muted.

"At the time, the proper thing for Toby to do was to seek

permission to pay his addresses. Hugh felt he was not within his scope and wrote to his father which necessitated the solicitor's presence."

The marriage settlement was most certainly encouraged by her aunt and uncle Bradford no doubt. In the end, it would prove an unnecessary journey for Mr. Waddle.

"You could not have known of his arrival but in some way, the timing of your confession was most opportune. In a solitary moment, everyone's perception of you and Kitty, your position in the household had been altered. It was rather shocking."

An odd notion came to her... Kate did not believe the news had come as a complete surprise to him. But how could he have known?

"With your announcement, it would seem that Mr. Waddle's presence would be no longer needed since *Lady Catherine's* marriage arrangements has turned out to be Toby wishing to marry Kitty."

"Of course," Stephen went on. "Mr. Waddle arrives expecting to hear of Lady Catherine's suitor... You must see that *the suitor* must make himself known."

Kate's pique finally subsided and she met his gaze. "So you stepped forward."

"*Needs must*, Kate," Stephen continued to explain his actions in a calm and thoughtful manner. "Toby is enamored with Kitty, and Hugh cannot have a *tendre* for Lady Catherine, it would be unseemly."

"True, and his primary interest lies with Alicia." Kate wasn't sure if he knew this bit, and by his expression he had not.

"My cousin?" Stephen must have been the last person to have known. "He never let on ..."

"I believe he plans to discuss their marriage with his father now that he is present. It works out well for him, as well?"

Was Stephen cross with himself that he had not noticed what

his two companions had been up to? Had he not paid attention? Where was his mind all this time?

"I will be the first to wish them happy." Ever the gentleman, Stephen would prove gracious.

"Yes, they seem to rub along more than tolerably well together." Kate could only imagine since she had refused to observe their private moments in the rain under the protection of the rotunda.

"In any case, there was an expectation of an offer for Lady Catherine. I do not see how else this situation could have been resolved. We have spent an inordinate amount of time together. I believe I understand you well enough that you do not wish to marry."

"You would be correct, sir."

"It might be expected that you might decline my offer without harm to either of our reputations. It is not an unusual thing that might happen to anyone."

"Do you think so?" What he is suggesting did seem to make sense. Then they could all go back to their own lives ... back to the way things were. That sounded quite agreeable indeed. She'd always enjoyed their friendly association.

"We need never participate in a *sham* engagement." That would have been ridiculous. Kate could not imagine anything more abhorrent. However, a sham *offer* seemed acceptable.

"No. It would be a simple matter of you refusing to marry, which I gather is true."

"No offense to you but there is not a gentleman of my acquaintance that I care to wed." With her recent experience of this last Season, Kate would not entertain such thoughts. She had spent months, very aware of those who wished to maneuver her into such a position.

"I am of a similar mind ... if only I could convince my mother of my sincerity." His lips pressed into a fine line of determination and he nodded. "I am in complete agreement."

"It seems that one's family is the last to accept the inevitable." Kate sympathized with him that his own parent should place him in the position that her aunt had. Kate could not imagine her mother pushing her, insisting she marry because it was expected.

"True. It is not to say either one of us may feel differently in that regard but for now, I would agree that we are quite content and there is no reason to alter our current arrangement. We could enjoy our evening walks, discussion of books, and plans of future travels."

"I would like that very much." It seemed to Kate that Lord Stephen was indeed a kindred soul.

"I will caution you not to give a rapid refusal to my offer." He sounded as if he spoke from experience. "Your friends and family members, quite unsolicited, will offer *helpful* suggestions as to why you should change your mind. You will bring down hours and hours of why you have come to that incorrect conclusion and *all* the reasons you should change your mind."

"I don't like the sound of that at all."

"No. It is not pleasant. The more consideration you *appear* to give my offer, the longer you will avoid the ultimate conflict."

"I see." Kate smiled. She had not the experience he had at avoiding such a situation with grace. Hers was an overtly hostile effort of planting her heels and refusing. Kate knew no other way in dealing with her aunt. "I will take your recommendation, my lord, and think on the matter." She spoke a bit louder so her words may be heard by the others, "I find you quite agreeable and will consider your offer of marriage."

There was a slight rumble of excitement from those in the room from Lady James, Alicia, and Hugh.

Stephen slipped her hand into his and brought it to his lips. "I could ask for nothing more—and I hope for the best." He kissed the back of her hand and smiled.

Kate expected they made quite a nice impression of an uncertain young couple teetering on the precipice of matrimony. She had hoped it appeared that way … if only for the present.

Kitty returned with Tobias, arm in arm. She fairly came into the drawing room floating on air! Both were smiling, they could not help but smile. Their infectious joy spread about the room and soon all the occupants were quite taken with their sudden appearance.

"Goodness, me!" Lady James said upon Kitty and Tobias' entrance. "I do not believe I have ever seen a couple smelling more of April and May."

"I have been made the happiest man!" Tobias decreed, gazing into his beloved's eyes.

Kitty felt her neck warm and face flush. She tightened her hold on Tobias' arm.

"Kit-ty …" Alicia drew out her name in a sing-songy manner, taking in the aspect of the couple.

"Is it true? Are you and Mr. Drayton to be married?" Alicia was quite bold to come out and ask directly.

"Well … we must first have the blessing of someone quite important. Without it… I am afraid …" Kitty shook her head, unable to go on.

"Who? Who must give you their permission to wed?"

Kitty's tentative gaze moved to Kate. "You have been my friend for so very long. Yours is the only opinion that matters to me."

"Me? I shall not stand in your way." Kate came forward and reached out to take hold of Kitty's hand. "I do wish you happy, dear friend—all the happiness in the world."

"But Tobias and I are to live far away." Kitty's voice softened.

She released his arm and slowly moved away from him, toward Alicia and Kate. Toby seemed to be swept into a similar conversation with the gentlemen who stood off to one side.

"That's what one must do if one marries, Kitty," Alicia added and Kate only nodded. "You must follow your husband."

"But how? Kate—you have been everything to me—friend, sister, constant companion. I do not know what I should have done without you."

"I do not think that Miss Maddingly would have turned you out. On the contrary, I believe she was a bit vexed that I had convinced you to leave with me. She had lost her best music teacher."

That skill may be to Kitty's benefit ... offering music lessons while Tobias attended Oxford might be their livelihood until they set out on their own. They would make do.

"We shall write to one another, dear friend." Kate did not sound bereft at all and offered her a cheerful smile. "We will tell one another all the details of our day just as we have always done."

The thought made Kitty smile. Kate had the right of it. They would go on just as they had done before only through written communication. Kitty was willing to make this change, to make a new life with Tobias. Her gaze drifted to their new friend Alicia Emerson. "We shall all write to one another."

"Of course, we shall," Alicia quickly agreed.

"Tobias is so kind and ... quite wonderful really." Kitty thought very highly of her future husband. "I had wished you would be happy for me."

"Kitty... How could I not be?" Kate took hold of Kitty's shoulder and gave it a little shake. "What manner of friend would I be if I did not stand by you? When is the wedding to be?"

"We have not discussed that yet." Kitty realized neither had a domicile or much money of their own. "This is all very new." As destitute as she—they were, Kitty could not help but remain opti-mistic about their future.

"I would never stand in the way of your happiness, Kitty." Kate leaned forward and gently embraced her friend, holding her close. "Never. Ever."

Eighteen

Alicia had left with Hugh, followed by Kitty with Tobias. Stephen seemed reluctant to leave Kate's side but Lady James insisted he accompany her. Kate was expected to join them in the front parlor while the other gentleman removed to the library.

Kate was no longer enjoying herself. Sad and miserable had replaced happy and content she'd felt the day before. How could everything have altered so drastically in such a short period of time?

"*Catherine?*" Called a familiar voice. "Might I have a word with you?"

"Of course, sir." Kate had expected Mr. Waddle would seek her out but had not expected it to happen so soon. Was he not present for her benefit? His periodic presence had been a constant in her life.

"Might we take a stroll outdoors?" he suggested. The solicitor could always be relied upon to advise, lend guidance, or scold her when needed by Miss Maddingly during the schoolroom years.

"I would suggest the back garden, however, it is still very damp, unsuitable for walking. Pity, that. It is quite something I have never seen before. You might have enjoyed it."

"One back garden is much like another, and I have seen many in my day." Mr. Waddle waved his hand about, showing impatience with the outside.

"Thank goodness this rain has let up." Kate could honestly express that thought without musing if she had said something she ought not have. "It did not last long and it was quite unexpected."

"It has served its purpose, drenched the countryside, made the roads difficult to travel, and delivered a general malaise to the surrounding area. I could have done without it. At least it could have held off until the arrival to my destination."

"But it has left the air fresh and crisp. I find its aftermath quite refreshing." Kate could see nothing wrong with a brief downpour. "We could step onto the back terrace if you would like."

The solicitor glanced around before answering. "Very well. Let us step outside, shall we?" He opened the door and allowed her to precede him. "It seems that felicitations are in order for your companion Kitty." He made certain the door had properly closed and was shut behind them.

"Yes. She and Mr. Drayton seem very well-suited. I do not think I've ever seen her happier than when she is in his company."

"It is a fine thing when one's friends are settled, is it not? One can take great pleasure in their comfort."

Kate thought so, no one was more deserving. Kitty's happiness had given her great pleasure.

"I am much more interested in speaking with you and finding out about your young man."

"*My* young man ..." *Lord Stephen ... were they about to tread down* that *path ... so soon?* The topic unsettled Kate.

"Lord Stephen *has* made his offer, has he not?"

"Yes, sir, he has." Her pulse raced and she hoped the flush that washed into her face could be explained by the cool, brisk outdoor air.

"Who can blame him?" Mr. Waddle smiled and nodded his head. "You are quite the young lady—grown. And …"

"And …" What should Kate say? From her most recent scrape —she had just escaped the near disaster of revealing her identity with her reputation seemingly intact. The deception might have worked out very badly for her if it were not for Stephen. The Emersons seemed to have taken it in stride. Kate was not certain she would have been so forgiving. "What is it that you would like to know?"

"I would like to know if you are in mind to accept him." Mr. Waddle could not have been more direct. Kate should have been able to give him an equally direct answer.

But she could not.

Kate's refusal to commit was not because Stephen had advised her to remain indecisive. She felt as if she had somehow come up against a brick wall. The marriage proposal was not real, she knew that.

"I find him agreeable, sir, and I like him very much" —All of that was true— "but *marriage*… I had not thought that he would go so far as to—"

"I see … caught you by surprise." Mr. Waddle took a deep breath, inhaling the fresh air and it seemed to restore him. "There is no hurry, my dear. You have time to decide but I caution you not to wait too long. Lord Stephen may find himself discouraged and withdraw his offer or fade into the distance."

Withdrawing his offer was exactly what she had expected but to think that *he might go away* …

"There is no harm in taking a bit of a holiday while you decide … you and me both. Lord James has promised me some sport while I'm here, and I might as well take advantage of it. He seems like an amiable fellow—and there is still business to attend to… We'll see how well we get on." It was as if he were losing himself in thought. "I think your parents would be very proud if they could see you now."

"My *parents* ..." Never having known them, Kate hardly ever gave them a thought. She couldn't even remember them. Nor had she ever seen an image of them.

"Robert and Sophia," Mr. Waddle said their names softly. "I can see both parents in you." He fell quiet and studied her. "You bring to mind your father's staunch determination. He wasn't one to allow anyone to tell him what to do. He had his own ideas about things." The solicitor chuckled at the memory.

So Kate took after her father.

"And you've always had your mother's looks bout you. Especially since you're now a grown young lady. You two share more than just the color of your hair and eyes."

And Kate resembled her mother. She thought of her brown eyes and her brown hair, always thinking them common. They weren't so ordinary anymore ... they were features inherited from her mother.

"Your exuberance—love of adventure ... you are very much like your mother. It's a quality the current Lady Bradford finds difficult to tolerate. I find it refreshing and quite out of the ordinary."

"I understand your reticence for not accepting Lord Stephen's offer. You have hardly been able to make your own decision, being too young to choose. Now that you are a young lady, soon to be of age, you will have the freedom of being the mistress of your own destiny."

That sounded quite grand.

"You have been denied your parents ... your parents' love for your entire life. There was little I could do about your upbringing but, with your parents' forward-thinking, they placed their fortune and every unentailed asset aside for you."

"And you've kept it safe. You've been my champion, sir. I thank you."

"Your property and your funds will soon be at your disposal. No one will dictate to you. You may do as you please. I am very proud of you and I think your parents would feel the same. I don't pretend to be your friend, nor am I your parent. I was, however, their friend and knew them for a number of years."

Listening to all this was making Kate feel no longer a child and very independent. She was no longer to suffer the whims of her aunt and uncle.

"After hearing your first marriage proposal, I feel very sentimental. I have no daughters of my own, you understand. I am happy to be here for council, if you should need me. Yet, I—" His voice faltered and he blinked his moistening eyes. "I cannot but think your parents would be very happy … relieved to know you are not to be alone. "

"What do you mean?" Kate had always enjoyed keeping her own company.

"They would not wish to see you spend your life without the love of a husband or of a family. They did so truly love one another and they adored you." He gazed upon her, showing a rare moment of affection. "Your father indulged your mother's every whim. They had just returned from Paris when that unfortunate accident on their return to Jessup Hall happened."

Of course, Kate had heard the story. It was how she had lost her parents.

"Your mother wished for a new wardrobe before embarking on their next journey. Did you know the three of you were soon to be off to India?"

"*India!*" Her parents were taking her across the ocean … many oceans.

"I *know* they would have wanted you to find the very same passion for life, in whatever form you wished it to be … as long as you were following your heart's desire." Mr. Waddle's words were ones Kate had never heard before. They were sentiments and wishes from her parents. "Only you can decide if your future includes Lord Stephen."

With Stephen? That might not be an option because his offer of marriage wasn't a true offer. Part of her was saddened. She could not have it both ways ... a life with Stephen but not married to him ... Kate had to make up her mind. From what she could see, a future without him felt quite empty.

"I do not understand how Grimshaw has managed to attract so many guests." Lord James paced before his desk in the library. "What are we to do with them all?"

Stephen, who sat next to one of his stacks of books he had set aside for his own enjoyment, did his utmost to keep his attention fixed on his uncle and away from the titles printed on the spines. It would be rude to browse through a book in pleasure while unease and worry plagued his relative.

"I have promised Mr. Waddle some sport during his stay and I expect you will join us. If your friend Drayton and the young Waddell were to attend that would make a very nice outing." Uncle James motioned with a wave. "If they can all manage to keep themselves amused the better!"

"Of course. I shall do my utmost to entertain our new guest." Stephen sighed at the necessary intrusion. He could not, in all good conscience, allow the burden of the visitors to rest squarely on his uncle while he closeted himself in the library.

"Didn't want to say anything while Mr. Waddle was around but ..." Lord James glanced over his shoulder at the door, checking to see that the solicitor was not present to overhear. "I'm not at all certain what that exchanging positions business with those two young ladies was about ... they seem nearly identical to me—both pretty, both well-behaved ... one is very much like the other."

Surely his uncle must have been aware of the disparity of social standings between the two ladies. Kate and Kitty were two sides of the same coin. Their upbringing may have been the same, perhaps observing them from afar, their exterior may have appeared similar ... and to Lord James, it did not matter.

"Yes ... well ... there was a bit of an issue..." Stephen would rather not get into specifics if he could help it. If his uncle asked for an explanation, he would oblige.

"And why is this the first I've heard of you *making an offer of marriage?* Gracious, Stephen! Is that not why you left The Towers to avoid the parson's mousetrap?"

"Well, yes ..." How could he explain that *his* was not a true offer of marriage and it was best not to make a confession to his uncle. "Sir... I am not expecting that she will accept."

"What do you mean *not* accept? How could she not accept you?" Lord James motioned to Stephen as if urging him to take a good look at himself. "Does she not know how remarkable it is that you should take notice of her? For *you* to consider marriage is ... well, miraculous, really. *You* who have never entertained a step in the matrimonial direction—you are a changed man."

Uncle James' words, his praise left Stephen quite speechless.

"Such growth and maturity ... all happening before my eyes ... quite smitten you must be." His voice choked with emotion and he placed his hand upon his chest, over his heart. "I can see that you two share quite a few similarities and that a union between you would make for a very comfortable arrangement. I expect that she might break your heart if she does not accept."

Break his heart?

Why would his uncle think that? Kate would not intentionally hurt him. He rather thought she was fond of him, as his uncle had mentioned, and the easy manner in which they seemed to get on indicated they shared some kind feelings for one another.

Stephen found Kate quite delightful. She often had unconventional opinions that rather surprised him. The days were never boring with her about. Then with a bit more thought, he realized that this life at Grimshaw, could not go on forever. Kitty and Toby would soon marry and what would Kate do? He did not know and he was fairly certain she had no idea either.

Would she plan to travel? Go to the places they discussed, and do the things they both wished to experience? She certainly could not go alone, not a young, single female. Someone must look after her— Perhaps Mr. Waddle would send along his son to make her arrangements, but Stephen did not care for that. Hugh should not be the one accompanying Kate. Stephen wanted to be with her, at her side, the one whom she relied on. If only he might convince her that he belonged there.

He had the oddest feeling. The thought of being alone, waking up one day without seeing her felt so empty. Lonely. Then he realized his life spent without her would be unbearable.

He'd never had this feeling before … the craving for another. Was this *love?* The ache of anticipation of being without her?

This was not the emotion … the *condition* he'd heard or read about. It felt far from exhilarating and wonderful. To be quite honest, Stephen felt, on the whole, quite miserable.

"Ah, Mr. Waddle, do come in!" Lord James' voice woke Stephen from his revelry.

"I have no wish to disturb you if you are occupied." The solicitor was hesitant to enter.

"No, no." Lord James waved him in. "We were just discussing my nephew's future."

Stephen shifted uncomfortably. He hadn't expected he'd remain with the two older gentlemen.

"Yes. Marriage arrangements are the topic of the day, are they not?" Mr. Waddle chuckled. "It is fortunate that you are present, Lord Stephen. I beg that you remain."

"Of course, sir. Is there anything I can do for you?"

"Would you care for something to eat perhaps?" Lord James

gestured to the refreshment off to one side. "A glass of claret? Dinner is still some hours off."

"No, thank you. If you would indulge me in a short, insightful conversation, if you please, Lord Stephen, to determine your character."

"My *character?*" To be placed under scrutiny for a potential marriage that would never come to pass.

"If you are to marry my ward, I want to assure myself that you are …" Mr. Waddle seemed to be mindful of the words he chose.

"Good enough for her, I imagine." Stephen smiled. Why would he not?

"I ask because I must. There are those who are—"

"A rascal, a vagabond, a scoundrel?"

"*A fortune hunter.*"

"Do you think my nephew a fortune hunter? How dare you, sir!" Lord James roared. "If this is the opinion you hold of my family—"

"I mean no offense but you must understand as Lady Catherine's guardian, I ask—for I must set my personal feelings aside in these matters."

"My lord, Mr. Waddle is only doing his duty," Stephen replied, trying to ease his uncle's rare show of anger. "I understand that you were friends of the previous Lord and Lady Bradford and you want what is best for Kate."

"I will have that glass of claret, if you please." Not that he had changed his mind but Mr. Waddle had managed to remove Lord James from their immediate vicinity.

"Yes, allow me to fetch it for you." His lordship tottered off to the far side of the room to see to the request.

"I must confess that Catherine does not seem to me much in mind to marry." Mr. Waddle addressed Stephen once again, glancing at him as if to measure his thoughts on the matter. "I had hoped for her sake, for her parents, that she had found someone who would love and care for her."

"She and I have enjoyed hours, afternoons, days together and as you may learn, share many of the same interests. Would you like me to speak of my affection? Of how I cherish her?"

"Your affection for one another is not in question." The solicitor shook his head then shrugged. "You both are young and obviously in love... I can see what transpires between the two of you for myself."

He could? "I can only make my offer known, Mr. Waddle. I cannot press my will upon her to accept."

"Naturally." Mr. Waddle seemed to accept Stephen's hopes and doubts on the matter. He wondered if it had occurred to the solicitor he might have wasted his time by traveling to Grimshaw. As her guardian, he must have some notion of Kate's opinion on the matter ... or the opinion Kate *wished* him to believe.

Stephen was coming around to thinking that remaining unattached wasn't what he wanted, not anymore. It wasn't that she occupied the hours of his day or images of her swam in his mind as if he were a hopeless romantic. No. He had held her in great esteem since the day they met. There was respect for her inquisitive nature and appetite to learn. Stephen liked her very much. There was more than a bit of affection he had for her. He wished to have her near—to be never parted from her. He wanted to protect her, make sure nothing bad ever happened to her.

The more he thought about how dull and empty his future without Kate would be, the stronger he felt marriage to her was exactly what he wanted.

This was the feeling of *love* that had been written about in so many poems and books. Not only was it the misery he'd felt earlier, there was some satisfaction and joy that mingled with the affection making the feelings muddled and complex. And now he felt that incongruous collection of emotions for himself. He, without a doubt, could use no other word than *love*. Put simply ... Stephen loved Kate.

As the drawing room had previously had a nice fire laid, tea was served there instead of the front parlor. The guests returned where smiles were plentiful, the company was agreeable, and conversation was easy. Kitty had chosen the sofa near Kate where she sat with Tobias. Alicia and Hugh, when they arrived, seated themselves on Kate's other side.

The numbers were uneven, but not for long, Lord Stephen soon appeared in the doorway.

"Gentlemen," he said with a bow. He met Alicia, Kitty, then Kate's gaze. "Good afternoon, ladies."

"Please come in and join us, Lord Stephen," Kitty beckoned, budging up to Tobias to make room for him so he might sit next to Kate. He lowered himself into the vacated seat, staring at her, in what Kitty thought was a most peculiar manner.

"Do allow me to pour." Alicia rose to near the tea tray and glanced at Kitty and Tobias before settling her gaze on Hugh. A flush of color washed up her neck and stained her cheeks.

"Do allow me to help," Hugh offered, mimicking his lady, following her to help arrange the cups on their saucers.

They were very sweet together. It was obvious to Kitty that the two made small gestures and exchanged brief glances that made any chores in which they took on a mutual expression of affection. She glanced at Lord Stephen and Kate, sitting beside him, and wondered if Cupid dared aim his arrow at the pair. Perhaps Kitty was wrong and a match between them was not meant to be.

It would be a shame really. Kitty thought Kate and Lord Stephen got on rather well. Kitty thought Kate might even be more than fond of him … she might have found him agreeable. They were of like minds in so many ways and had spent numerous hours searching for *that* book. Perhaps that was too much to hope for.

"I beg your pardon," said a footman appearing in the doorway. "Miss Emerson, Mr. Waddell, your fathers' request that you join them in the library."

Alicia turned to stare at Hugh and their weighted silence permeated the room.

"Gracious, it is so soon ..." Alicia had the sense, and coordination, to return the full teapot to the tray without incident. There was only the smallest tremor from Hugh as cups and saucers he held rattled uncontrollably until Alicia took them from his possession.

"*A-l-licia*?" The previously confident Hugh even had a bit of a shake in his voice. He glanced at her in uncertainty.

"Everything will be fine." She smiled, calming him. "Let us be on our way." They strolled toward the door together.

"What do you say we remove to the music room and pass the time there while we wait?" Kitty stood and laid her hand upon Tobias' arm. "We shall meet you there, Alicia." She called to her friend before stepping out the door.

Alicia took several seconds to gaze at the occupants as if to memorize this moment. Kitty silently wished her every bit of good luck that their fathers had come to an agreement. She was certain they had for no two people deserved more to be together.

"An excellent idea, my dear. What of the tea? It'll grow cold."

"We shall call for a new pot when we return." Kitty stepped toward Tobias, preparing to progress to the music room. "Perhaps we will need something special for a real celebration."

"That will be splendid," he replied. Then Tobias became quite unmovable when he turned back to call his friend. "Stephen ... *ehm, Stephen*?"

Kitty, who held onto Tobias, was brought to a sudden halt. She peered around him to see what had captured his attention. He stared at his friend and Kate sitting together. Earlier she had been very conscious of covering her exposed shoulders and had now relaxed her grip, allowing the wrap to drape at her waist.

"What is that, Tobias?" Kitty saw that Lord Stephen held some sort of sphere in his palm. He and Kate gazed at it together and it seemed they were absent from all else. "What is that he has in his hand?"

"It's the pocket globe Stephen carries with him," Toby kept his voice soft. "It looks to me that Stephen is offering Kate the world."

Nineteen

Kate had leaned close to Stephen, their shoulders touched as they stared at the pocket globe together. It seemed to hold some sort of magic spell over her when she gazed upon it. It symbolized her hopes and dreams.

The miniature globe was truly lovely to look at. The oceans were green in color and composed most of the sphere. The continents were drab-colored and black lettering identified the land masses. Small and compact, it rested comfortably in the palm of Stephen's hand.

"Is it not your dearest wish to visit distant lands?" He had brought out the object and placed it before her as if he attempted to mesmerize her.

To travel the world had been a dream. "That was only talk. I did not mean— I cannot possibly …" Kate would wish to consider such things but now was not the time. "It is quite apparent that Kitty and Toby will be starting their life together soon."

"Yes, and I am happy for them." But Stephen did not look away from the globe.

"As am I," Kate agreed. "But I am very selfish and had hoped that she and I would travel together." Kate felt her world falling apart without her friend. Kitty had always been there and to contemplate a future without her … it was so very sad.

"I had not thought Kitty the adventurous type," Stephen commented. There was something in his expression that told her he knew more than he was letting on. What was he *not* telling her?

"It does not matter. Travel abroad was ever only a fanciful notion. I must be realistic and I cannot manage alone, therefore…" And it was never her intention to replace Kitty with the handsome Lord Stephen out of fear of being alone or desperation.

"Even after reading about all those women who travel to faraway lands?" Stephen hadn't read those books but Kate had and she had told him about them. "I must admit it has always been something I would like to do but I am without means, I'm afraid."

Stephen, Kate had learned, was the youngest son of a marquess. His modest allowance could not fund his travel and adventure … the very same dreams Kate had. But they'd spent many enjoyable hours discussing intriguing places of interest. Those times had been great fun, but now she could imagine that her time at Grimshaw Court would soon come to an end.

Perhaps Stephen might be agreeable to a letter exchange, writing to one another, and a social visit or two in the future. Would that seem so outrageous? It might be perceived as a bit unorthodox, but so many of Kate's actions were believed to be far from the norm. It saddened her that she would be losing a great friend if they lost contact for he understood her so well, and in some ways better than Kitty ever could.

Kate understood that he wanted no female entanglements and the best that could be said of their association was that they were *friends*. And who would not welcome thoughts from a kindred soul who understood one's ambitions?

"I have learned that I have a much greater interest in visiting distant lands but I do not know if I am that brave to venture there on my own," Kate confessed.

"*Not* brave? I think you a very determined and quite an ambitious young lady." Stephen, as ever, staunchly came to her support and she admired him for that. "There is nothing you cannot do once you set your mind. What of your house in the country? The small one with the library—the large book room you wish to stock until they reach the ceiling?" He stared at her as if she were the one dampening his dreams.

"I expect that could be achievable when I come of age." Might Stephen be of some help? Be *willing* to advise her? But she did not wish to read too much into the meaning of his words. "Yes, I suppose I must have someplace to live ... with or without Kitty ..."

It was a harsh realization but one with which Kate must come to terms. She had relied on Kitty most of her life. With having so much in common, their orphan status, their upbringing, it was as if they were almost one and the same. Up until now ... *now* Kitty was to spend her future with her husband Tobias. It was a path Kate had no intention of following.

The faint run of an *arpeggio* drew Kate's interest. It was familiar and brought Kitty to mind. Kate thought she must have been dreaming ... was that Kitty at the keyboard? Kate blinked, moved her gaze from Stephen, and looked around at the empty drawing room.

"Where is everyone?" Stephen said, echoing Kate's very thought.

"Kitty is in the music room." Kate knew without a doubt. "Can you hear her play?" Kate and Stephen stilled, sitting quietly to listen.

There it was again. The faint notes lilted through the air.

"I think we must have missed something important." Kate felt a bit guilty that she had been so absorbed in conversation with Stephen they had missed the departure of the two other couples.

Stephen stood, closing the pocket globe with one hand and

holding out the other to help Kate to her feet. "To the music room
… shall we join them?"

"Yes, please." Kate took his arm and he escorted her down the
corridor. He was all consideration, and it was very easy to read
more into his actions than mere civility and kindness. She had no
wish to burden him with her silly girlish, romantic notions that
had floated into her head. Kate herself was doing her utmost to
ignore them.

They entered the music room with a calm and deliberation
that they should not be caught out. Kate hushed Stephen when
they stepped inside and they seated themselves on a pair of chairs
just inside the doorway, ensuring Kitty's concentration would not
be broken.

Their unnoticed arrival seemed successful for there was no
interruption in the music and neither Toby nor Kitty glanced in
the latecomers' direction. Stephen had no intention of speaking.
He was quite satisfied to spend the length of whatever musical
piece was being currently performed, gazing into Kate's lovely
face and expressive brown, intelligent eyes.

There was nothing for it… Stephen knew without a doubt that
he loved Kate. He was aching to tell her so.

He could not sit here and merely admire her. How could he
stare at her without his attention being misconstrued? *Such a
mooncalf!* He had to tell her how he felt. He must do what he
could to win her over. If she would not accept him as her husband
then perhaps she might accept his presence in some other capacity. They had sat there for some many, many minutes before he
leaned closer to her to begin.

"*Kate,*" he whispered into her ear. "I understand that you have
unconventional notions, tending to veer from the norm."

"What are you suggesting?"

"I had some thoughts regarding you purchasing your own house," he began, keeping the volume of his voice low. "I hope you do not take this as an intrusion."

"Not at all. Do continue, please."

"Well… I was thinking that once married, Toby and Kitty will reside in a small home near Oxford until his studies are complete. That allows you time to search for a country house with the very large book room you desire."

"A country house?" she echoed not quite following his reasoning thus far.

"*Your* country house," he emphasized. "I believe you would also wish it to have a church for your new rector or vicar and his wife."

"Do you mean for Kitty and Tobias?" Her eyes widened with her growing enthusiasm.

"Kitty could return to your side as a neighbor and it would provide a living for the two," Stephen proposed. "If the thought of travel continues to lure you, I am certain they will be more than happy to watch over the property while its owner returns from her travels."

"If Kitty remained with Tobias to oversee the house… That sounds quite good, sir. However, it remains that I still cannot travel alone …"

"You may change your mind by then. Or perhaps … you know, I would dearly love to accompany you but … one must consider how it would appear, there are expectations of society one must maintain."

"Do you think to become my companion? A *male* companion—I like the sound of that." Kate smiled and pressed her hands over her mouth to keep from laughing out loud. Even she had not thought of that outrage that would send society's tongues wagging. Her eyes sparkled with unshed tears … not ones of sadness but of amusement—*hilarity*! The corners of her eyes narrowed as she fought to subdue laughter. Kate tried to maintain the quiet but he must have made it quite difficult.

No, it was not a jest. Stephen was not beyond suggesting such a thing. He would do what he must to keep in her good graces and remain in her company … even if it was on her terms. In a bout of desperation it occurred to him… *If not* a companion, *then perhaps as a secretary?*

He would pen her correspondence, arrange her travel, manage her wardrobe if need be.

"Stephen … you are so very funny!" Kate chuckled and shook her head.

"Don't you see how perfect it would be for us? You would no longer be alone and I can imagine you, and your guardian, might feel satisfied that you remain under my protection." Stephen could not see how anyone could argue with that … but he dearly wished their association between them could be, would be, might be much more. "Kate—in all seriousness … do you not see? See *me*?"

"What? Oh, don't be ridiculous, of course, I see you." Her laughter had subsided and she stared at him.

"Do you not see that my happiness is linked to yours?" Then Stephen confessed, "I do not care for my sham offer of marriage any longer."

"You don't?" Kate wondered if this meant he wished nothing to do with her. Stephen would tell Mr. Waddle that there never was an understanding between them—that this whole episode had been a farce.

"I find that my emotional, impulsive side knows far better than my thoughtful, rational side as to what I truly want. Perhaps it is not my head so much as my heart." He held his hand to his chest as if to ease an ache. His fingers pressed into the embossed fabric of his waistcoat.

He could see that nothing could have surprised Kate more.

"Will you accept, Kate?" He gazed with heartfelt sincerity. "Will you *truly* marry me?"

"Stephen... I—I thought we had agreed on this ..." The joy and relief in her eyes had expressed earlier now creased in anguish. "I thought you did not wish to— You cannot mean ..."

How could he do this to her? Stephen had been all that was understanding, but... Kate turned her head away from him, taking a deep breath, and exhaling quickly. He had stepped in, albeit quite unexpectedly, when *Lady Catherine* had needed a suitor, she would have never asked it of him but she welcomed his interference.

But *to marry*? It was not what she'd wanted. Kate thought very well of him. He was good company, oftentimes making her laugh —not only at him but at herself. Lord Stephen had never said a harsh word to her and always treated her with care and reverence, whether they were among others or in private.

Her circumstance, her fortune, was not known to him when they first met. Theirs was coming together for the love of books and travel. But one did not marry because of similar interests, did they? Kate had never thought she'd marry. To hand over the running of her fortune, property, her life to a man was unthinkable. But *this* man...

Lord Stephen was a tall, lean, handsome figure but whatever affection she felt for him had nothing to do with his outer appearance. His wavy hair, and light brown eyes... Yes, she had noticed them ... were so very agreeable. To look upon him lifted her heart and when they were together she felt *complete*. She did not wish to admit, even to herself, of the time they would all leave Grimshaw. Kitty and Tobias, Alicia and Hugh were to marry, leaving Kate and Stephen to go their separate ways.

The thought was very lowering. Was she never to see him again? Never?

That she would never again share his company... Kate could not like it. Surely they might do other things than merely search for a book, they had spoken of so much they had wished to achieve … *together*.

Kate hadn't meant it, nor could he, not really, it was only *talk*. However, she liked it far less when she might attempt those very same undertakings alone.

When he smiled, the expression reached all the way to his eyes. The manner in which they crinkled when some amusing notion caught him, she found most becoming. She gazed at him, trying her best not to allow his warm and gentle smile melt her heart any further. For if she allowed herself to dwell upon losing him forever.

"Dearest, Kate … is this not what we both want?" His voice softened. "It is what *I* want. Without you, I am not whole and I have no wish to live my life as a shell of a man. You give me purpose—a reason for greeting each morning with the hope of seeing you and being by your side, taking on whatever adventure you wish to embark."

"Please… *please*… do not say such kind things." Kate did not wish to say the words or feel the ache inside her … she had to resolve the struggle. To reject him would be impossible for she held him in the highest esteem. To accept his offer would be the end of her independence, surrendering all she would have gained by reaching her majority but without him by her side. "You will make me fall in love with you … and you know I do not wish to …"

"If you are to fall, then I will catch you, dearest, for I am already in love."

"Tobias?" Kitty called to her intended.

"Yes, *my heart*?" Was he not the most wonderful man to refer to her in that manner?

"Would you do me a kindness and sit next to me and turn my sheet music?"

"*Sit next to you?* Why, certainly." Tobias retrieved a chair at once and placed it next to Kitty. He sat close enough to perform the task she had asked and they both enjoyed the proximity which they shared.

Kitty began to play, but for all her efforts it seemed that her young man was more besotted in her presence than paying attention to the music before her. *Goodness!* Had he not even realized she did not play the notes as written?

She had switched to another—an entirely different piece, one she could play by memory, one she had played in this house, at this very instrument numerous times without him taking notice. Their only audience, Kate and Lord Stephen, had not commented. Upon further inspection, Kitty could see that they were not paying attention at all. She could have been playing scales for all they knew.

So on she went. Kitty had concluded her finger exercises and moved on to a simple piece. Why should she put so much effort into playing only to ignore Tobias? He sat next to her, and gazed at her in an adoring manner. She returned his adoration, meeting his gaze with hers and a warm smile while her fingers moved on their own accord. How Kitty *loved* him. How lucky she was that they were to marry.

Then the most shocking—*wonderful* thing happened! They were kissing—Kate and Stephen. It was not that he kissed her or she kissed him ... but they were kissing one another! How had that happened? Kitty thought it wonderful.

"Tobias, *they* are kissing!" Kitty said, alerting her beloved but not disturbing the two lovers, and her hands, fingers pressing the keys of the pianoforte did not dare to stop and disturb them. Kitty was delighted she could provide a heartfelt, sentimental melody and not the staccato of scales as a musical backdrop.

"What is that you are saying, dear?" Tobias replied through his dreamy haze of adoration of his wife-to-be. "Yes, of course, I would be delighted to kiss you." He leaned forward, mesmerized by Kitty, and touched his lips to hers.

Kitty's eyelids fell shut. She was absolutely transported and could not form a single thought in her head. The feel of Tobias' lips on hers was all-encompassing, filling her heart, her mind, her body. Her fingers stilled on the keyboard and the room fell quiet.

An unnatural shrieking echoed down the corridor into the music room. The two couples, who were previously kissing their respective betrotheds, leaped apart by the disturbance of a soprano-pitched, clear-sounding note that could only belong to Alicia.

Their attention focused on the door of the music room where Alicia and Hugh entered arm in arm with the most glee-filled, exuberant expressions.

Without a word said, nothing could have been more clear—they were to be married!

"Father and Mr. Waddle have come to an agreement!" Alicia unabashedly threw her arms around Hugh's neck and pressed her cheek against his, nearly knocking her beloved off his feet.

"*Alicia!*" he cried, holding on to her perhaps more for physical self-preservation than an expression of joy.

"That is wonderful, Alicia!" Kitty, with Tobias by her side, moved from the pianoforte toward the two.

"May I be the first to wish you happy!" Tobias and Kitty approached the other newly engaged couple.

Hugh set Alicia on her feet, allowing his arm to linger around her waist. The men shook hands in congratulations.

Kate and Stephen had left their chairs and approached. "May I offer you my felicitations, Cousin?"

"Thank you, Lord Stephen," Alicia replied.

"And to you, Mr. Waddell," Lord Stephen said with a nod.

"Thank you, my lord," Mr. Waddell nodded, wearing a great grin.

"Are you to live in London?" Kitty asked. "A wife must follow her husband, does she not?"

"I expect so," Alicia replied shyly. "We have not discussed where it is to be as of yet."

"After you have settled, you must come to the country to visit. There will be plenty of room!" Kate proclaimed. "We shall have a grand time!"

"To your country house? I thought you had not expected to entertain guests." Lord Stephen must have knowledge Kitty had not. She had no notion that Kate wished to purchase a country house ... although Kitty now understood it was quite possible for her friend had the means to do so.

"*Guests?*" Kate retorted, staring at Lord Stephen in the most quizzical manner. "Alicia and *Hugh* are to be ... *will be* family. Her mother is my aunt's sister."

"*Hugh*, is it?" Lord Stephen started at the use of Mr. Waddell's Christian name. "That is another matter entirely. Quite acceptable, I'm sure. They are not guests but *family*."

"However, I expect there may be some difficulty finding a property with an adequate-sized book room for my needs. We may need to build a new one."

"*We?*" was Lord Stephen's pointed reaction to the usage of the pronoun. "I had not realized *I* had a part in all this."

"Oh, Stephen, do keep up," chided Kate. "Were you not telling me you *loved* me? Did you, just now, wish to confirm the offer of marriage you made earlier? Or do you wish to withdraw your offer?"

Kitty had not heard of his declaration of love nor the renewed offer of marriage. She felt her face warm when she recalled she might have been occupied by Tobias' kiss at that time.

"I have no wish to change my mind," Lord Stephen teased. For clearly, he *had* told Kate he loved her—and Kitty had seen the kiss for herself. Kate *had* accepted. Her friend was also to be married, and Kitty could not be happier for them!

"I would hope so," Kate huffed in exasperation. "You've kissed me before these people—in public. I would be shocked and scandalized if we were not betrothed, sir."

"Really? *You*?" He chuckled and made a valiant attempt to maintain his composure. Lord Stephen must have known almost nothing shocked Kate and that becoming embroiled in a scandal meant very little.

"Married? You and Miss Kate—*Lady Catherine?*" Mr. Waddell, who must have been well-occupied with the entanglement of his own, Tobias and Kitty's engagement, hadn't expected matrimony in Lord Stephen's quarter. "Then felicitations to you are also in order!"

"Yes, I believe they are." Lord Stephen smiled. He appeared truly glad of it.

"And to you, Miss Kate, as well." Mr. Waddell offered with a smile and bow of his head.

"Thank you, sir." Kate appeared shy. She had never been *shy* in her life. Kitty could see something different in her friend's eyes. Hope? Joy?

"To return to the discussion of the *country house* …" Lord Stephen addressed the topic in a serious manner. "What else do you have planned? This is *your* house to build … pray, continue."

"*Stephen* … it is to be yours as well." Kate had wholly accepted him, Kitty could see that for herself. "*Our* house, our home. As my husband, I expect you will have a say in its renovation."

"Well …" he began. "I do not believe there is a single *book room* in the realm that will accommodate all the volumes in your collection."

"*Collection?* What collection?" Kitty must have missed this most current portion of Kate's future plans. As far as she knew, Kate's current collection of books was very limited.

"That is true for the present but I expect to add to my collection soon." Kate was not one to hold back once she had made up her mind.

"So there is time to build an additional space?" Lord Stephen's inquiry was not at all unexpected.

"I expect so," Kate replied.

"And there is your wish to travel abroad," his lordship reminded her.

"Oh, yes," Kate's face fairly glowed at the prospect.

"I would say our wedding trip will be of extended duration."

"That sounds wonderful, Stephen."

"And you will ship all your acquired books, works of art, and whatever you deem to collect, home to *our* estate." Lord Stephen was certainly growing accustomed to his upcoming marriage. "But there are many arrangements to be made before we depart, my bride. First, we must marry, then there is the matter of purchasing this home in the country."

"We shall ask Mr. Waddle to make inquiries as soon as he returns to Town," Kate told him.

"Well done, my love. It may take some months to find the right property." Lord Stephen seemed to be laying out the groundwork needed to plan their future. "After we take possession and move in, we will require a steward to manage the estate and care for it while we are abroad. A competent steward. Someone who can manage a vast property and with experience in dealing with legal issues. Someone we can trust completely."

No one spoke for many moments. Then all eyes focused on Hugh Waddell.

"An excellent choice. Do you not agree?" Lord Stephen remarked pointedly.

"I— I— don't know," he stammered. "I had thought to follow in my father's footsteps and become a member of the firm but ..." Hugh glanced at Tobias. "What do you think?"

"It would be a great change for you ... financially and to strike out on your own... I believe you must give this serious considera-tion," Tobias replied. He, and Kitty, would not have such an opportunity, not with the path he had chosen.

Hugh glanced from Tobias to Lord Stephen, all three seemed to sense the importance of maintaining the bond they had forged at Grimshaw, a life long connection.

"I insist that our estate have a parish church," Kate informed them. "I am hoping that Kitty and Tobias will live there too."

"Will she?" Lord Stephen sounded surprised. "She *and* Toby?"

"A parish church of my own?" Tobias whispered in disbelief. "And a parsonage ..."

"*Tobias*," Kate said softly. "Kitty is like a sister to me, you *must* understand the closeness of our friendship." Kate glanced from him to Lord Stephen. "The music room in the house will be available to her. A music room has *always* been meant for her. The pianoforte is *her* instrument. Whenever she wishes to access the pianoforte she is most welcome."

"Thank you, Kate." Was all Kitty could manage ... she was so very touched and so very close to tears.

"Come now, you lot—" Lord Stephen cleared the heavy emotional webs in his throat and continued. "Since no property has been purchased, no decision needs to be made at this time, none of us should be so serious." He smiled. "Until then ... we have weddings ... marriage celebrations ... plenty of merriment ahead of us all!"

Twenty

The three betrothed couples left the music room and swept down the corridor toward the drawing room for tea. Alicia and Hugh led the way, quickly followed by Kitty and Tobias. Kate and Stephen's slightly delayed departure was due to their wish to find some moments alone together.

They gazed at one another, smiled, held hands, and shared a few kisses, a bit of laughter, and a few warm words. Both were eager to exhibit their affection, and neither seemed to regret making the admission of love to the other.

Stephen ran his finger along Kate's exposed skin from the base of her neck to the end of her shoulder. She smiled, shivered and scolded him for causing any number of unnatural feelings to well inside her. They both wondered what had taken them so long to realize what now seemed so obvious.

It would not do to keep the others waiting, and the two did not tarry long. They were in time for the arrival of Mr. Waddle whose bellow could be heard in any number of areas within Grimshaw.

"I heard there was to be refreshments." He glanced about the drawing room for signs of a grand celebration. "There should be champagne—my ward has become engaged to marry! That is cause enough for a party of some kind, if you ask me. If Lord Bradford were here he would *insist* on it."

"Well, sir. Lord Bradford is *not* present and we are not prepared for that luxury. If *he* wishes champagne to be served at his niece's betrothal then *he* should have provided it." Lady James informed them all, busying herself with the customary tea tray.

"Allow me to help, Mama," Alicia moved forward and assisted with the many cups and saucers to be assembled.

"I shall, as well. Pray, excuse me, Tobias." Kitty followed Alicia moments later.

Kate glanced at Stephen and shrugged, "I suppose I should as well…" It was the thing to do.

"Might I inform you, my lady, that our own children are to be wed to one another?" Mr. Waddle did not need to remind her. "That would be reason enough for festivities, in my estimation."

"I beg your pardon, Mr. Waddle, but this is not London and we cannot conjure bottles of champagne at a moment's notice."

"It is quite disappointing that we must wait, I must say." The solicitor appeared a bit deflated. He was clearly excited about the impending nuptials surrounding them all.

Three weddings! It was quite amazing.

"I suppose you are correct, I beg your pardon, Lady James." He bowed respectfully. "I shall send news of Lady Catherine's engagement to Lord Bradford and perhaps he will see fit to supply enough for all three couples!"

"We are to be in-laws and I can forgive *family* nearly anything —you are absolved, sir." Lady James could now relinquish the task of setting out the china. "If his lordship sees fit to contribute to the Wedding Breakfast, it would be much appreciated. If he deems to attend the ceremony, I shall relay my gratitude in person. Do not forget that he *is* my brother-in-law so I am familiar with his generosity."

After Kate's stay in London, she knew any gratuitous display

from that quarter would be a reflection of their joy at relin-
quishing their familial duties, once and for all.

"We are nearly ready to serve tea," Lady James announced.
"Do set the biscuits and tea cakes within reach of the guests, will
you, dear?" She indicated the several treat laden plates to Alicia,
who did as she was bid. My lady turned to Stephen, "Will you not
see if you can locate Lord James and ask if he would care to
join us?"

"I would be delighted, Aunt," Stephen bowed and with a
slight lift of his arm, offered his escort to Kate, silently asking if
she would accompany him.

"Excuse me," she whispered to Kitty and Alicia. Kate placed
her hand upon Stephen's arm and they quit the room together. All
the times they had strolled the corridors never felt like this. He
headed for every darkened corner, every doorway that had a hint
of a shadow, and drew her to him, into his arms for a stolen kiss.
Not a *stolen* kiss for she gave them willingly.

After making their way down one side of the house, Kate
scolded him. "You are not even looking for your uncle. He might
be in any of these rooms."

"There is no need. I know exactly where he is," Stephen said,
chuckling and drawing her near to inhale the intoxicating citrus
scent lingering on the soft skin of her bare neck. When she was
close enough, he whispered, "He is in the library, of course,
goose."

Stephen and Kate made their way into the library ... the book
room. They need not venture far for his uncle would be found at
his desk with pen in hand.

"Would you mind if I..." Kate motioned toward one of the tall
bookcases lining the wall, smiled and shrugged.

"Go on," he whispered, urging her on. She could, as he had, be distracted for hours. "Don't get lost, it will take only a moment to retrieve my uncle."

Kate stepped away and Stephen continued into the room toward the large desk.

"Uncle! We are here to fetch you for tea at the behest of Lady James," Stephen announced.

"Tea already? Well, if my lady calls for me, I suppose I must attend." Lord James retired his pen and stretched before standing. "My boy! My boy!" Lord James came up alongside his nephew and clapped Stephen on the shoulder repeatedly punctuating every word. "Your mother will be so proud to hear that you are to be married."

"I think you mean *relieved,*" Stephen corrected. "Oh, yes, Uncle, her ladyship has wanted to see me married this age!"

"Well, yes, she was rather anxious, wasn't she? But there is no need really, Greg is now married and will fill his nursery soon enough."

"If only it were enough for her." Stephen could not see the value in having the heir *and* the spare both having nurseries brimming with little boys. "She thought I was wasting my time at University and dearly wished I would marry a daughter of one of her friends."

"Was it as bad as all that?"

"She began by removing us to London. She searched for a proper aristocratic daughter and I thought I had met every female attending the Season. Not until I arrived at Grimshaw had I realized she had missed one."

"Which *one* would that be?"

"Lady Catherine Jessup, of course." Stephen delighted in saying her name—and it would not be her name for that much longer. Kate would soon be known as Lady Catherine Emerson! There could not be another female like Kate in London—in all of England! "I expect that Mother and Lady Bradford do not occupy the same social circles and that was how my darling Kate had gone by undetected."

"Have you written to her ... your mother? *Will* you write to her? She would want to know the good news as soon as possible."

"Everything has happened so quickly and I must admit I want to take some time to enjoy myself." Stephen was in no real hurry. "I daresay my mother will want us to return to Woodley Towers for a spectacular ceremony, wedding breakfast, and feast."

"Oh, no ..." Lord James vehemently disagreed. "You must be married here with Alicia, Hugh, Miss Kitty, and Mr. Drayton. They will be quite disappointed if you run off and marry elsewhere. The *ladies* have plans, you see."

"I had not considered..." Stephen began and had no notion what Kate might think appropriate. Return to London for a Society wedding? It wasn't her style but Lord and Lady Bradford might insist. Mr. Waddle may have his own ideas. A Special License perhaps?

"Have the banns read on Sunday, passing the weeks with after dinner promenades, musical evenings," Lord James held out his hand gesturing at the surrounding Grimshaw Court, the perceived grandness of it all. "For you, and your fiancée, evening by the fire with your nose in a book—and hers as well, I believe."

"Yes, she is fond of books." Stephen chuckled. "Actually, she is very—"

"Are you talking about me?" Kate appeared at exactly the right moment. She approached the two men with a newly-discovered volume that interested her in hand.

"Find something that caught your interest in the library, did you?" Lord James teased.

"Always," Kate smiled then moved her gaze to Stephen. "This is where I first met Lord Stephen."

"We were just speaking of the wedding arrangements," Lord James repeated for her benefit.

Why was everyone so quick to wed? Stephen had only been

engaged to Kate for the last hour, why did they need to rush to the altar?

"I have no preference, my lord. Whatever my guardian Mr. Waddle and Stephen deem appropriate, I shall abide by their decision." Kate added, with a glance to Stephen, "There is no hurry."

"Have you no thoughts as to the ceremony?" Lord James seemed more confused than upset.

"Not one."

"That is most irregular." Lord James scratched his head and raised his brows, seeming bewildered. "I understand that it is the wish of the two other couples to have banns read in our local church and married after the final reading. Would you like to join them?"

Kate's face brightened with delight. "That sounds most pleasant. What do you say, Stephen?"

"I am agreeable to that." As long as they were to marry, he cared not how or when.

"Splendid. And where will you take your wedding trip, lad?"

Stephen met Kate's serious gaze and knew *exactly* what was going through her mind.

"If you don't mind, sir. I believe it is her wish—*ours* that we continue to search for the second volume of *Gulliver's Travels.*"

"What? Are you saying you both want to spend the first days of your marriage here at Grimshaw Court? In *my* library?" Lord James shook his head. "Why in heaven's name …"

"A moment, if you please." Stephen walked to the small table that stood between the two chairs near the hearth that he and Kate occupied in the evenings. There sat the empty cover Kate had found and he snatched it up to show his uncle.

"Oh, that ghastly—" Kate firmly closed her eyes and turned her head away, drawing her shawl tight around her shoulders once more.

"Do allow me to explain, sir." Disappointment washed over Stephen at the mere thought of the incident when the empty spine had been discovered. This was Lord James' library and he had every right to see the bits and pieces that made up this grand room. Stephen held out the spine of the book that he and Kate had searched for. "Look here." He turned the cover, displaying the golden-colored title for his uncle to see.

"Oh, *that's* where the spine is ..." Lord James exclaimed with some surprise.

"*Uncle?*"

"Do you know of the missing contents?" Kate gazed at Lord James, nearly pleaded, wanting to know more.

"Do you know where it is? Where it has gone?" the words slipped out of Stephen.

"Well, of course, I know. This is my library." He retook his seat behind his desk and leaned back in the chair, taking in the drawers on either side and then stared at the drawers of the credenza behind him. "Hmm ... where is it?" He clapped his hands together and rubbed them several times as if it helped him think. "I do recall seeing it recently around here somewheres ..."

Where? Where? Stephen nor Kate said a word. They waited patiently for Lord James to remember. He opened one drawer and then another and another ... "Ah—here it is!"

At last! Neither Stephen nor Kate reached out for it. They stood there staring ... it seemed to be unbelievable that what they had looked for was right here. So very close to them—so close. In the very same room all this time.

"Is that it?" Kate pressed into Stephen's side to have a better look.

"Thought you might want it back ... wrote your name all over the front ..." Lord James held it out for both to see.

Stephen Emerson

Yes, he had. And for once he was very glad of it. Stephen wouldn't even have cared if Kate had scolded him. The pages were perfectly bound together and had merely come free of their spine.

"Here, take it." Lord James offered it to his nephew. "It's yours, ain't it?"

"Thank you, Uncle." Stephen smiled and took the intact insides of *Gulliver's Travels* in his hands.

"I'll be off now," he said, rising from the chair. "You two come along when you are able." Lord James quit the room, leaving Stephen and Kate alone.

Stephen turned to Kate and held the book contents for her inspection. He thought she might want to hold it for herself.

"We no longer need stay at Grimshaw Court, my love. We may go anywhere you like … across the globe."

"But we have so much to do before then … the purchase of our estate, seeing to the relocation of Alicia and Hugh and Kitty and Tobias."

"Yes, yes. We shall do all that but we must continue to make plans for our travel. Do you not realize that it all takes time? One cannot decide then leave on a whim."

"True," Kate stared at the book in his hand. "I suppose *first* we must marry before we continue on to what comes next."

"While we are waiting for that auspicious day, would you like it if we have the two parts of this book reunited?"

"It seems right we have that done ... just as it is important that we are together." Kate smiled but had concerns regarding the restored volume. "When the book is returned, may we share it? For I would like to know the end of *that* story before we are to begin our own."

The End

About the Author

California-born Shirley Marks lives in Silicon Valley with her husband and unpredictable Australian Cattle Dog-mix.

Shirley dreams of returning to London, Paris, and Florence to research settings, develop new characters, and imagine stories to weave together for her upcoming novels.

When at home, she spends time reading, writing, gardening, and trying to get the odd knitting project completed.

Shirley writes Traditional Regency Romance stories (clean/sweet), Romantic Comedies, and a couple of paranormal novels.

You can visit Shirley at:
www.ShirleyMarks.com

www.ingramcontent.com/pod-product-compliance
Lightning Source LLC
Chambersburg PA
CBHW030115180626
46812CB00002B/424